THE ADVISOR

NICO ARGENTI #2

KEN TENTARELLI

ISBN ebook: 978-1-7331773-3-7

ISBN paperback: 978-1-7331773-2-0

Law arises from human reason. The political and civil laws of each nation should be determined by applying this human reason.

-Montesquieu 18th century French judge and philosopher

CENTRAL ITALY CIRCA 1465

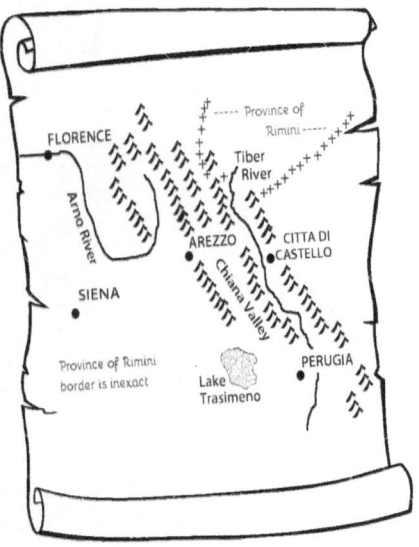

FLORENCE

Arno River

SIENA

Province of Rimini
border is inexact

Province of
Rimini

Tiber
River

AREZZO

Chiana Valley

Lake
Trasimeno

CITTA DI
CASTELLO

PERUGIA

1

PIETRA BASSA

"Being a nursemaid for a tax collector is not a job for a knight, and I intend to prove it." Rufio Scalari, Knight of Rimini, recited the mantra again and again as he rode through the withering August heat. Sweat glued his uniform to him and him to his saddle.

Hours of crisscrossing the countryside had sapped vitality from both the soldiers and their horses. When they left camp in the early morning, they sat erect in their saddles with shoulders squared and eyes alert. Now they slumped and looked out with blank expressions, each soldier in the column focusing only on the man ahead of him. Uniforms that were crisp and clean in the morning now hung as limp as the soldiers wearing them. Road grime and a film of dust muted the bright colors of their tunics.

The town they were about to enter was the fourth, and thankfully the last, on their list for the day. Three days ago, a lone courier had traveled the same route to serve notice that officials representing the Lord of Rimini would be coming to the town. He didn't say when the officials would arrive, nor did he mention the purpose of the official visit. The courier served only to incite anxiety among the townspeople. His announcement was the first step in a carefully planned process.

The knight, soldiers, and tax collector were performing the second step in the process, informing citizens of the newly increased tax rates, intimidating them, and overcoming any resistance or objection to the expanded taxes. Several days later, the soldiers would return to perform the last step, the actual collection of the levies. This process had been proven to work exceedingly well.

The tax map listed this town as Pietra Bassa. As the troop came near, they saw that Pietra Bassa was hardly a town; it was a village, a small one at that. It had no central piazza and no recognizable center. There was only one public building, an old timber and fieldstone church.

The knight stopped at the first house he encountered along the road. In a garden nearby, an old man tended a collection of plants; some were vegetables, others appeared to be little more than weeds. The old one had no tools and used his leathery hands to pull at the weeds and gently prop up the delicate seedlings.

"Where can I find the prior?" the knight barked.

The old man looked up; confusion spread across his face; he said nothing.

"Speak up, old man, tell me where to find the prior," the knight repeated.

In a barely audible voice, the old man replied, "There is none."

The knight growled, "There must be a prior. Who's in charge of this town?"

"No one is in charge."

"Senile old idiot." The knight spat the words as he turned his horse to ride in the direction of the church.

A monk wearing a black Benedictine robe stood outside the church, fingering a strand of rosary beads and watching the approaching soldiers. When the knight was close enough to hear, the monk spoke first.

"Welcome to Pietra Bassa. A rider said you would come. He was here yesterday... no, it was before yesterday that he was here. Yes, I am sure it was before yesterday."

With hostility already building in his voice, the knight demanded, "Where can I find the prior?"

The monk broke into a broad grin and responded, "Pietra Bassa has no prior."

Every town had a prior, or priors. Of that, the knight was certain. Surely someone, or some people, must tell others the rules that they must obey. But as the knight scanned the town, his conviction wavered. Pietra Bassa was hardly even a village; it was just a group of people living near each other.

Looking down from atop his mount, the knight commanded, "I want to address all the people of the village. Go fetch them."

The monk nodded, picked up his cane, and ambled away from the church toward the nearest house. The knight quickly realized that at the rate the monk was moving, it would take until nightfall before the monk returned with all the villagers.

He turned and addressed the military leader, "Captain, we can't wait for this old fool; dispatch your men to summon the villagers."

The soldiers dispersed to fetch the villagers, who slowly began wending their way toward the church, each from a different direction. The villagers had seen soldiers before, but they did not understand status or rank. However, it was clear to all that the one who stood in front, the one with the fanciest uniform, was the leader.

The citizens of Pietra Bassa numbered six men and eight

women; two men leaned on canes, one woman bent so much that she saw only the ground directly in front of her, and two elderly couples linked arms to support each other. They formed a single line a respectful distance from the knight.

The knight's announcement was brief. "Taxes have been increased. The taxman will tell you how much to pay."

The tax collector, the only one of the contingent not in uniform, stepped forward. He withdrew a sheet labeled 'Pietra Bassa' from his folio and began reciting the names listed. Hearing his name, each man acknowledged his presence with a grunt until the tax collector said, "Zaramucci." There was no response.

After an awkward silence, the monk said softly, "Which one?"

The taxman looked down at the sheet he was holding and announced loudly, "Guglielmo Zaramucci."

At the mention of the name, one woman began wailing. People on either side steadied her and wiped at her tears. The monk sought to explain her outburst by saying, "Guglielmo was taken."

The tax collector registered suspicion. "Taken? What do you mean, taken? Who took him?"

Raising his eyes toward heaven, the monk answered, "The Lord."

The taxman withdrew a charcoal stick from his pocket and crossed out the name Guglielmo Zaramucci. He read the next name on his list, this time being sure to read the full name, "Giulio Zaramucci."

This time there was no crying; instead, a voice to his left called out, "He's gone."

The taxman turned to see the speaker and asked, "Did he, too, go to the Lord?"

A woman spat on the ground in front of her, then stamped down hard on the spittle with her shoe.

"The Lord wouldn't want that lazy bastard. He went off with some bitch, probably his cousin, although I don't know why. At his age, he doesn't remember what to do with a woman, and if he did remember, he couldn't do it. Believe me; he can't do it."

"Angelina," the monk interjected, "we must not speak ill of anyone. It is God who will deal with sinners."

The taxman crossed out the last name on the list, Giulio Zaramucci, and unfolded the paper to reveal the column that specified the tax amounts. Next to each name was the same notation, 'see special notes.' He searched through the sheath of papers in his folio until he found a page labeled 'Notes.' Halfway down the page, a line read 'Pietra Bassa dispensation.' This was the taxman's first assignment in the field. Previously, he had been a low-level clerk in the office of tax assessment. In a move to speed up tax collection, he and many other clerks were sent into the field with no training; consequently, he had no idea what 'dispensation' meant. He held the sheet up so the knight could read it and see for himself that this visit to the village was a total waste of time. The people of Pietra Bassa weren't required to pay taxes.

The knight threw the sheet at the taxman, who shrank back to avoid the knight's wrath. He balled his hand into a fist, but instead of striking the taxman, turned to the troop leader and barked, "Captain, get your men mounted. We are leaving."

As he re-mounted his horse, the knight muttered to himself. His benefactor, the previous Lord of Rimini, had knighted him as recognition for his exceptional service. If that lord were still ruling the Province of Rimini, the knight was certain that he would sit with the royal court, but the bastard had died. The current lord did not appreciate his talents and granted him no position in the royal court. His only recourse was to establish a mercenary band of men loyal to him. Over time, he had done so. To assure the men's loyalty, he had secured highly profitable commissions for his small private army. Although this current task was profitable, it was pitiful. Even his men believed that shepherding an incompetent tax collector was humiliating. He vowed to prove his worth to the current Lord of Rimini, or find new commissions elsewhere.

The befuddled villagers watched the soldiers as they prepared to leave. The entire village was summoned to hear an important announcement, but no announcement had been made. As the villagers drifted slowly back toward their homes, they wondered why it took so many soldiers just to read their names from a list.

The captain's eyes followed one villager, then he looked beyond to the villager's house, hardly more than a hovel. Two scrawny chickens were pecking on the hard ground beside the house, but there were no goats, no sheep, no livestock of any kind. In a small garden beyond the shack, plants struggled to survive in the parched soil.

"These pathetic people have nothing," the captain said, speaking to himself. "They can't pay taxes, yet their poverty means nothing to the tyrant who rules the Province of Rimini."

The soldiers eased their mounts out of the churchyard and onto the dirt road. They had visited four villages today, and this one was their last. They were tired, ready for a potent drink and pampering by a busty barmaid. As the knight moved onto the road, he glanced back and observed that the road did not end at this village. It continued onward, rising gradually into the mountains. He eased his horse alongside one of the villagers and asked, "Where does that path lead?"

"Pietra Alta."

"Pietra Alta? Is that another village? How many families live there?" the knight asked.

"I don't know. I've never been there," the villager replied.

"Who is this village does know? Someone must have been there."

"None of us have ever been there."

"If no one has ever been there, how do you know there is a village? How do you know its name?"

"Sometimes a wagon comes down the road from the mountain. It comes maybe one time in a month, but the wagon doesn't come to Pietra Bassa. Maybe it goes to a city. I don't know."

Turning in his saddle, the knight faced the departing soldiers and declared, "Captain, turn your men around. We're going to Pietra Alta."

The captain sought to appease his grumbling men, telling them, "If we don't do this now, we must return tomorrow. If we finish today, you can rest tomorrow."

The way was narrow, barely wide enough to accommodate two horses abreast. Weeds sprouting in the track supported the villager's claim that the road was rarely used. The knight, riding in front of the soldiers, could discern slight depressions made by wagon wheels. He reasoned that if wagons could use the road, then surely the horses should have no difficulty. For an hour they plodded ahead while shadows of the high mountain peaks lengthened until all, even the knight, questioned how much farther they could go and still be able to return to camp by nightfall.

When they came over a small rise, spread out before them, was not just a tiny village but a good-sized town stretching across an expanse of flat land set in a saddle between lofty mountain peaks. Nearly twenty houses were visible, with perhaps an equal number on the far side of a nearby hill. Near each house were pastures where animals grazed. Sheep stood in some meadows, cows wandered through others, and flocks of goats roamed through still others. Green fields held tall grass that would be harvested to feed the animals in winter. Large barns dotted the landscape. There were fewer barns than houses, suggesting that home owners shared the barns.

Ahead, a small cluster of buildings close to the road formed what appeared to be the town center. One building was a livery with sound pouring out its open door, the rhythmic pounding of metal against metal. As the soldiers drew near, the noise ceased, and a thickly muscled man emerged from the building. He glimpsed the soldiers, gave a courteous nod, then turned and walked away around the far side of the building. He didn't seem concerned by their presence. Smoke rose from behind another of the buildings. The knight dismounted and walked around the building to investigate.

A short, beefy man with slight traces of grey in his other-wise brown hair stood tending a clay oven filled with loaves of bread. He deftly maneuvered a long-handled peel to withdraw the loaves that were cooked to perfection. Those he placed on a table to cool. Other loaves he rotated, so they would bake evenly.

As he had done at Pietra Bassa, the knight asked, "Where are the priors?"

The baker looked up, startled to see a knight trailed by a column of soldiers. In response to the knight's query, the baker responded, "Pietra Alta has three priors. I am one."

The knight sighed, releasing the frustration that had been building since the debacle in the village at the base of the mountain. Finally, a place with civilized behavior, he thought, and said, "We are here by order of the Lord of Rimini to inform you of the new tax assessment."

The knight motioned for the taxman to join him and indi-cated that he should speak. The taxman sifted through his folio, looking for a Pietra Alta listing. While he did so, the baker responded to the knight's statement, "We've never paid taxes to Rimini. Pietra Alta is not in the Province of Rimini."

The pressure of the day returned to the knight in an instant. He stared at the taxman, expecting the bureaucrat to contradict the baker, but the taxman said nothing. He remained silent while he continued fumbling through the pages in his folio, desperate to find a sheet labeled Pietra Alta.

Worried that tension was building to a critical level, the troop captain withdrew a map from his saddlebag. Before he could unfold it, the knight snatched it from him with such force that it tore the paper in two. On the smaller piece, the one he still held, the captain located Mount Freccia. He rotated the sheet slightly to orient the map with the highest mountain peak in the distance to the north. Mount Freccia, with its arrow-shaped summit, was a distinctive landmark easily recognized by everyone in the district. The captain held out his piece of the map and fit it together with the part that the knight was holding. The composite drawing showed that there were two prominent mountains to the south. From where the captain was standing, he could see only one of those peaks. He could not tell whether the visible peak was Freccia Majore or Freccia Minore. The map showed just a single road, the road they had traveled, and a small dot labeled 'Pietra Bassa,' the village they had come from at the base of the mountains.

Pietra Alta did not appear on the map, nor did the territorial boundary of the province of Rimini. The Province of Rimini claimed all territory to the summit of Mount Freccia during a border dispute six years ago. Pietra Alta may have been in the annexed area, but without it being marked on the map, there was no way to be certain.

The knight's patience was at an end. Pointing a quivering finger at the taxman, he ordered, "Read him the names."

The terrified tax collector stepped backward, away from the

knight. He had been searching through his papers and could not find a listing for the town. He replied sheepishly, "There is no sheet for Pietra Alta."

"Damn it," the knight bellowed and pounded his fist onto the table so violently that muffins and loaves of bread danced across the table. One muffin slipped from the edge and was saved only by the quick acting baker, who snatched it in midair.

The knight ground his teeth together. How can I represent authority to these peasants when the bungling bureaucrats cannot do their jobs? How can this taxman not have a sheet for the town? How can map makers omit this place? Their only purpose in life is to show where towns are located. Bureaucrats, tax collectors, map makers, they're all fools.

Knight Scaleri spun around and snapped at the captain, "Gather your men, captain. We're leaving."

He spat final menacing words to the baker, "I will return."

2

CASA ARGENTI, FLORENCE

When Nico Argenti was nine, his parents both succumbed to the plague that ravaged the Italian peninsula. Thousands died of the disease, but others survived, even though physicians had no cure for the disease. All that anyone could do was pray. Young Nico was sent to live with his uncle Nunzio, who treated Nico with the same love and care that he had for own his son, Donato. Nico and Donato, just a few years older than Nico, became like brothers.

Nunzio owned a restaurant called the Uccello, which passed to Donato several years later when Nunzio retired to a villa and vineyard outside the city. Under Nunzio's care, the Uccello had built a reputation as the finest restaurant in Florence, and Donato worked tirelessly to preserve that standing. Donato expanded the Uccello into a highly successful dining club, the first establishment of its kind where members could enjoy an outstanding meal or just sit and relax in comfort.

When Nico was young, his father had accumulated savings to pay for Nico's tutors. Nunzio placed the remaining funds in an account at the Medici bank. Proceeds from that investment covered Nico's tuition and expenses at the esteemed law school of the University of Bologna.

Newly graduated, Nico again was living with Donato, Donato's wife Joanna, their young son Giorgio, and their adopted daughter Alessa in the Argenti family palazzo.

Joanna was mending a pair of Giorgio's leggings, and Donato was listening to Giorgio reading one of Petrarch's sonnets when Nico entered the room. Giorgio's tutor believed students must extend the time he spent with them by doing additional study done at home. The tutor claimed that study at home not only reinforced their lessons; it also brought parents closer to their children.

Nico chatted quietly with Joanna until Giorgio finished his recitation. Then Nico pulled a sheet of paper from his pocket and announced, "This letter just arrived. It is from Alessa. She will be returning to Florence soon."

As a young child in Morocco, Alessa had been kidnapped, auctioned by a slave trader, and pressed into servitude on an ocean-going freighter. Donato rescued her from that life and brought her to Florence, where she became like a daughter to him and Joanna, and like a sister to Nico. Nearly a month ago, Alessa, who had grown into an attractive young woman, was invited to visit Venice by Nico's friend Simone. Simone had developed a warm friendship with Alessa while he was visiting Nico in Florence. Alessa and Simone traveled to Venice with a Venetian diplomat who met Alessa during his official visit to Florence. The ambassador had invited Alessa to accompany his diplomatic convoy when he returned home to Venice. He had been eager for Alessa to meet his daughter, who was the same age.

Nico read Alessa's letter aloud,

Nico,

You have been to Venice, so you know its beauty, charm, and welcoming people. The two most welcoming to me are Simone's sister Veronica, who everyone calls Roni, and Ambassador Bembo's daughter Diana. The two girls – or women, I never get that distinction right – are keeping me active constantly with delicious dining, parties with their friends, and exploring the city's fascinating buildings. I feel as though I've known them forever. During my first week in the city, I kept getting lost among the maze of canals whenever I ventured out, but now I can wend my way from bridge-to-bridge like a native. Everyone is urging me to stay longer, but I don't want to draw excessively on their hospitality, so I am preparing to return to Florence.

Venice is an exciting city, but I do miss you, Donato, and Joanna, and I look forward to seeing you all very soon.

Your sister, Alessa

"Nico, will you go to Venice to escort her home?" Joanna asked.

"No. That was our original intent, but her letter says that Simone will be returning to the university. She will travel with him from Venice to Bologna. From there, Simone will arrange for her to continue the remainder of the way to Florence with one of the students or professors who frequently travel between the two cities. It is fortunate that Simone will be making Alessa's travel arrangements because I am not able to leave Florence at this time."

That statement surprised Donato and Joanna. Both looked at him apprehensively waiting for an explanation.

"The other news I received today is that the Magistrates and Notaries Guild formally approved my membership application."

"Congratulations!" Joanna and Donato exclaimed simultaneously.

"Now you are officially a lawyer able to practice anywhere in the Florentine Republic," Joanna added.

"Almost. The guild is accepting six recent graduates as new members. We cannot practice law until we are officially certified at an induction ceremony conducted by the consuls of the guild. The consuls have not announced the date of the ceremony, but it will be held soon, so I should not venture far from Florence."

"What happens after the induction ceremony? When will you learn what openings there are for new lawyers?" Joanna asked.

"Guild rules prevent any candidates from being recruited before they are inducted, so there is no way for me to know what openings exist. The normal practice is for government commissions and legal tribunals to recruit new guild members immediately after the induction ceremony. Until then, the openings are kept secret. New inductees are permitted to accept any of the positions offered to them."

"You know all the tribunals and commissions, so you must have some preferences. Which do you find most appealing?" Joanna asked.

"I've tried not to think of the possibilities or to pick a favorite. I will be pleased with any assignment."

Joanna gave Nico a friendly poke. "You can only tell that fable to yourself, Nico. There must be some positions that appeal to you more than the others."

Nico refused to be baited. He just sat silently with a closed-lip smile growing across his face.

"Chancellor Scala has taken an interest in you. Might the Chancery have openings? Donato asked.

"The Chancery employs a large staff of notaries to compile and maintain records. Those are the only guild members in the

Chancery. The Chancery does not have a tribunal, so it does not use lawyers or magistrates."

Joanna decided her probing was not successful in getting Nico to reveal his feelings, so she changed the direction of the conversation. "How will you spend your time before the induction?"

"I would like to renew contacts with my old friends. Being away and studying for the past six years has disconnected me from almost everyone."

Since returning to Florence, Nico had spent time with a few of his old friends, but the one he was most eager to spend time with was a special new friend, Bianca Cellini. Nico met Bianca through a friend of a friend. Bianca had created a successful business designing and making stylish women's dresses. Although many of her clients were aristocratic young women of Florence, Bianca lived in the city of Siena, where her family and her business were located. Unfortunately, the distance between Florence and Siena limited the time that Nico and Bianca could spend together, but despite the separation, they were developing a warm relationship.

As if reading Nico's mind, Joanna said, "I suppose you can find a reason to travel to Siena."

Nico smiled. "I'm sure I can, and this time I will try to stay out of trouble."

3

PIETRA ALTA

Fapane, the town's baker and one of its priors, had no doubt that the intrusion by a knight and a band of soldiers did not bode well for Pietra Alta. The knight's final words, 'I will return,' represented a threat, one that the town priors needed to address before the intruders returned.

Pietra Alta was a self-sufficient town that asked nothing from the neighboring provinces. The natural bounty of the surrounding mountains provided the town with more than it could ever receive from any duke or lord. Streams cascading down from the high peaks brought water to the crops and animals. Slow melting snow cover each spring turned the land rich and fertile. The highest peak, Mount Freccia, gave shelter from winter storms and icy north winds. A few times each year, the town folk sent a wagon filled with animal skins and a lamb or goat to the markets in Rimini. There they exchanged their goods for spices that had been brought by ships from the east to the port of Rimini.

While Fapane finished his baking, he dispatched his son to summon Albizzo and Pandolfo, the other priors of Pietra Alta.

"Tell them we will meet at the bakery after dinner," Fapane directed.

Pietra Alta had no church. Its religious needs were met by an elderly priest named Pandolfo, who lived in a room behind the butcher shop. Pandolfo served the community in many ways. Pietra Alta had no school or qualified teacher, so Pandolfo became the person who taught children of the town. He also served as one of the town's three priors. Albizzo was one of the few people not born in the town. He came there as a young man many years ago from Piemonte. He brought a loom with him and used it to weave cloth. Women of the town spun sheep fleece into yarn that they brought to Albizzo for weaving. Even though he was a foreigner, he gained the respect of the townspeople who showed their trust in him by electing him as a prior. Shortly after dinner, Albizzo and Pandolfo arrived at the bakery, where Fapane recounted his meeting with the soldiers.

"How many soldiers were there?" Pandolfo asked.

"About ten, but they did and said little, even their captain stood aside. The knight did all the talking. I believe that his intent was mainly to intimidate us, first me, and then the entire town. I tried not to show alarm, but I admit to you that I was frightened. The knight claimed that Pietra Alta is within the Province of Rimini, so we should pay taxes to the Lord of Rimini. He was humiliated when the town did not appear on his map, and they had no tax records for the town. I was afraid his anger would make him violent and that he would direct his fury against our town. Instead, he just gathered his men and rode off, but he did give me a warning that he will return."

"Did he say when they will return?"

"No, only that they will, and I believe he will do so if only to reclaim his lost dignity."

"What made them come here?" Albizzo pondered.

Neither of the other two men responded.

"We need a plan," Fapane said. "And the first step in the plan must be to answer that question. We should send someone down to Pietra Basso to see if the people living there know anything."

"We could block the road," Pandolfo suggested. Albizzo and Fapane looked at him incredulously. Seeing their skepticism, Pandolfo added, "We could block the road so the soldiers cannot reach the town. The old ones tell of the road being blocked many years ago to protect the town from bloodthirsty mercenaries."

"If we did that, we would be completely cut off," Fapane countered.

"We would only be cut off from Rimini to the east. The road west toward Arezzo would be passable," Pandalfo explained.

"We do not know if that road is passable. No one has used that road for at least five years." Albizzo said. "The last person to use it was an itinerant musician. He walked here from Arezzo and planned to continue walking all the way to Venice, at least that is what he said. Surely you remember him. He wore strange clothes, wide pantaloons, and he spoke with an unusual dialect. He played the lute and sang songs in exchange for meals. He stayed here just one night. I remember that because he slept in my barn, and the following morning he had breakfast with my wife and me. His singing delighted my children, and then he was gone. He never returned."

"There is another possibility," Pandolfo offered. "My grand-father says there is a path, not more than an animal track, that can be taken down toward Urbino. Mercenary armies never found the path, so these soldiers probably won't find it either. If we block the road, we might still be able to use that path."

"We can hold that idea," Fapane said, "but it would take

time to block the road. There might not be enough time if the soldiers return soon."

The three priors sat silently, looking from one to another. It quickly became clear they had no other thoughts to offer.

"Let's gather the townspeople in the morning," Fapane proposed. "They need to be made aware of this situation, and some of them might suggest a course of action that we have not considered."

The following morning all the adult citizens of Pietra Alta, both men and women, gathered in the field behind the cluster of shops at the town center. Prior Fapane described the problem to a line of worried faces. A few people shouted protests saying the town should refuse to pay any taxes, but most citizens realized that doing so would only invite the knight's wrath. No one was foolish enough to suggest that the town directly challenge the soldiers.

One person recommended that they seek protection from the duchy to the south, the Duchy of Urbino, but most people believed that the Duchy of Urbino would not be willing to confront the Province of Rimini for any reason. They certainly would not enter into conflict merely to support Pietra Alta. And if Urbino were to challenge Rimini, there was a danger that Pietra Alta could become a battleground where armies from the two states burned houses and raped women in a bloody fight that left only charred remains of their town. When no other suggestions were forthcoming, Fapane said, "I have a cousin who lives in Florence, where there are skilled lawyers who settle disputes by using the law rather than by fighting. Yesterday I sent my son with a note describing our plight. Maybe a lawyer in Florence might know of a legal recourse we can use to press our case."

"Florence is a great distance away. Do you expect your son to walk to Florence?" someone asked.

"No, I sent him to Arezzo. I pray someone there can deliver the note to Florence."

Very few townspeople thought his action had merit, but the group dispersed slowly without suggesting any other ideas.

4

THE APENNINES

Tommaso spent his entire young life in his hometown and the surrounding highlands. He had never even ventured down to the nearest village at the base of the mountain. On rare occasions when travelers passed through Pietra Alta, he listened spellbound to news of the outside world and their descriptions of fascinating cities like Perugia and Siena. He dreamed that one day he might visit a city himself, and today he would realize that dream. His father entrusted him to deliver a vital message to Arezzo. "The very future of our town depends on you," his father had said. Of course, Arezzo was a much smaller city than Florence or Siena, but it represented the entire full world to Tommaso.

With pride and confidence, Tommaso set out on a narrow path leading away from the town. A little-used road extended down the mountain, but father had warned against taking the road to avoid any risk of encountering soldiers. Tommaso often hunted on animal paths near the town, so he was skilled in following even veiled tracks through forest and brush. He was not familiar with this particular path, but that was of no consequence. Father had said that any path leading down the mountain would eventually take him to a road that would bring him to Arezzo. He had reassured Tommaso, 'Soldiers will not be on the road near the city. Anyone you meet will be able to point you to Arezzo.'

He was barely out of sight of the town when he came upon numerous animal tracks crisscrossing the forest. At first, it was easy to determine which of the paths was leading down the mountain, but the farther he went the more difficult the choices became. He followed one track down a slope for a considerable distance until it changed direction and began climbing. He hoped the path would resume its downward slope, so he continued ahead. The trail kept rising and gradually it became steeper and the ground became rockier. Reluctantly he admitted that he had made a bad choice and reversed direction.

Once again, he found a track that headed down the mountain. When he neared the location where earlier he had spotted an intersecting trail, he heard a sound ahead. Bird and small animal sounds had been with him since he entered the forest, but this sound was different; something more substantial was making it. Tommaso was not fearful of meeting an animal because he had encountered bears in the forest many times. When bears are given a respectful distance, and they are not surprised, they are generally not aggressive. His concern was that the sound might be that of a hunter. Once h had nearly been shot with an arrow by a careless hunter and did not want to repeat that experience.

Tommaso stepped off the trail and crouched down behind the trunk of a large cedar tree. Animals could detect his presence by smell, but he would be unnoticed by a person passing by. Moments later, he saw movement on the crossing trail, a white-tailed deer. The deer did not pause to look for berries; it moved as if heading toward a known destination. It had not walked far before trees and bushes obscured its entire body, even its bobbing white tail. For the short time that the deer was visible, Tommaso judged that the path it had taken seemed to be heading down. He opted to follow it.

After proceeding a short distance, Tommaso noticed that the tree canopy ahead was thinning. Possibly he was nearing an open field. Tommaso marveled when he saw not an open field, but a vast expanse of water. He had only seen drawings and heard stories about things called lakes. In Pietra Alta, the only bodies of water were small man-made ponds created for animal watering. This lake was so large that the slight breeze caused its surface to shimmer. Drawings he had seen had not captured the changing reflectance and colors of the ripples. For several minutes he stood in awe of the sight.

The trail he had been following ended at the lake where the deer and other animals came to drink. He needed a new course. Looking out over the water, the land to his right rose from the lake toward distant mountains. To his left, the ground seemed to fall away; he needed to find a path in that direction. The view across the lake also let him see that the sun was moving close to the horizon. Backtracking had taken time, making Tommaso fearful that he might not reach Arezzo by nightfall.

He chose to walk along the lake shore to further appreciate its beauty and to search for a suitable path. Before finding a trail, he came upon a small stream flowing out of the lake. Water always flows downhill, so he elected to follow the stream. Although his progress was downhill and generally straight, Tommaso had to step carefully to avoid slipping on wet rocks or trip over tree roots.

The sun had just disappeared below the horizon when he reached a narrow dirt road that broke out of the forest and paralleled the stream. Walking in the road was much faster

than trudging through brush or along the stream. A single
wagon track in the soft dirt said the way was little used, perhaps
by a woodcutter. In time the narrow road intersected a wider,
more heavily used road. Tommaso decided that this must be
the road to Arezzo. The wagon tracks he had been following
turned to the left as they entered the main road. Based on that
scanty evidence alone, he guessed the city lay in that direction.
He found no travelers whom he could ask to verify his
assumption.

Houses began to appear along the road, little cabins at first,
then larger farm houses, and eventually clusters of houses and
shops. He had reached the outskirts of Arezzo. Near one
dwelling, two young boys were kicking a ball back and forth to
each other.

"Can you tell me where to find the forester?" Tommaso
asked.

The boys looked at him quizzically and then at each other,
but they did not respond.

Is it possible they speak a different language in this province, Tommaso wondered?

He tried again. "Is there a place where they cut trees into
boards?"

This request did elicit a response. One of the boys raised his
arm and pointed. "Go on that street to the water."

Following the boy's direction, Tommaso walked the length
of the street to its end, where a building stood next to a stream,
perhaps the very same stream he had followed earlier. Beside
the building was a large pile of logs, and in front of the building
sat a wagon loaded with cut wood. There were no horses
harnessed to the wagon and no workers in the building. It was
late, and the light was fading; work at the sawmill had ended
for the day. Delivery of the urgent message would have to wait
until morning. Adrenaline had fueled Tommaso during his

hike, so he had not stopped to eat. He still had the food that his mother packed for him, cured meat, dried fruit, and nuts. He settled down on a soft pile of sawdust, and before he finished eating, he was asleep.

At first light, he arose and walked toward the wagon. A giant of a man stepped behind him, grabbed him by the collar and hoisted him into the air. Tommaso's feet dangled, his toes unable to reach the ground. He could not see the face of the man who barked into his ear.

"What are you doing, boy? I have not seen you before. Are you trying to steal something? If you took anything, I'll paddle your ass until it bleeds."

Disoriented, Tommaso did not reply. Tears filled his eyes. The commotion drew two other men.

"Go easy, Toro, he is just a boy," one of the men said.

Toro lowered the boy. By now, tears were streaming down Tommaso's cheeks. He was so shaken that his legs could not support him; he slumped to the ground like a wilted plant. The second man, the owner of the sawmill, helped him to stand.

"Who are you?"

"Tommaso," was the boy's feeble reply.

"Where are you from?"

Tomasso pointed upward toward the hills rising to the east. "I live on that mountain at Pietra Alta."

The Apennine Mountain range extended hundreds of miles, forming the backbone of the Italian peninsula with countless towns and villages scattered alone its length. The woodcutter was not surprised that he did not know of a place called Pietra Alta.

Gradually Tommaso's tears stopped, and his sensibilities returned enough for him to speak. "I must find the person who brings wood to the carpenter in the city of Florence. This message must be delivered."

He unpinned the flap of his pocket, withdrew the note, and handed it to the woodcutter who read the name written on the letter and the message within. As he read, he walked toward the front of the mill, where a worker was harnessing two horses to the wagon. Tommaso followed behind him.

The mill owner turned to face Tommaso and said, "This wagon is already loaded and will be leaving for Florence soon. The driver can deliver the message, or you can go with him and deliver it yourself."

Not even in his most beautiful dreams had Tommaso imagined traveling to such a magical place as Florence. He realized that this might be the only chance in his lifetime to visit the city. His decision was a painful one.

"I must return home. Father will worry about my safety, and I need to tell him that the message has been delivered."

The woodcutter gave an understanding nod, then placed a hand on the boy's shoulder. "You look like you could use something to eat. Come with me. My wife always cooks more than enough food at breakfast. I'm sure she will have something for you."

As they walked to the woodcutter's house, he asked, "If there is a response to the message, how can we communicate it to Pietra Alta?"

A concerned Tommaso gave a hesitant reply, "I don't know. Father never told me that part."

"Well, you found your way here once, maybe we will see you again. We can talk about that more after you've eaten."

While Tommaso wolfed down a stack of wheat cakes slathered in honey, the wagon carrying the message from Pietra Alta set out for Florence.

5

THE UCCELLO, FLORENCE

With clock-like precision, honed by years of gathering for their weekly luncheon, six men arrived simultaneously at the Uccello. They chose Tuesday, or Martedi as they knew it, for their weekly meal because Martedi was named for Mars, the fierce god of war. It stoked the ego of the six shopkeepers to think of themselves as fierce men. Two of the six, the carpenter and the butcher, best fit that image with their muscled arms, broad shoulders, and calloused hands. The baker, with the delicate features of a Venetian, and the barber, with the blue eyes of a Bohemian, were fierce only in their imaginations. The remaining two, with their unremarkable Florentine faces, became fierce only on the rarest of occasions.

Over time their weekly meeting had established certain traditions. One tradition held that the chef of the Uccello would determine the menu of their mid-day meal. His choices never failed to win their approval. As soon as the six were seated, Donato, owner of the Uccello, greeted them and announced that the day's menu featured cinghiale, wild boar. That revelation triggered their second tradition, which called for one of their members to select the wine. On that Tuesday, the choice fell to the barber. He had consumed enough wine in his days to have gained a level of expertise, but picking a wine to pair with cinghiale could be tricky.

"How is the cinghiale prepared?" the barber asked.

"Arrosto con erbe," Donato replied. To aid the baker, he added, "We have a red wine blend from the Veneto that is an excellent complement."

The baker nodded his acceptance of the suggestion. It would not have been his first choice, but he had to admit that Venetian vintages excelled in recent years. Moments later, a server appeared and moved around the table, filling their glasses without the slightest interaction with the men. He placed a second opened bottle on the table and set a third bottle at the ready on a nearby serving table.

The conversation bounced among the usual favorite topics: the weather, politics, and women. The stable owner shared that his wife was in Lucca visiting her sister. He referred to that news as his good fortune. With his face beaming, he said, "It is truly a delight to go home every night and not have her telling me that I smell like horse shit. I may not bathe until she returns."

That was just the opening his friends needed. The butcher began the assault saying, "Enjoy it now because by the time she returns, your whole house will probably smell like horse shit. She'll make you sleep in the stable with the horses."

The jeweler added, "Long before she returns, we'll be telling you that you smell like horse shit."

Soon they were all laughing so much they could barely speak. The baker slid his chair slightly, moving it away from the stable owner. He regained enough composure to add, "Ah, the air is better over here."

The banter persisted until the barber noticed the carpenter's silence and downcast expression. "Vittorio, you are too quiet. Are you troubled?"

Vittorio shrugged his shoulders. "Maybe more puzzled than troubled. This morning a forester from Arezzo delivered a load of wood to my shop. He gave me this note."

The carpenter withdrew a sheet from his pocket, unfolded it, and explained, "The letter is from my brother-in-law. It says that soldiers came to his town to demand that everyone pay taxes to the Lord of Rimini."

"Why did your brother-in-law send the note to you? What does he expect you to do?"

"That is why I am puzzled. I am not sure what he expects me to do or what I should do."

"Does he have any other relatives, or are you the only one?" the jeweler asked.

"He has no brothers and no sisters other than my wife. I have never been close to him. He visited us here in Florence only twice, and we have never visited him."

"What did your wife say? He is her brother."

"The note came just as I was leaving to come here. I haven't shown it to my wife yet."

"Don't show it to her," the barber suggested. "Burn the note and forget you ever saw it."

"If I did that, I would have to pay the devil when she learns of it. One of you is sure to reveal this to your wife. And the way women talk, the whole city will know of this before long. My wife is sure to hear of it."

"Does your brother-in-law live in Arezzo?" the baker asked.

"No, he lives in a town called Pietra Alta."

The butcher said, "Pietra Alta? I've never heard it. Where is it?" All nodded, signifying that they too had never heard of the town.

"It's a small town in the Apennine mountains."

"Well, is it in the Province of Rimini or not? If the town is in Rimini, then they can't object to paying taxes."

"The note says that the soldiers claim the town is in the Province of Rimini, but the townspeople do not believe it."

"How is it possible that they do not know?" the barber asked.

The butcher gave a possible answer, "The town must be in the Papal States. That whole territory is a horror. The Pope claims to have control of all the land, but all he does is appoint dukes, lords, and governors, then he stands aside while they do whatever they please. They fight with each other while the Pope sits on his throne in Rome and does nothing. The poor citizens have no recourse; they are batted around like a pallone ball. I'm always the first to complain about our government, but at least we know which towns are in our Republic.

"Here in Florence, we keep records of everything in the archives. It will not surprise me if they record in the archive every time a member of the Signoria urinates. The town must have a record that tells whether they are part of the Province of Rimini or not."

"The town may not have an archive," the stable owner offered. "If it is indeed part of Rimini, the records might be in a central archive of the Province. Or they might even be in Rome in the archive of the Papal States."

All fell silent, thinking about what counsel to give their friend. The baker beckoned Donato, who was standing across the room, to join them. The baker slid his chair aside to make space, pulled over an empty chair from a nearby table, and motioned for Donato to sit with them.

"You have a brother who recently graduated from the University of Bologna. He is a lawyer, is he not?"

"Yes, Nico Argenti. He is my cousin, not my brother. He is a lawyer, a graduate of Bologna, but he has not yet been admitted to the Magistrates and Notaries Guild. His induction should happen within a week or two."

They explained the carpenter's dilemma to Donato.

"Might your cousin Nico know how to determine whether Pietra Alta is part of the Province of Rimini?" the baker asked.

To Donato, this sounded like a straightforward question. "I don't know," he answered, "but surely there is no harm in asking him."

6

CASA ARGENTI, FLORENCE

Joanna cracked two eggs into a well in the mound of flour on the table before her. She used a wooden spoon to swirl the combination into pasta dough that she would make into cannelloni sleeves. When the shells were ready, she would fill them with a spinach and cheese mixture. Making cannelloni was a time-consuming process, but the result would be a delicious dinner enjoyed by all members of the Argenti house: her husband Donato, their son Giorgio, their adopted daughter Alessa, Nico, and, of course, herself. Tonight she would make a version of cannelloni using basil pesto sauce, a favorite in the Argenti household.

Joanna had pinned up her long brown hair, but one wayward strand escaped and was determined to settle in front of her eyes, first one eye then the other. Her hands were covered with flour, so her only recourse was to blow the offending strand aside, again and again.

As she began kneading the dough, a voice behind her asked, "Joanna, do you find this style appealing?"

Joanna turned to see a smiling Alessa twirl around to showcase a beautiful crimson dress. At that very moment, Nico and Donato entered the room.

"I certainly find it appealing," Donato answered, a wolfish grin on his face.

Joanna shook the loose flour from her hands and walked to where Alessa was standing. She circled completely around Alessa to view the entire dress before commenting, "The dress is lovely, and the chermisi color is perfect for you."

She glanced to the side where Nico and Donato stood transfixed.

"I doubt that my husband even notices the dress, though his eyes haven't moved beyond your exposed breasts."

"They are not completely exposed," Alessa responded.

"I assume you got the dress in Venice."

"Yes, it is the latest fashion; all the young women in Venice are wearing this style. They call it scollatura."

"Scollatura may not be the most appropriate name because it is certainly revealing much more than your neckline," Joanna opined.

Looking to his wife, Donato said, "You would look great in a dress like that."

He walked behind Joanna, put his arms around her waist, and began nibbling at her ears. "We should visit Venice on our next holiday," Donato suggested in a conspiratorial tone.

Joanna retorted, "Alessa said young women are wearing that style. What she means by young means those with perky breasts, not sagging ones."

Donato slid his hands up from her waist toward her breasts, but she was quicker. She pushed his hands downward, but she did not try to twist free from his embrace.

"In Venice, even older women ..." Alessa began speaking but stopped before saying more.

"After seeing you in that dress, I'm surprised Simone let you leave Venice," Nico quipped. "His father must be making him behave. The Simone I know would have never let you go."

"Simone never saw me wearing this. I wore it only once at a party that his sister Roni and I attended. Roni's dress was light blue, which complemented her light skin color perfectly. It had larger pleats and was cut lower than this one."

Neither Nico nor Donato had ever met Roni. They struggled to imagine any woman being able to wear a dress cut lower than the one Alessa was wearing.

With a touch of sadness in her voice, Alessa lamented, "I don't suppose I'll ever get a chance to wear this in Florence."

"Probably not. Florence is much more conservative than Venice. We have always been more conservative," Joanna said as she returned to her pasta making. Then with a smile, she added, "At the risk of encouraging my husband's animal tendencies, perhaps we can visit Venice next spring for the Carnevale."

All the talk of dresses and fashion drove Nico's thoughts to Bianca. Bianca was one of the very few women to have started her own business. Her niche business designed and created unique clothes for women by drawing on her knowledge of the latest Paris fashions. Nico was introduced to Bianca by one of her customers, Francesca Pitti, the daughter of the influential banker Luca Pitti. Nico and Bianca immediately formed a warm relationship; unfortunately, they only get to see each other infrequently when Bianca came to Florence to meet with one of her clients.

Encouraged by the prospect of returning to Venice, Alessa departed with a bounce in her step to change into her usual clothes. As Alessa reached the doorway, Joanna glimpsed a thin gold chain around one of Alessa's ankles. That was another new addition, possibly also a fashion item obtained in Venice.

She would ask Alessa about it later. The eyes of the two men had never dropped low enough to notice the anklet.

Donato began preparing the spinach and cheese filling that Joanna would need for the cannelloni, and Nico dropped into a chair to watch him. As he worked, Donato recounted the conversation he overheard earlier at the Uccello.

"One of our regular luncheon customers read a letter he received from his brother-in-law, who lives in a small town called Pietra Alta. The letter said that recently soldiers went to the town to demand payment of taxes to the Lord of Rimini. Citizens of the town were surprised by the demand because they had never paid taxes to Rimini in the past. He said that the people of Pietra Alta are mostly farmers who are in no position to challenge the demands of armed soldiers. The town did not appear on the soldiers' map, and the tax collector could not find a list for Pietra Alta. The knight said that he would return to say exactly how much each person must pay. The brother-in-law of my customer is one of the town's priors. He sent the letter that my customer read to us during lunch. We wondered whether there are any laws that the town can use to defend itself. None of them are lawyers. Since you are a lawyer, Nico, they would like to know your opinion. Do you think the town might have a legal defense?"

"I have never heard of Pietra Alta," Nico answered. "Without knowing its location, I cannot offer any advice. However, I find it strange that the people of the town do not know whether they are part of the province of Rimini."

Nico paused as his attention focused on Joanna, who had started making the cannelloni sleeves. He became absorbed in watching her roll the pasta dough into thin squares and then form them into tubes ready to accept the cheese and spinach filling. After observing for a few moments, his thoughts returned to the legal issue. "If the town is near the province of Rimini, then it is probably in the Papal States."

"Is that significant?" Donato asked.

"It might be. As you know, the Florentine Republic and all the towns within it comprise a single state. The Papal States are different. As the name implies, the Papal States are not a single state, but a collection of states of various types. There are duchies, districts, provinces, and even independent towns. For example, Perugia is an independent town, and there are certainly others. Perugia has a governor appointed by the Papacy, but I doubt that a small town like Pietra Alta would have a Papal governor, and if it did, surely the people in town would know of him. Most likely, Pietra Alta is administered by locally elected priors. In theory, those priors answer directly to the Papal Secretariat in Rome. That is the theory. In practice, the Papal Secretariat is much too busy to become involved with every independent town."

"Rimini is a large province ruled by a lord. Wouldn't it have records that tell what towns are within its territory?" Donato asked.

"Not necessarily. Dukes and Lords tend to have short reigns. About twenty years ago, a fifteen-year-old boy named Oddantonio became the Duke of Urbino when his father passed. In less than two years, he was assassinated and replaced by his stepbrother. In such turbulent times, records are easily lost."

"Does that mean there is no way to determine the town's status?" Joanna asked.

"Again, not necessarily. The Papacy in Rome administers all territories within the Papal States. A variety of events can elevate someone to power, but only the Papacy can confer the title of Lord or Duke. Duchies may not have good records of their territorial boundaries, but when the Papacy grants a title, it keeps records of what that grant encompasses."

Nico began laughing, and when he stopped, he explained the reason for his laughter. "I recall a class at the university about the laws of the Papal States. Whenever the students believed that we understood the laws, the professor would mention another complication. Most of the students decided that the laws of the Papal States were intentionally contrived to be an incomprehensible maze of orders and regulations. I felt fortunate as a Florentine that our legal structure is straightforward and simple compared to theirs."

"From what you have said, it sounds as though the status of Pietra Alta might be found in Rome," Donato speculated.

"That would be the best place to look, but even in Rome, the search would be difficult. I haven't mentioned all the ways that Papal State boundaries get changed."

Joanna posed a leading question. "If the laws of the Papal States are that complicated, how can people from a small town in the Apennine Mountains possibly cope with the legal morass?"

Donato followed her lead. "I agree, Pietra Alta needs an advisor. Their only hope is to get the advice of a brilliant young lawyer who is well versed in the laws of the Papal States."

Nico could tell where the conversation was heading. When Joanna and Donato agreed on an issue, they were relentless. They came around the table and sat on either side of Nico. This seating arrangement was the prelude to their attempt at persuasion. Nico had experienced their firm pressure before. He felt like a pallone ball as he turned his head side-to-side in reaction to one statement after another being hurled at him by the pair:

"Until you receive a magisterial appointment, you have time to fill," Donato began.

"You shouldn't let your knowledge fade through disuse," Joanna added without wasting a heartbeat.

Then back to Donato. "The people of Pietra Alta have no other recourse."

Joanna's turn again. "Any advice you could give them would be helpful."

Nico had to admit that the situation was intriguing, but he was not eager to become entangled in a protracted action with people he did not know in a town far from Florence.

"For a lawyer to give sound advice, he needs a full understanding of the issues. The report that your friend gave you based on a brief note is hardly sufficient for any lawyer to form an opinion."

"The issue seems clear enough," Joanna countered, "either Pietra Alta is part of Rimini, or it is not. The priors of the town can certainly provide any other relevant facts."

"Surely you are not suggesting that I travel to Pietra Alta, wherever that is, to meet with them."

That statement told Donato and Joanna that they had overcome Nico's objection. All that remained now was to formulate a plan.

"No, of course not," Donato replied. "Let me speak with my customer, Vittorio, and see if they might send someone to meet with you, or perhaps Vittorio can act as an intermediary."

7

THE CHANCERY, FLORENCE

One of Bartolomeo Scala's duties as Chancellor was ensuring that the Florentine government operate smoothly by uncovering and eliminating obstacles. He did this with a team of 'listeners' who gathered information from all parts of the Republic and all levels of society, from its aristocrats and wealthy bankers to its peasants and derelicts. They brought the collected data to the city of Florence, where it was assembled and analyzed in the Chancery offices. They were so skilled in their jobs that little happened in the Florentine Republic unknown to the Chancellor.

Nico climbed the stairs to the second floor of the Palazzo della Signoria, the administrative center of the Republic. He took the corridor to the right, leading to the separate wing at the rear of the building that contains the Chancery offices. Nico slowed when passing one conference room to see men gathered in front of a map that filled an entire wall of the room. He listened briefly as the men discussed possible ways that the Bisenzio river might be re-routed to augment the city's water supply. From the short snatches of conversation that Nico overheard, it was clear that no easy solution existed to their problem. He continued along the corridor until he reached Chancellor Scala's office. Although the door was open, and he could see the Chancellor standing in the room, Nico felt it appropriate to knock before entering.

As soon as Scala noticed Nico, he motioned for Nico to enter, and then he quickly scanned the room to see if anything was visible that the young lawyer should not see.

The Chancery offices included spacious conference rooms and massive document storage rooms. In contrast, the leader of the organization, the Chancellor, occupied a relatively small office. The only furniture was a desk set against one wall and three simple wooden chairs. The most distinctive feature of the room was the two walls covered with small slips of paper arranged in columns. A label above each column identified the nature of the information below. Some column headings bore the names of towns, some had the names of neighboring states, and others listed complex legal issues. Scala spent much of his time absorbing the information displayed on the walls and deciding how to deal with any looming problems. Scala saw that the column summarizing a difficulty in the Kingdom of Naples might eventually affect Nico, but the information tabulated on the wall was too sketchy for Nico to realize that possibility.

"You seem to be very busy right now; perhaps I should return at a better time."

"I am always busy, at least I like to think so, but I often find interruptions can be helpful. When I think about a single problem for a long time, I am not able to generate fresh ideas. Interruptions and other breaks in concentration help me address problems from a different perspective." Casting a warm smile, Scala added, "So, consider your presence here as helpful."

Scala turned one of the chairs to face Nico. "I spend more time standing than sitting, but please sit if you wish." Nico sat and then Scala followed.

"I asked you here because there is a recent development that you should know. Several government officials in the Duchy of Ferrara stand accused of corruption. To assure an impartial trial, the Duke of Ferrara has decreed that independent magistrates should conduct the tribunal. He has requested support from the Magistrates and Notaries Guild here in Florence. The guild is honoring his request by dispatching its proconsul and two consuls to preside over the tribunal.

"Witness interviews are expected to last more than a week, then several days of deliberation may be needed to reach a verdict. Consequently, your induction into the guild will not occur until the guild officials return."

Nico slumped visibly in the chair.

"You are eager to begin your career, so I am sure that you view this news as a disappointment. That is understandable; however, the setback is only temporary. The only consolation I can offer is that in the overall scale of your career, two weeks is a short time."

Scala paused to let Nico process the news; then he continued in a softer voice. "I cannot reveal any details at this time, but other events are unfolding that may lead to a new opportunity which could be a good match for your interests. I expect this possibility will become clear in two or three weeks."

Scala's words lifted Nico's spirit. He looked up and waited to hear more, but Scala said nothing further. Nico gripped the arms of the chair and lifted himself slightly, preparing to leave, then sank back into the chair. Scala already knew the other issue that was occupying Nico's thoughts, so he said nothing as he waited patiently for Nico to raise it.

In a hesitant voice, Nico asked, "I know the Chancery keeps

the all official records and archives for our republic here in Florence. Does the Papal States store all of its official documents only at the centralized archive in Rome, or are copies also kept elsewhere?"

"Ah, I assume your question relates to the Pieta Alta dilemma," Scala said.

Why am I not surprised that he knows about the Pietra Alta issue? He knows everything, Nico thought.

Without waiting for Nico to confirm his assumption, Scala continued. "The Papal Archive does maintain copies of all documents at a central repository. Copies are often kept in the provinces as well. Unfortunately, as you know, situations in the Papal States can be volatile, so one can never be sure that the records held in the provinces are accurate. The only official records are those held in Rome."

"Are there copies of Papal States records here at the Chancery?"

"We have some records, but we only maintain the ones that concern interactions between the Florentine Republic and the Papal States. We do not keep records of agreements that the various Papal States make with each other, so we have no documents that could help clarify the status of Pietra Alta."

"Then it would be necessary to travel to Rome to obtain such records?"

"Normally, that would be so; however, there is a new archbishop at the cathedral in Lucca. Previously he was the director of the Papal Archives in Rome. I would not expect him to know about all the small towns in the Papal States like Pietra Alta. But he certainly would know about events in Rimini.

"Chancery couriers travel throughout our Republic constantly, and they frequently deliver inquiries on behalf of the Chancery, but this matter could be sensitive. Members of the clergy, including the archbishop, assigned to positions in our Republic, also have responsibilities to the Papacy. Most of them cope with the dual loyalty honorably, but some, thankfully only a small number, are little more than spies for the Papacy. Both Rimini and Pietra Alta are within the Papal States so that a suspicious clergyman might view any official interest in their relationship as irregular. I have no experience with the archbishop, so I do not know how he might react. We cannot take the risk that his speculation might result in a simple query expanding into an international incident."

"Yes, I understand. Lucca is not far, certainly much closer than Rome. I have not been to Lucca since my parents took me there when I was a small boy. I have a vague memory of visiting its famous cathedral at that time, but that was long past. I would enjoy a journey to Lucca to see the cathedral again and to speak with the archbishop."

"The quandary that grips Pietra Alta is intriguing but take care not to become involved in a protracted dispute because your induction into the guild will occur in about two weeks, after which your attention must be on beginning your career."

Nico nodded his acceptance of the Chancellor's caution as he rose to leave.

8

LUCCA

Bluffo earned his nickname at such a young age that only Nico and a few other close friends could still remember his given name. As a youngster, he enjoyed playing card games, and it was his penchant for bluffing that earned him the label Bluffo. Everyone he played with knew his inclination to bluff, so the practice had no bearing on his winning or losing; it was merely his style of play.

During his teen years, Bluffo spurned the latest trends popular among his peers, adopting his own styles instead. He let his hair grow long and pulled it together in the back. Boys said to each other, never to Bluffo himself, that the long hair made him look like a girl. But when the hair became a horsetail reaching to his shoulder blades, women began to notice. They viewed it as the mark of a confident man, a virile man.

The scar above Bluffo's right eye added to his rugged appearance. The story, one he did not deny, claimed that the mark was inflicted during a tavern brawl. Only Nico and a few others knew that confrontation with another patron did not cause the mark. It occurred late one evening when an overly indulgent Bluffo had an encounter with a door as he exited the tavern. Bluffo was sure his good friends would never sully his reputation by revealing the truth.

Equally impressive to the women was his always neat appearance and courteous demeanor. Credit for those characteristics was due to Bluffo's father, who honed them because customers of the family business valued those qualities. His father was grooming Bluffo for the day when he would inherit the business. Bluffo was already responsible for crucial aspects, such as the deliveries to valued clients. Nico sat beside Bluffo on the loaded wagon during the ride from Florence to Lucca. In appreciation for the transport, Nico promised to help Bluffo unload the shipment when they reached their destination.

"How often do you travel to Lucca?" Nico asked.

"There is a shop in Lucca that uses our silk cloth to make fancy dresses and tunics. In the past, one of our workers made deliveries to the shop every week, and about once a month, my father would make the journey so he could meet with the shop owner and take the new orders. Last year father became too ill to travel, so I went in his place. On my first visit to the shop in Lucca, I discovered that father had been keeping something from me. He had never told me that the shop owner has a daughter, a lovely and charming daughter."

In a burst of raucous laughter, Bluffo added, "Since Easter, I have been making the trip almost every week."

"Does this mean you are finally in a serious relationship?" Nico asked.

"It is too soon to know. For now, we are just enjoying each other's company."

"I remember your father as being a clever person. I watched him once setting the threads on a loom. Several of us were watching, and none of us could follow his technique, but when he finished, that loom produced the most intricate designs I have ever seen."

"He taught me everything I know about this business, and he still knows more than I ever will. He built the business and grew it despite fierce competition from established shops in Milan that dominated the silk trade. He will leave big shoes for me to fill."

Bluffo's voice trailed off as he suddenly remembered that Nico's parents had died when Nico was young. Nico averted the awkward moment saying, "I understand. My uncle Nunzio is my role model. I am still learning from him."

Nico's intercession let Bluffo continue. "Age is taking a toll on my father's body, but his mind remains sharp. Recently he discovered a way to dye silk in a manner that creates beautiful patterns. Clothiers in Florence can use all of that silk we can make, but the shop in Lucca is one of our first customers. Loyalty is important to us, so we keep making deliveries to them. Now tell me, what draws you to Lucca? I hope it is not to visit the daughter of a shop owner."

"No, my objective is a different one. I am hoping to gather information regarding a legal matter. There are documents in Rome that have the information I need, at least I believe they do, but I am optimistic that I might also be able to obtain copies in Lucca. If the information is there, I can avoid a long trek to Rome. Before his recent appointment, the Archbishop of Lucca was the administrator of the Papal archives. He may have the documents I need, or he may be able to help me obtain them."

"You are a Florentine magistrate; what commission are you associated with that relies on evidence from Rome?"

"I am still waiting for my induction into the guild, so I do not have a commission or tribunal assignment. My interest is not an official inquiry; I am seeking information about a town that believes it is being pressured unjustly to pay taxes to the Province of Rimini."

"My father heard something about that incident at lunch recently, but I don't recall the details of what he said." Bluffo flashed a wide grin in Nico's direction as he added, "Father is always gathering tidbits of information, and most of them are of little interest to me. How did you become involved?"

"My cousin Donato and his wife have sweet tongues. When they are in total agreement on any matter, they are difficult to resist. They argued I should be a legal advisor to help the people of the town. Thank heaven that Donato and his wife are rarely in total agreement with each other, or I would have no free will whatsoever. They assailed me with reasons to get involved until I could no longer resist."

After a thoughtful pause, Nico continued, "In truth, I do find the problem intriguing, and, as I said, I do not yet have an official appointment to occupy my time."

For several minutes they rode without speaking, listening to the squeaking of the wagon wheels and the breeze whistling through the trees. Bluffo broke the silence, "I hardly know where Rimini is located, but last spring I met a young couple who said they came from Rimini. They were passing through the city on their way to the Chianti region, where they planned to buy a vineyard. He said the land called to him, so that was where he intended to start his vineyard. There was such joy in his voice when he spoke. They were a pleasant couple, and I got the impression that he is a hard worker. I hope they find happiness in Chianti."

Nico and Bluffo passed the remainder of the trip sharing memories. Bluffo's eyes shifted from the road ahead to the distant past, and he began reminiscing. "Nearly every day from early spring until All Saints' Day, we were together on the pallone field. We never thought about the future. We never dreamed that life would set us all on different paths."

"I have been away in Bologna for the past six years, but you must still see our friends who remained in Florence. What became of Lodino? He always looked to you as his protector. No one ever troubled him when you were close.

"He was like a mouse," Nico recalled, "small but a fast runner. He darted from place-to-place and could change direction instantly. When he got control of the ball, no one could catch him."

"I felt sorry for Lodino because he was smaller than everyone else. Then, a few years past," Bluffo raised one arm in an upward sweeping gesture, "he grew like a weed. Now he is almost as tall as I am. His self-confidence grew in proportion to his height, and soon he formed a relationship with a young woman."

Nico stuck on the words 'formed a relationship,' a nebulous phrase open to interpretation. Had Bluffo said friendship, romance, or even liaison, the meaning would be clear, but relationship made him wonder. However, before Nico could ask about the meaning, Bluffo added clarification.

"She was a sweet thing and smart. She read poetry to Lodino, always bawdy poetry, beginning with tales from Boccaccio's Decameron, then moving to Ovid's Art of Love."

Bluffo responded to Nico's sudden change of expression, saying, "Yes, I too thought it was obvious that she was trying to seduce him, but Lodino missed the temptation entirely. Rather than noticing her form, he developed an appreciation for the poetic form. He is now at the University of Florence studying literature. I rarely see him anymore."

"What became of the girl?" Nico asked.

"I was told that she moved to Naples." Bluffo began laughing, a deep throaty laugh. "From what I know of Naples, she will have no difficulty finding men willing to seduce her."

Their reminiscing gave Nico an idea. "We should get the team together. Some of the boys must have interesting stories to share."

Bluffo nodded. Both men knew it would never happen. They could not recapture the joys of the past.

They stopped only once where the Via Cassia, the road they were traveling, crossed the Torrente Ombrone river. There they enjoyed a lunch that Bluffo had bought from a street vendor in Florence. The river crossing was midway between Florence and Lucca, and it offered a pretty view of the river, so it was a favored stopping point for all travelers. Two other wagon drivers had pulled from the road at that location to enjoy their mid-day meal. One cart was empty. Its driver said he was headed to a nearby farm. The other wagon was carrying a load of wood from the forests of the nearby Pistoia Mountains to Florence.

When they arrived at the clothier in Lucca, Nico helped unload the wagon as he had promised, and then he set out for the Lucca Cathedral a short distance away. Nico expected to find the bishop at the archdiocese offices, but he decided to visit the cathedral before calling upon the bishop. The cathedral, almost two hundred years older than the one in Florence, housed the crucifix known as the Volto Santo. Legend said that Nicodemus had begun carving a wooden crucifix, and while he slept, the face of Christ was rendered in place miraculously.

Inside, Nico found a few other visitors also admiring the Volto Santo. Whether the legend was true or not, the carving was a beautiful work of art. None of the onlookers spoke a word as they gazed up at the Holy Face. One elderly woman rocked back and forth slowly, her eyes glistening with tears.

The cry of a baby broke the silence and caught Nico's attention. He followed the whimpering to a side chapel where a family clustered around the baptismal font. In their midst, a priest trickled water onto the head of an infant. Red piping on the priest's garb marked him as a bishop, the very person Nico had come to see. To avoid intruding on the private ceremony, Nico stood silently near the statue of Saint Martin, the cathedral's patron saint, and watched the priest welcome the infant into the faith with the sacrament of baptism.

How effortless it was, Nico thought, for a priest from Rome to perform a baptism in Lucca. Church practices are the same everywhere, the same sacraments, the same gospels, the same prayers said in the same Latin words, so there was no obstacle to relocating members of the clergy from one location to another. In Nico's chosen profession, it was not so. The laws of all the Italian republics derived from the Code of Justinian, but each jurisdiction adapted the rules to its own needs. At the university, Nico and students from other nations learned the same basic precepts. As a Florentine magistrate, he would experience how Florence interprets those guidelines. But even years of practicing law in Florence would not give him the localized knowledge needed to serve on tribunals in Milan, Rome or elsewhere.

After the ceremony, the proud parents thanked the priest and carried their calmed child from the church. A procession of family and friends accompanied them from the church to the family's home, where a dinner was held to celebrate the happy occasion. The bishop moved toward a side door that led to a piazza and the archdiocese offices beyond. Nico stepped into the aisle alongside the priest. "Your excellency, would it be possible to speak with you?"

When the priest turned toward him, Nico noticed that the bishop had no wrinkles in his forehead nor creases at his eyes. He was younger than his counterparts at churches in Florence.

"If you are a member of the flock who obeys the teachings of Our Lord, then, of course, you may speak with me. Walk with me to my office where you can speak while I remove these vestments."

9

DIOCESE OF LUCCA OFFICES

They exited the cathedral through a side door and crossed the piazza toward the diocesan office building.

Nico introduced himself and said, "I watched the baptism. I have never seen a happier family."

"As it should be. One day their infant may become a voice who spreads the word of the Almighty, or he may become a holy warrior who punishes evil-doers. Now, though, I think he will be reassured when he is taken from this strange place and returned to the comfort of his own cradle."

Nico was struck by the bishop's choice of words, 'punishing evil-doers.' Perhaps the bishop misspoke. Nico recalled hearing members of the Church refer to opponents of its crusaders as infidels, but not as evil-doers.

When they reached his office, the bishop motioned for Nico to be seated before removing his vestments and settling himself into a chair behind a massive ornate desk.

"The cathedral here in Lucca is beautiful and the diocese a prominent one. It must be an honor to be named its archbishop." Nico said.

The bishop reacted to Nico's words with a cold stare.

"Two of your presumptions are flawed. First, I am not an archbishop; my posting here is only temporary. And second, for someone else, this assignment might be an honor, but not for me. God calls people for many different reasons. He did not call me to minister to the masses; I was chosen to organize the affairs of His church. Records at the Papal Archives bear witness to those who have served his Commandments and to the glorious history of His church. Before being sent here, I was the administrator of the archives, and that is where I belong."

Nico hesitated to interrupt the outpouring. He sat quietly, listening to the bishop's words, a mixture of ire and sadness.

"Unfortunately," the bishop continued, "the Papal Secretariat does not always display wisdom when making assignments. I am hopeful that the Secretary will rectify his flawed judgment and return me to the archives."

The bishop held such strong and unusual views that Nico was reluctant to mention the matter that prompted his visit. He began slowly recounting the situation as Donato had described it to him. At the mention of Rimini, the bishop tensed, causing Nico to pause. The bishop filled the silence. "The son of Satan. The one you ask about is the spawn of the devil."

Without another word, the bishop took a key from a desk drawer, rose from his chair, walked to a cabinet, which he unlocked, and then withdrew two documents. He handed them to Nico. Nico opened the first folder. It contained a proclamation issued by the Holy Father detailing sins committed by Sergio Malcranio, the Lord of Rimini. As Nico read the document, he mouthed some of the key phrases.

"...such great lust that he violated both of his daughters. ...he ignored the sacrament of marriage raping nuns, peasants, and noble women without restraint. ...he had people murdered, including young boys and girls. ...he poisoned his wife while committing adultery with another woman. ...he is a barbarian whose cruelty knows no limits."

While Nico studied the paper, the bishop sat with his arms folded tightly across his chest, his body tense and defiance in his dark eyes. Nico continued absorbing the long list of crimes and sins cited in the paper. A stunned and speechless Nico set the first folder on the desk and looked down at the second folder resting in his lap. Could it possibly contain words more damning than those he had just read?

With trepidation, Nico opened the second folder. It held a single sheet, a letter to the Holy Father from Federico da Montefeltro, the papal legate of the Duchy of Urbino. The letter charged Sergio Malcranio with beating, then poisoning, his first wife and molesting his children. Nico's hands felt clammy as though they had become tainted by merely touching the denunciation.

He replaced the letter into its folio and handed both folders back to the bishop. When the bishop reached out to take the folders, Nico noticed that that the bishop wore an unusual ring. It had braided strands of silver and gold topped by a silver oval set with a gold Constantine Cross. Nico had seen the signet before; it marked the person wearing it as a member of the Priors of Constantine, a secretive fraternity of clergy whose mission was to punish sinners and to prevent their sins from causing pain to the innocent.

"Now that you know the extent of Malcranio's sins, do you believe that you, a Florentine magistrate, can stop these atrocities? Do you believe that laws alone can stop this follower of Satan?"

Nico had been assuming that by locating the relevant official record, he could reconcile the differing views of Pietra Alta and Rimini. If the Lord of Rimini was evil, as evidenced in the documents he had just viewed, then malice could be motivating the claim against Pietra Alta. Nico had no answers to the bishop's questions, but he clung to his ideals.

"I spent six years at the University of Bologna with students from many places. We all came to believe that everyone deserves justice, that includes the citizens of Pietra Alta. People of the Florentine Republic prosper by living under the rule of law. Is it foolish of me to think that law might bring justice to the people of Pietra Alta?"

"No, it is not foolish, but all men do not share that lofty goal. Those men scoff at ideals like justice, just as they reject the teachings of the Almighty. Rimini has such men. Malcranio is the worst among them, but he is not alone.

"Nevertheless, your intention is righteous. Your ideal is in keeping with the prophet Isaiah; he bid us to 'seek justice and correct oppression.' So tell me, why have you come to speak with me? What do you wish of me?"

"Pietra Alta is within the Papal States. The Papacy keeps account of the boundaries of districts and duchies in its territories. Before you came to Lucca, you were an administrator of the Papal archives, so I am hoping you can help me determine whether Pietra Alta is within the province of Rimini."

"The Papal Archive does keep careful records, but there are too many records and too many towns for me to remember them all. I can petition a colleague to search the archives to determine the status of that town. Tell me, though, what will you do with that information?"

"I can convey it to the priors of Pietra Alta. If it shows that the town is not in the province of Rimini, the priors will certainly want to protest the unjust taxation."

"And how would they lodge their protest?"

"In one of the courts in the province," Nico answered.

Although the bishop believed there was little chance that a court ruling would dissuade Malcranio, he did not voice his opinion. Perhaps he was too pessimistic. Maybe God will stand by this idealistic magistrate, and if not God himself, then a brotherhood of his warriors.

In the silence that followed, Nico asked, "If Lord Malcranio has performed such atrocities, why is he not dealt with by the Church? Why has he not been recalled as Lord of Rimini?"

The bishop exhaled forcefully and shook his head. "His time is coming."

Recalling a passage from Isaiah, the bishop said, "Woe to those who enact evil practices. Their devastation will come from afar."

He thought, but did not say, *and if the Church does not act, then the Priors of Constantine will deal with the evil tyrant as we dealt with his father.*

"I am sorry our meeting must end so soon, Nico of Florence, but I must attend to another matter. I look forward to hearing how your undertaking unfolds, and if the Papal Archives contain the information you seek, I will have a copy sent to you."

The bishop escorted Nico out of the building, and they parted ways in the piazza. Nico did not look back to see the cleric fondling his silver and gold ring as he said aloud, "Malcranio's vile behavior has persisted or too long. His domain cannot be allowed to expand any further."

Crossing the piazza, Nico thought, *The Papal Archives contain a massive number of documents. Why does the bishop have copies of these particular documents? Does the cabinet hold testimony to more evils like these, more candidates for the ninth circle of Dante's Inferno? Are these the files that drive the actions of the Priors of Constantine?*

The documents that the bishop shared with Nico did not answer his question about the status of Pietra Alta, but they did suggest that its problem might be more challenging to resolve than he had anticipated. Justice begins by having courts render judgements based on the laws. For justice to prevail, governments must then implement those court rulings. At Bologna, Nico had learned that jurisdictions ruled by tyrants have little regard for court judgements.

Nico left the piazza and walked to the San Gervasio city gate, where he looked for someone who could take him back to Florence. Many merchants travel the Via Cassia between Lucca and Florence, and it is customary for them to accept travelers for a modest fee. Nico quickly found an available wagon with an affable driver. The cart was bigger than the one driven by Bluffo. It was piled high with goods, but a thick cloth covering, secured by heavy straps, made it impossible to identify the merchandise.

A curious Nico asked the driver, "Is your business in Lucca or Florence? What are you carrying in the wagon?"

The driver chuckled, "I have business neither in Lucca nor in Florence, and I have no idea what kind of merchandise is mounded up behind us. I am simply a wagon driver. For a fee, I transport goods for merchants in both cities. I am making my second pass to Florence today, and I hope to return to Lucca with another full load before sundown."

Shortly after they left the city, the wagon driver let the reins loose and reached under his seat to retrieve a flute, which he began playing. The horses had made the journey many times and needed no guidance to find their way. Nico was left alone with his thoughts that echoed the words he had read, murder, violence, torture, thievery. Could anyone possibly be that evil, and if so, what hope was there for the people of Pietra Alta?

10

BLUFFO'S SHOP, FLORENCE

Nico sat up in bed and rubbed the sleep from his eyes. Through his bedroom window, he saw that sunlight extended halfway down the Torre del Medici telling him it was already mid-morning. He had hoped to awaken, but despite a restless night disturbed by dreams of an evil tyrant, he'd slept longer than usual. At this hour, Donato and Joanna would already be at the Uccello, and Giorgio would be with his tutor.

If anyone else remained at Casa Argenti, it would be Alessa. She never slept late. Nico listened for any sounds of singing or music that would reveal her presence. She had always enjoyed music and had recently begun learning to play the lute. The house was quiet. As he descended the stone steps to the dining salon, all he heard was the echo of his own footsteps.

In the dining salon, a pitcher of almond milk and a fruit filled dolce awaited Nico on the table. He pressed a finger into the dolce then licked the fruit spread from his fingertip. It was raspberry, one of his favorites. He was about to take a bite of the sweet when Alessa appeared in the doorway, holding a sack of dirty laundry. Before Nico could turn to greet her, she said,

"Nico, something is troubling you. Were you haunted by a fugitive from the underworld, or chased by demons during the night? I sense that you were restless."

Whenever one of them, Alessa or Nico, was in distress, the other could sense the discomfort even if they were a considerable distance apart. Alessa claimed it was mystical, caused by their *nafs* becoming entangled. They never spoke of their mystical connection to anyone else. They could not understand the phenomenon, so how could anyone else possibly explain it.

Alessa dropped the laundry sack to the floor and slid herself into a chair across from Nico. She reached across the table to his plate to retrieve a crumb that had fallen from his raspberry dolce. As she popped the morsel into her mouth, they both shared conspiratorial smiles knowing that taking food from another person's plate was a behavior that Joanna did not condone. She frequently scolded her son Giorgio for doing that. If Joanna were there, she certainly would have chastised Alessa for setting a bad example.

Nico responded to Alessa's concern saying, "As usual, you are very perceptive. I did not sleep well."

He told her of his visit to Lucca and the documents shown to him by the archbishop.

"I cannot comprehend why anyone would torment people, especially the lord of the province. He has countless wealth. What more could he want? What would drive him to do such things? How can his subjects tolerate his actions?"

Alessa understood Nico's reaction, but as one who had been abducted and sold into slavery, evil did not surprise her. Before responding, she closed her eyes to recall images from the village of her youth.

"People find ways to live with fear. Fear never leaves the mind, yet somehow, the heart is still able to overpower the mind. That is the only way the heart can experience joy. To truly understand the plight of those victims, you must speak with one of them. You must speak with someone from Rimini."

Nico lived in a safe republic. He would never know the suffering that Alessa and others like her had endured. He did agree, though, that to achieve any measure of understanding, he must speak with someone from Rimini. Nico remembered something that Bluffo told him, which became the germ of an idea.

"Yesterday, Bluffo told me that a couple from Rimini bought a vineyard in the Chianti region. The Chianti hills are not far from here, so I could go there to meet with the couple. The problem will be finding them. There are several towns in the Chianti region, but there is little chance that I could locate the newcomers from Rimini just by roaming from town-to-town. I need to talk with Bluffo again. Maybe there is more he can tell me about the couple that will help me find them."

"Is Bluffo the person with the long hair? The horsetail?" Alessa asked.

"Yes, that is he. He is an interesting person. You should come with me. Bluffo works with his father, and together they operate a business that makes silk cloth. They sell fabric to designers who make dresses like the scollatura you bought in Venice."

"That could be interesting," Alessa said as she rose from the table and fetched the laundry sack. Upon reaching the doorway, she turned back to Nico, who was finishing the last of the dolce. She couldn't resist any opportunity to tease him. She broke into a grin. "I didn't buy the scollatura; it was a gift." She left Nico to ponder who had given her such a lavish gift.

As soon as Nico finished breakfast, he and Alessa set off for Bluffo's shop. Alessa left the sack of dirty clothes at the neighborhood launderia on their way across town to the Santa Maria Novella district, where the silk shop was housed in two buildings near the river. Loud clacking sounds emanated from the first building. Nico deduced the source of the sounds to be weaving looms. He decided to enter the second building, and there they found Bluffo carefully comparing two swatches of silk. When their shadows reached his peripheral vision, he turned and looked in their direction.

"Nico, I hadn't seen you for three years, now our paths cross twice in as many days."

Bluffo lifted the two swatches and held them up for Nico and Alessa to view. "Do you see any differences between these?"

Nico's eyes flicked back and forth between the two samples several times before he responded. "No. They look identical to me."

Alessa took one sample in each hand and pulled them close, then she raised one of them. "This one looks smoother; it is a finer weave."

Bluffo smiled broadly. "You have a keen eye. The difference is so small that very few people can detect it. Our most experienced weaver made that one."

He asked Nico, "Who is this observant, and lovely, lady of yours?"

"I agree she is lovely, but never say she is my lady. Her spirit is hers alone."

Bluffo bowed slightly in her direction as he said, "As it should be. Everyone should guide their own essence."

Nico introduced Alessa, adding that she accompanied him to see the workings of the silk shop. "Neither of us has ever seen how silk is made," he informed Bluffo.

With a radiant smile, Bluffo said, "We don't actually make the silk. Silk strands are made by tiny worms."

Seeing them startled by his words, as he expected they would be, he continued, "Yes, most people find that strange. The cocoons of silkworms have been gathered in China since ancient times. Now many countries in Asia have silkworm farms Most of our silk strands come from India. We spin the strands into thread and then weave the thread into cloth. Come with me and I will show you."

Bluffo led them to the other building where teams of men and women were operating spindles and looms to produce silk fabric.

"Yesterday, you mentioned that your father had devised a unique means to dye the silk, but all of this fabric is white," Nico said.

"Come this way."

Bluffo escorted them to a courtyard between the two buildings where large expanses of colored silk fabric were drying on racks.

"These are beautiful," Alessa exclaimed.

One rack held fabrics with rosy pink along one edge, gradually darkening to a cherry red, and then to dark ruby at the opposite side. Cloth on another rack transitioned smoothly from a light sky color to a deep sapphire blue.

"These are my father's latest innovation. I am certain you would enjoy meeting him, but he is in Prato, making a delivery to a customer. No one has more experience with silk than my father, and he loves telling stories. For decades, maybe even centuries, people have tried to produce these dye patterns, and all had been unsuccessful. Silk fabric tends to stick to itself when it is dyed, and that causes unattractive color splotches. To avoid that problem, silk thread is normally dyed before it is woven; doing so produces fabrics of uniform color. My father found a way to keep the fabric from sticking, so we can dye fabric in a way that creates these smooth color gradations. No other shop has discovered his secret, although I'm sure they are all working hard to duplicate his method."

"Are they free to copy . . . to steal his idea?" Alessa asked.

Nico responded, "There is a kind of protection called a patent that can protect designs and processes from being copied. The Signoria granted a patent to Brunelleschi, the engineer who designed the cathedral dome. That is the only patent ever issued by the Florentine Republic, so it is not likely that a patent will be granted for a silk dyeing process. Perhaps someday the Signoria will grant patents more freely. Until then, there are no protections. Anyone who discovers how to duplicate the dyeing process will be free to use it."

Turning to Alessa, Bluffo asked, "Do you make your own clothes?"

"No. I never learned how to weave or sew."

Saying the words brought back to Alessa the painful memory of being abducted before her mother could teach her the many things that every girl should learn. She struggled to suppress the memory by shifting the focus of their conversation.

"Nico has a friend who operates her own design business. She does excellent work. All of her creations are unique."

Bluffo looked toward Nico and raised an eyebrow.

"We were together many hours yesterday, yet you mentioned nothing about this friend. A woman operating her own business is rare. How could you not have mentioned her? I am certain our fabrics would delight her. Tell me, what color is her hair? And her eyes?"

"Her hair is like spring honey and her eyes are blue, but the clothes she designs are for customers, not for herself."

Bluffo adopted what seemed to Nico as a knowing smile as he instructed one of the workers to cut a length of fabric and package it for Nico to take to his friend. "With this material, she must make something for a special person to wear to a special occasion."

Both Nico and Alessa found Bluffo's comment to be cryptic,

but before they could question him, Bluffo turned to Alessa and said, "And what is it that I can do for you?"

She thought for only an instant before replying. "I have never seen the cathedral at Lucca. Maybe the next time you travel to Lucca, I can join you."

Bluffo thought Alessa would choose a fabric color when he posed his question, but he accepted her suggestion without hesitation.

"Next week. It will be my pleasure to show you the beauty of Lucca, the cathedral, the Volto Santo, and a restaurant with braised quail so succulent it rivals that at the Uccello."

Nico had told Alessa about the shop keeper's daughter who inspired Bluffo's weekly excursions to Lucca. She used that knowledge to tease Bluffo, saying, "That is very generous of you, but is there not already a lady in Lucca who deserves your attention?"

Bluffo was unfazed. "I shall invite her as well, and her cousin. I think you might enjoy meeting him."

Bluffo turned back to Nico. "Now tell me the real reason for your visit today. As much as I would wish it were so, I doubt that you came here only to have me meet this charming woman."

"Yesterday, you told me of your encounter with a couple from Rimini. I wish to speak to them. I am hoping you can tell me something that will help me find them."

Bluffo leaned against one of the drying racks, folded his arms across his chest, and closed his eyes in deep thought. He muttered a few incomprehensible phrases aloud as he tried to recall his conversation with the couple. After a time, he stood straight. "I am sorry, but I did not hear the name of the town that was his destination. The only name I remember was his, Gheraldo."

Disappointment shown in Nico's eyes until Bluffo added, "I

met the couple at the Topolino Rosso," which Nico knew was an osteria, a small family-owned restaurant, only two blocks from Bluffo's silk shop.

"I was having lunch with Stephano Buccola; you must remember Stephano, he used to play pallone with us until he tripped in a rabbit hole and broke his leg. He never played after that. Now he is the chef at Topolino Rosso. When I arrived at the osteria, Stephano was talking with the couple. They departed shortly after I arrived, but they may have had a lengthy conversation with Stephano. If so, he might be able to help you.

A worker emerged from one of the buildings, walked to where Nico was standing and handed him a surprisingly heavy package containing silk fabric.

"There is more than enough fabric here for your friend to make a full-length cioppa," Bluffo said. "Tell your friend that I am eager to see her creation."

Nico thanked Bluffo for the information and the fabric.

"I am going to Topolino Rosso to speak with Stephano," Nico told Alessa.

Rather than going with him, Alessa decided to remain at the shop, so Bluffo could show her fabric in other colors that workers were readying for delivery to his customers.

11

RIMINI

During his fourteenth year, Sergio Malcranio's childhood ended with the death of his father. Young Sergio inherited the title Lord of Rimini and became the de facto leader of the small band of mercenaries that his father had assembled. Even as a boy, he had observed his father and learned a powerful philosophical tenet, one that a future philosopher might claim as his own: given a choice between being feared and being loved, a leader must always choose to be feared.

Young Lord Malcranio resolved to expand the small band of soldiers into a formidable mercenary army as the surest path to achieve the power he craved. Despite a lean treasury, he grew the size of his force with the same approach that Julius Caesar used successfully: he shared the spoils generously with his men. In Malcranio's case, spoils were the contract fees paid by foreign states to employ his resources. Most foreign governments avoided the cost of maintaining a standing army by hiring mercenaries when a need arose, and Malcranio happily filled the need for those who had sufficient finances to pay him generously. His only loyalty was to gold florins. He sought no friendships and nimbly switched allegiances to garner the most lavish payments. In time he became the most infamous mercenary captain-general on the Italian peninsula.

Malcranio's father had married twice, and neither of his wives was the mother to his four children. Like his father, Sergio also married twice. The first unfortunate woman was poisoned, and rumors say his second wife was strangled to advance his affair with Isolla, his mistress. Malcranio's fascination with Isolla was difficult for anyone to understand. When Malcranio's brother introduced him to Isolla, he remarked, 'she isn't beautiful.' All members of his court agreed that the parade of young maidens through Malcranio's castle proved Isolla did not satisfy all of his physical desires. However, she clearly had some quality that held his attention.

Members of the ruling court close to Sergio and Isolla said that she had an inexplicable insight to his thought process. Whenever he pondered an issue, she reached his conclusion before him – as though she were a mirror that could reflect his image before he even stood before it. This insight let her steer his decisions. They, the members of the ruling court, credited Isolla for Malcranio's interest in sponsoring scholars and artists. Until Isolla entered his life, Malcranio had displayed no interest in intellectual or artists pursuits.

The Treaty of Lodi, which was adopted by all the major Italian city-states, brought an era of peace to the Italian peninsula. It brought forth the first years without war in the memory of any living person. Minor disputes still erupted from time-to-time, and Malcranio's mercenaries welcomed the opportunity to engage in those feuds on one side, or the other, or both. However, contracts for their services were neither large enough nor long-lasting enough, to support the sizable army that Malcranio had assembled and trained.

He would never consider reducing his force, so that left few recourses. One measure was to increase taxes enough to pay his men. His mercenaries proved effective at persuading citizens of the province to accept the increased levy. Six troops of cavalry, each led by a knight, were dispatched throughout the province to inform everyone of the increased tax levies. Then, two weeks later, the soldiers returned to collect the amount owed. If farmers were forced to sell all their livestock or property, or if laborers were forced to sell family heirlooms, it mattered not to Malcranio.

Those consequences paled in comparison to the suffering endured by anyone who defied the tax edict. Those who objected to paying were not punished individually. Instead, if one person in a village refused to pay, Malcranio's army made the entire village bear the consequences of his action. One community afflicted by a severe epidemic had its sole physician taken to prison because one person refused to pay the tax. Desperate members of the village exiled a troublemaker and confiscated his property to appease the tax collector. Word of this incident spread quickly throughout the province and served as a warning to others who might consider resisting.

When tax increases alone could not support the sizeable mercenary army, Malcranio devised a scheme for seizing territory from unincorporated towns and also from small towns in the neighboring Duchy of Urbino. He directed the bulk of his military to positions along the Urbino border. From those positions, scouts went into the adjoining territory to identify towns that were both poorly defended and wealthy enough to make them beneficial additions to Rimini's coffers. Any new acquisitions would become entirely new sources of funds. The Duchy of Urbino was in no position to challenge Malcranio's superior military strength. The Papacy, in far off Rome, should have exercised dominion and controlled its renegade appointed

Lord of Rimini, but it ignored the situation and the cries for help from the Duke of Urbino.

Just outside the walls of the port city of Rimini, Malcranio built the castle that bore his name. The old city walls would have been ineffective against attack by a well-equipped military unit, but the thick stone walls and guard towers of the castle made it a fortress easily able to withstand any assault. Deep within its most secure central area were the rooms where Sergio and Isolla resided. Close to the castle's single entrance was the long narrow room known as the great hall, where Sergio met with his court advisors.

At one of the hall's narrow ends, a raised platform held Sergio's seat of power, an oak throne carved with intricate designs, adorned with silver medallions, and upholstered with hand-embroidered velvet. The platform height was arranged such that when Sergio sat on the throne, he projected authority by always looking down upon anyone standing before him. On the wall behind the throne hung a huge tapestry depicting a larger-than-life-sized rendering of Sergio Malcranio, with his sword raised menacingly, routing a band of enemy fighters. The decoration was a gift from the Doge of Venice, who had contracted with Malcranio and his mercenaries to protect a Venetian colony on the Dalmation coast from a tribe of barbarians. Venice had the most formidable navy in the Mediterranean, but they did not maintain an army, choosing instead to hire mercenaries whenever the need arose. After being ferried across the Adriatic in Venetian ships, Malcranio and his men showed their prowess by driving the troublesome tribe away from the colony and across the Dinaric Alps. But the warm accord between Rimini and the Venetian Republic did not last. A short time after his Dalmation victory, Malcranio's belligerence destroyed the relationship with Venice that had taken decades to establish.

The tapestry was positioned a short distance in front of the wall and hid a small doorway through which Malcranio could enter the great hall without having to use the main entrance. All advisors and ministers of the court were expected to be in the room and seated before Malcranio entered. Members of the court sat in a single row of seats along one of the room's long walls. The most senior ministers sat closest to Malcranio. Junior advisors occupied the far end of the row. Isolla was the only person other than Malcranio permitted on the raised platform. She sat on a thick cushion placed next to Sergio's throne.

Malcranio entered, settled into his throne, then scanned the uneasy room. Despite the elevation of the platform that held his throne, he did not appear stately. He was short with a small bony frame. Ruffles on his robe covered his neck, so his squarish head looked to be held in place by two protruding collar bones. The slightest displeasure could turn the animus smoldering behind his eyes into blazing fury. He scanned the room, fixing his sights on one empty chair. From its position in the row, Malcranio could tell it belonged to a minor functionary, but one whose name Malcranio had never bothered to learn. The attendance of all ministers was mandatory. Death was the only excuse for being absent.

Malcranio turned to Novello, his younger brother, who served as the Provincial Secretary. "The one whose ass belongs in that chair, replace him."

He barely finished speaking when the door at the far end of the room opened. A man stepped into the room and shuffled toward the empty chair. He reached halfway when Malcranio bellowed, "Cazzo! Shut the goddamn door!"

All eyes locked onto the man who turned, retraced his steps, and pushed the door closed. Everyone, including the man himself, knew he would never attend another session. No one said a word; they barely breathed until Malcranio's anger dissipated enough for the court business to begin. Malcranio regularly received progress reports from the knights who led his tax collection missions. Novello conducted those reporting sessions.

Five knights delivered their reports without incident before Novello summoned Rufio Scalari, the sixth and final man. Rufio had been knighted by Sergio's father more out of pity than for any accomplishments. The noble Scalari family had deep roots in Rimini and an excellent record of serving past lords of the province. Rufio, however, lacked the competence of his ancestors. When the escorting guards conducted him to the great hall, he entered and approached the throne with an unsteady gait rather than with the confident swagger of the knights who preceded him. He walked the length of the room, then stood with his mouth hanging open but saying nothing.

"Speak up. What are you waiting for? Speak up," barked Malcranio.

Before considering the consequences of his words, Rufio blurted out, "Yesterday the men under my command informed the people in three towns of the new taxes. I could not give information to the villagers in Pietra Bassa because the tax record lists only 'dispensation' for all the villagers."

Malcranio looked away from the knight and toward the row of ministers. He focused on the provincial treasurer, the person responsible for maintaining tax records. In a booming voice, Malcranio demanded, "What is 'dispensation'?"

The words echoed throughout the hall. The treasurer, seated about halfway down the row, stood and made his way toward the throne. As he walked, the poise he initially felt upon standing dissipated with every step.

"Your father determined that some villages are so poor that they are unable to pay taxes. He granted them dispensation. They pay no taxes," the treasurer explained.

For a moment, Malcranio said nothing. He wanted to blame someone for the failure to fill his coffers, but realistically, he could not blame his dead father.

Rufio sensed that he was not the object of Malcranio's wrath, so he summoned the confidence to divulge his second finding, "There is another town, Pietra Alta, for which there is no tax record at all."

That remark caused sweat to run down the treasurer's face. He had never heard of Pietra Alta. He could not possibly know the tax status of every village in the province, but other men, including Lord Malcranio's cousin, had been imprisoned for similar failings. This time his guardian angel must have been standing beside him, for he was spared punishment when another minister, the Provincial Engineer, the one who oversaw the official cartographers, called out, "Pietra Alta is not within the Province of Rimini."

How did the Provincial Engineer happen to know this fact, the ministers asked silently looking from one to another.

"Where is it? Is it in Urbino?" Malcranio demanded.

"It is within the Papal States, but it is an independent village. It is not part of the Duchy of Urbino."

Malcranio toyed with the gold rings on his fingers. "So, possibly a new source of revenue," he mused.

Upon hearing Malcranio's words, the treasurer relaxed and resumed breathing normally.

The engineer explained further, "Pietra Alta is a small isolated village located high in the Apennine Mountains. Approximately twenty families live there. They are all farmers who manage to maintain a meager existence."

The treasurer said nothing. He merely wondered how this man, this engineer, could know such details of a small remote village.

Malcranio was about to order that Pietra Alta be annexed

and taxed accordingly when Isolla leaned toward him and whispered, "Would it not be better to send your men to wealthier places?"

Malcranio absorbed the idea from Isolla, then turned and gave a new order to the military minister, "Do not waste everyone's time trying to pull gold from dirt. See to it that the soldiers visit towns that are more able to pay." With a wave of his hand, Malcranio dismissed Rufio and the treasurer.

Rufio had mixed feelings as he exited the great hall. He was pleased to have escaped blame for the aborted tax mission, but if he did not return to Pietra Alta, how could he avenge the humiliation put upon him by the priors of that village? Anger within him turned to determination. Despite any new orders, he would return to Pietra Alta. That town would be taught to respect a person of his standing. He had already dispatched a handful of men, men loyal to him, to observe the town's priors so he would know if they were planning any measures to oppose him. If Lord Malcranio would forego the collection of taxes, then Rufio and his men would garner tribute in another form.

12

TOPOLINO ROSSO, FLORENCE

Topolino Rosso was only a short distance from Bluffo's silk mill. It occupied a small storefront between two larger shops on a narrow street and was one of many osterias scattered throughout the city that served simple meals to neighborhood patrons. Nico pushed open the door, stepped in, and immediately detected the aroma of something delicious being prepared in the kitchen. Nico scanned the interior, and as he expected, it was clean and sparse, like all other family-owned restaurants. The walls were bare, and the dining area was small, with only five tables.

A young girl carried steaming bowls of soup to two patrons seated at one of the tables. Nico was not good at judging ages, but he guessed the girl to be no older than fourteen or fifteen years. She wore a wreath of pink flowers in her hair that complemented her rosy complexion. The way she carried the heavily laden serving tray to the table suggested that she already had considerable experience as a server.

She noticed Nico entering and gave him a friendly smile. He gestured toward one of the empty tables, and she nodded her approval. She was still smiling when moments later, she came to Nico's table and said, "Welcome to Topolino Rosso. I believe this is your first visit. How may I help you?"

Nico expected that this osteria, like most small restaurants in Florence, had a fixed menu with one, or at most two, selections each day. Cooks could accommodate slight variations at the request of customers, but patrons generally found that the cook's chosen preparation was always delicious. Judging from what the two men at the rear table were eating, today's luncheon fare was a hearty soup. It was too early in the day for Nico to have a full meal, but he felt obligated to order something.

"Is it possible to have a small antipasto and something cool to drink?" he asked.

"Yes, of course," the girl answered.

As she turned to leave, Nico said, "You presumed that this is my first visit. Are you able to remember all of your customers?"

"I try to remember everyone. It isn't that difficult because most of the customers are regulars from the neighborhood. We get very few newcomers."

Watching her head to the kitchen, Nico tried to imagine what she might have looked like when she was much younger. He recalled that Stephano, the owner, had a younger sister. Could that be she? It had been eight or nine years since he had last seen Stephano. His sister would have been only six years old, a child, at that time. If that were Stephano's sister, she had grown from a little girl into a young woman, so Nico was not surprised that he did not recognize her.

Many years past, Nico and Stephano enjoyed sports and studied together until the time when Stephano's father died from a strange illness. Physicians never did determine its cause. His symptoms were like those of plague victims, but he did not succumb during the time of a plague epidemic, and his sickness did not pass to anyone else, so the doctors remained puzzled. His father's passing left Stephano as the head of the family and the one to operate the family business. The new responsibility left Stephano with no time for sports or school.

The girl returned from the kitchen with a plate of pecorino cheese, smoked meats and roasted vegetables, and a glass of lemon water.

After she set the plate on the table in front of him, Nico said, "I was a friend of Stephano. I am Nico Argenti." Her brow furrowed as though she recognized the name but could not recall the context. "Are you Stephano's sister?" he asked.

She nodded slowly and continued to look puzzled.

"I know Stephano has a sister but she . . . you were too young to remember me. Many years past, your brother and I studied with the same tutor, Signor Gonzago."

Her expression softened. "My name is Salvaza, but everybody calls me Squeaky."

This time it was Nico who looked puzzled. His was a common reaction whenever she mentioned her tag name.

"I had a pet mouse with that name," she explained. "I fed him well and cared for him, but one day I did not latch his cage tightly, and he escaped."

"When did it happen?" Nico asked. "Maybe he will return."

"It was a long time ago. He is probably happier being free, but I doubt that the food he finds is as good as what I fed to him. A good friend said I could keep him with me in spirit by inheriting his name. I took his suggestion, and I've been called Squeaky ever since.

"Stephano is indeed my older brother. Would you like to see him?"

"Yes, is he here?"

"He is in the kitchen. I'll tell him Nico Argenti would like to speak with him."

She spun around, her dress billowing out as she twirled, and dashed to the kitchen.

Nico had barely tasted the antipasti when Squeaky returned. "Stephano is busy preparing tonight's dinner, but he is eager to see you. Come with me to the kitchen."

His few mouthfuls of the antipasti had aroused Nico's hunger, so he took the plate of antipasti and the glass of lemon water with him as he followed Squeaky into the kitchen. There Stephano stood before a large pot stirring its contents. Nico was about to speak when Stephano held up a hand to silence him. Stephano dipped a tasting spoon into the pot, then held it out to Nico.

"Before you say anything, taste this."

Unlike his cousin Donato, Nico had little culinary expertise, but the aroma was familiar to him. He slowly sipped the chunky sauce. "I had sauces like this one before, many times when I was at the university. Many restaurants in Bologna serve pasta with sauces like this."

He took another sip and tried to analyze the flavors. "This sauce is richer than the ones I remember, as though it includes some additional ingredients."

Nico didn't even try to identify the unique flavorings. Pride in his work compelled Stephano to elaborate further.

"Three months past, I heard a customer commenting to his dinner companion that pasta sauces in Florence did not compare to those in Bologna, and even in Bologna none compared with his nonna's recipe. I joined his conversation, and the following day, he returned to show me how to make the sauces in the style of his grandmother. I added some twists of my own. Now everyone who tries my creation agrees this is the best Bolognese sauce they ever tasted."

Nico nodded as he said, "I agree. It certainly is delicious."

Stephano removed his apron and ended the tale by giving

Nico a giant hug, lifting him into the air, and kissing him on both cheeks.

"It has been forever since we last met on the pallone field." Their recollection of warm memories began with an exchange of sports stories then turned to remembrances of family and friends. As they relived the past, Stephano tended to his sauce, and Nico nibbled at his antipasti.

Eventually, Stephano asked, "What brought you here today? I doubt that you discovered Topolino Rosso by chance."

"That is true. I had a reunion with Bluffo yesterday. He deserves the credit for pointing me to your door."

Stephano leaned in close to Nico and whispered in a conspiratorial tone, "I believe Cupid may have finally wounded the big man. He takes lunch here often. Every week he would mention the name of a different woman, and he even brought some of them here to lunch with him. As you know, Bluffo is not one who chases after women; he never did. It is the women who chase after him. Lately, though, he speaks of only one."

"A woman from Lucca?" Nico asked.

"Ah, he has already told you. I believe that this time Cupid's arrow may have landed him a fatal blow. I judge it to be a well-placed shot, though, because I have never seen Bluffo happier."

Stephano stepped back; a thoughtful expression spread across his face. "You still have not told me your purpose in coming. I am certainly happy to see you, but for what reason did Bluffo send you this way?"

"I wish to locate a certain couple from Rimini. Bluffo said that he met the couple here at Topolino Rosso, but all he could recall is that the man's name is Gheraldo. Bluffo thought you might be able to tell me more, something that could help me to locate them."

Stephano paused while stitching together in his mind the fragments of a past conversation. "As you said, his name is

Gheraldo. The woman's name is Masina. They were passing through Florence on their way to the Chianti region, where they hoped to buy a vineyard."

"Did they say their destination? The name of a town?"

Stephano thought deeply before answering. "No, they never mentioned the name of a town. Gheraldo did say that he had passed through the region previously. It was during that journey when he became enchanted by the Chianti hills and chose to make his new home there."

Nico waited for Stephano to continue, but there was only silence.

"Can you remember anything further? What inspired Gheraldo to choose the Chianti region?"

"He did delight in telling that story to me. He was passing through the region on his way to Siena and reached a town with a tall tower at the top of a hill. While they were stopped in the town to rest their horses, Gheraldo decided to climb the tower. When he reached the top, he was captivated by the sight of lush vineyards with row upon row of vines spread in all directions. A young girl had also climbed the tower. She stood on her toes to peer over the guard railing so she could view the scene. He asked the girl if it was possible to see Florence. He was curious whether the dome of the cathedral might be visible from their vista, but the girl told him that hills blocked the view in that direction. She pointed in the opposite direction to a village on the next hilltop and said it is the only town that was visible from the tower. I do not know whether she told him the name of the town, but if so, he did not tell it to me. He only said that she told him the village is across the border in the Republic of Siena. I wish I could tell you more, but that is all I know."

Squeaky entered the kitchen and announced the lunch orders from three new customers. Nico quickly found himself holding a spoon and stirring the pot of Bolognese sauce until Stephano finished preparing plates for the new guests.

"Donato has a staff to help him at the Uccello, but here at Topolino Rosso, you must be constantly busy as the sole cook. Do you ever have time to get out into the world?"

"The osteria is closed on Thursdays, so I get some time away. But even when I am here, customers bring the world to me. One of the regulars is the captain of a barge on the Arno River between Florence and Pisa. Every time I see him, he has new stories to tell."

Stephano paused and adopted a thoughtful expression before continuing. "This life is good for me, but I worry about Squeaky. Working here occupies too much of her life. She should have time to make friends and to learn about the world. Young men who come for lunch see that she is no longer a girl; she is becoming a woman. Some are reputable men, but others see only her nubile body. Squeaky has no sister or friend to give her the warnings that every woman should learn."

"I may be able to help with that," Nico asserted.

Stephano raised an eyebrow. "You?"

Nico chuckled. "Not me; Alessa, my sister. She has more experience with unsavory men than any woman should bear."

"Alessa . . ." Stephano reflected. "Yes, I remember her. She was about Squeaky's age when I saw her last, maybe even younger."

"She is now a strong independent woman," Nico said.

Nico promised to bring Alessa to the Topolino Rosso to meet Squeaky, and he thanked Stephano for the information about the couple from Rimini. He departed the osteria intending to talk with Donato at the Uccello. The few facts revealed by Stephano were more than he had before, but not enough for him to determine the town where he might find Gheraldo. During his travels to Siena, he had never passed through a town close to the border with a tall tower. Several roads rise from the Arno River valley into the hills leading to Siena, and out of habit, Nico always followed the same route. He needed to speak with someone familiar with the other roads. His first thought was of Donato because Donato traveled to many places in search of new tasty additions for the menu at the Uccello.

Nico walked only a short distance before realizing that Donato's travels took him to seaports, such as Naples and Genoa, which imported exotic foods and spices from Africa and the Levant. Donato had no reason to travel to Siena. Nico changed direction and turned onto a street that would take him to the Chancery Annex. There he hoped to find the mysterious Chancery official with a vast knowledge of the Florentine Republic, the one known as the 'connector.

13

CHANCERY ANNEX, FLORENCE

Administrative offices of the Florentine Republic were located in the Palazzo dei Signoria. As its name suggests, the Palazzo was also where the ruling body of the Republic, the Signoria, conducted business. As one of the government's highest administrative entities, the Chancery also had its principal offices in the Palazzo. However, all of the official records, which the Chancery maintained on behalf of the entire government, were processed and kept in a different building, the Chancery Annex.

Nico had never been inside the old tower building that housed the Chancery Annex, but he had passed the building many times when leaving the city through the Porta San Gallo gate to visit his Uncle Nunzio's vineyard. In the distant past, when feuds between families happened frequently, wealthy families fashioned their houses into towers for defensive purposes. The government had acquired one of those towers and converted into the Chancery Annex.

As Nico moved out from the center of the city along Via Gallo, he kept recalling the information Stephano had given him: a hill town with a tall tower, close enough to the border that it was possible to see a village in the Republic of Siena. If that report was correct, there was probably only one town fitting that description and the 'connector' would surely know its name. What concerned Nico was that the girl might have been mistaken when she told Gheraldo that the town they were seeing was in Siena. That fact was crucial because it could pinpoint the location of the town. There were many reasons for building tall structures, so merely knowing that the town had a tall tower was not sufficient. Nearly every town had a church with a tall bell tower. Nico believed that the 'connector' could tell him the names of all the towns in the Chianti region that had tall buildings, but it wouldn't have been feasible for Nico to visit every one of those towns to search for the couple from Rimini. His success depended on the girl having correctly identified the distant town as being in Siena.

The Chancery Annex appeared no different from any other building along Via Gallo. There was no sign or marking indicating it as an official government archive. A casual passerby might have assumed the structure contained shops and businesses similar to those in the buildings surrounding it.

Nico expected the entry would open to a small anteroom where a clerk would be stationed to ask his purpose. Instead, he entered directly into a large room filled with groupings of tables where men were processing stacks of documents. The room was much larger than he expected with generous space between the work tables. On one wall was a faded old fresco, most likely of a religious scene, although a layer of grime accumulated over the years degraded its hues and obscured the image. White doves, now visible only as white blobs, spotted the dirty blue sky. Below, a person stood alone in a greenish brown field. A fresco of a person with birds, who else could it have been but Saint Francis?

Before the building was converted for use as the Chancery Annex, it must have served another purpose. Possibly it was the home of an aristocrat who had lost favor with the ruling political party. Florence had a history of exiling opposition leaders and seizing their property. Even Dante Alighieri, one of the Republic's most esteemed citizens, had been cast into exile, Nico recalled.

Directly ahead of Nico, men were making notations on sheets of paper that covered the far wall of the room. To his left, three men seated side-by-side were marking the documents they were scrutinizing. One of the three men looked up as Nico entered. When he finished marking the record he was holding, he rose and stretched his lanky frame to its full height to dispel the kinks that came from a long session of sitting hunched over stacks of paperwork. As he came to where Nico stood, his boyish face showed him to be not much older than Nico.

"You may be in the wrong place; this is the Chancery Annex. If you are looking for the Chancery offices, they are in the Palazzo della Signoria."

"I wish to speak with the 'connector.' My name is Nico Argenti."

Usually, the mention of a covert Chancery operative, such as the 'connector,' evoked surprise, but that did not happen this time. The man reacted as though he was familiar with the name Nico Argenti and he found it entirely reasonable for Nico Argenti to be seeking the 'connector.'

"I am Galetto, one of the notaries. The 'connector' is away from the annex. I will have a message sent to ask if he is available."

"Would it be better if I return later?"

"He is not far. You can wait here for his reply."

Galetto beckoned for a clerk. He wrote a brief note and instructed the clerk to deliver the message to the 'connector.'

Nico scanned the room, taking in the flurry of activity. Like a colony of ants, the men were in constant motion, each performing his designated task without speaking. Papers rustling and footfalls on the stone floor were the only sounds in the otherwise silent room.

Seeing Nico's interest in their work, Galetto said, "One of the Chancery's responsibilities is archiving all official government records. In the past, we put all the records into boxes labeled with the date they were stored. That filing process was easy, but it was virtually impossible to find a specific document later. When someone came to look for information, they could give us the name of a topic, but no one ever knew the dates of various documents. Our previous Chancellor, Benedetto Accolti, devised the method we use now. It organizes documents by subject matter."

Galetto pointed to a table across the room where two clerks were organizing a tall stack of papers. "Those are new documents that just arrived this morning. First, the clerks assign a unique number to each document. Then they record that number and the source of the document on a list. I believe the stack of papers they are processing now is from one of the government commissions, the Tribunale della Mercanzia if I recall correctly. After they add the number and source to the list, they pass the document to one of the other notaries or to me. We read each document and highlight all the significant items mentioned in the document."

"What do you mean by 'significant items'?" asked Nico.

"Let me show you."

Galetto lifted a paper from the table where he had been working and held it for Nico to read. "These meeting minutes describe a proposal made to a commission by a representative of the University of Bologna. As you can see, I have highlighted the names of both the University and the representative. I understand you attended the University of Bologna; perhaps you know this person."

"I was a student in the law school at the University of Bologna, but I do not know this man."

Nico noticed that a smile of satisfaction spread across Galetto's face when he confirmed Galetto's recollection of Nico being a graduate of the University of Bologna. Nico wondered if there were records in the archive that had Nico Argenti highlighted as a significant item.

"Each of those sheets fastened to the wall," Galetto said as he gestured to the wall at the far end of the room, "is labeled with a different topic. Together they encompass every possible topic of interest. For example, somewhere on the wall is a sheet labeled 'University of Bologna.' One of the clerks will record the number of this document on that sheet. He will also record the document number on the sheet labeled with the name of the representative. It may sound like a complicated process, and I suppose it is, but if anyone in the future needs to retrieve all information referencing the University of Bologna, the numbers will let him recover all the relevant documents in the archive."

The tone of Galetto's words conveyed his pride in the system. Then, again revealing the extent of his knowledge about Nico, he added, "Magistrates, and soon you will be one, find this method extremely valuable. For the first time, they can recover prior decisions and rulings that might bear on the cases they are adjudicating in their tribunals."

"Would it be possible to recover information about Rimini?" Nico asked.

To answer Nico's query, Galetto led him across the room, where he scanned the array of sheets and quickly found a sheet labeled Rimini. The sheet contained a short list of numbers.

"Our Republic has no direct relationship with the Province

of Rimini, so we have very few records in the archives that mention Rimini. I suspect the documents that we do have are from our embassy to the Papal States in Rome. If Rimini were mentioned in passing to our ambassador during a meeting on a different topic, the ambassador's notes from the meeting would cite Rimini. When the notes were recorded here at the archive, a notary would have highlighted the citation as being significant."

Realizing that Nico's question was more than a hypothetical, Galetto added, "The archives are the property of the Republic, so they are accessible only for official government purposes."

While Nico perused the assortment of other sheets affixed to the wall, the clerk who had been dispatched earlier returned with a response from the 'connector.' The clerk went directly to Nico and said, "He is available to meet with you now. He prefers to meet at the Mugnone rather than here at the annex."

The Mugnone was a small river that paralleled the city walls outside Porta Gallo gate not far from the annex. Across a bridge on the far bank was a clearing that local teams used for their pallone games. It struck Nico that the pallone field was an unlikely choice of meeting place, but the 'connector' always had a reason for his actions.

Nico thanked Galetto for his hospitality and exited the Annex in the direction of the city gate. As he walked along Via Gallo, he reviewed in his mind the record keeping system described to him by the notary.

Record keeping was not a topic discussed during my six years at the law school, Nico thought. In class, we never considered where, or how, to preserve documents. I assumed, as did all the other students, that any information needed by a magistrate would be available whenever it was needed. Was the topic avoided because states do not have systems like the one at the

Chancery archive? Or have others copied the system created by Chancellor Accolti? I cannot imagine how magistrates and government officials coped in the past when record keeping consisted of merely stuffing documents into boxes. How fortunate I am to live in this modern age.

On the bridge crossing the Mugnone, Nico saw two men sitting with the 'connector' on a wooden bench adjacent to the otherwise deserted playing field. They were too far from the bridge for Nico to hear their voices, but he could see the 'connector' speaking and the two men nodding to acknowledge his statements. Before Nico reached the end of the bridge, the conversation had ended, and the two men stood. They were neat and very well dressed in the stylish, well-fitting clothes worn by business owners and bankers. Their neatly trimmed hair looked as though they had just returned from a barber shop. One man wore a gold ring that was large enough to be seen from a distance.

The 'connector' had been sitting between the two men. He wore no jewelry. His hair hung straight down to his shoulders. It was neat and casual, not styled. His clothes could have come from any table of the vendors in the central market. His face had the angular features common to most Florentines and had no distinguishing marks. He was a person that one could spend an evening drinking with in a tavern and then be unable to describe the following morning.

The two men walked across the clearing toward the bridge. They gave a courteous nod to Nico as they passed him. The 'connector' watched Nico as he approached and dropped onto the bench. With no preamble, the 'connector' said, "I imagine the purpose of this encounter stems from your recent interest in Rimini."

At one time, Nico would have been surprised by the 'connector's' insight; however, Nico had grown accustomed to members of the Chancery, especially the 'connector,' having an uncanny knowledge of all happenings in the Republic.

"I would like to speak with the couple from Rimini who recently bought a vineyard in the Chianti region. I understand that the town near their vineyard has a tall tower and that it is possible to see a village across the border in Siena from the top of the tower. I suspect that there is only one town that fits that description and I am hoping you can tell me its name."

The 'connector' answered without a pause, "Indeed there is such a place. It is the town of Castellina. The tower is part of a fortress built to defend the border from incursions by mercenaries from Siena. Fortunately, the Peace of Lodi has ended hostilities between Florence and Siena, so the fortress no longer serves a military function. It has no purpose other than offering an attractive vista to travelers.

"The most traveled road to Siena leaves the Arno River at Empoli and climbs into the hills, passing through the town of Poggibonsi."

"Yes," Nico affirmed, "that is the road I follow when traveling to Siena."

"There is another road that connects to Siena. That road begins here in Florence outside the Porta Romana gate. It passes through the town of Castellina enroute to Siena. The vineyard of Gheraldo and Masina is not far from Castellina."

Nico did not ask the 'connector' how he knew the names of the couple Nico was seeking. The 'connector' waited for Nico to pose any additional questions. Hearing none, the 'connector' said, "Here is advice you should heed."

The 'connector' leaned forward; his expression became serious and intense.

Nico tensed in anticipation.

"Do not travel to Rimini. That province is like a hidden animal trap ready to snare the unwary. The Papacy has an extensive network of informers and spies; there is none larger. They have been growing and refining their network of informers since the early days of the Roman Empire. The Papal Secretariat knows more of the unsavory plots in Milan than Duke Sforza and more of the schemes in the Kingdom of Naples than Ferdinand. But even the Papacy cannot predict events in Rimini. Lord Malcranio is unpredictable. He changes course on a whim without warning."

"Surely, even he is subject to the rule of law. The Papacy must have established tribunalss in Rimini, and those tribunals must be beyond the control of Lord Malcranio." Nico said.

"Courts of the Papal States do operate in Rimini. But the magistrates presiding in those tribunals must be exceedingly careful in the rulings they issue. Any ruling against Malcranio would put them in peril."

Nico had no further questions, and the 'connector' had no additional information to give. After a few moments of silence, the 'connector' rose to leave. He took a few steps and then turned around to face Nico. "It must be disconcerting to have your induction into the guild delayed, but I am certain the opportunities awaiting you afterward will be to your liking."

Nico was taken aback by the 'connector's' mysterious statement regarding his future. It echoed the comment made to him recently by Chancellor Scala. Nico kept telling himself he was not sure which of the openings for new lawyers might appeal most to him, yet the Chancellor and the 'connector' believed they knew. Was he that easy to predict?

Nico watched the 'connector' cross the bridge and pass through the city gate before he rose from the bench. As he returned to the city, Nico recalled an example he had studied while at the university. It was a classic instance of an authoritarian ruler compromising judicial integrity. That situation ended poorly for everyone involved. The monarch had magistrates imprisoned, and shortly thereafter, exploited peasants assassinated the sovereign.

In his mind, Nico replayed his conversation with the 'connector' and reached one conclusion: If Pietra Alta could not obtain a fair ruling in the courts of Rimini there must be another way, or another place, for them to find justice

14

PAPAL ARCHIVES, ROME

A long-standing practice of the Church was for novices studying for the priesthood to be nominated by their bishops for a temporary assignment at the Papacy in Rome. The newcomers benefitted from the unique experience of serving at the Church's seat of power. And the papacy profited, in turn, by having talented workers to perform its many administrative and operational tasks. Many bishops made these appointments because they too benefitted by having an ear at the church's center of power. Regular communication between the bishops and their appointees let the bishops know of any impending changes in advance of official announcements. Shrewd bishops found ways to use that knowledge to enhance their standing among their peers.

Bishops viewed the ideal assignment for their nominees to be at the office of the Papal Secretary. That office made the most important and far reaching decisions. From his appointee in the Secretariat office, a bishop could learn which of his peers had the most significant influence on decisions and directions that the church would follow in the future. Such knowledge had been used to smooth a bishop's elevation to archbishop and even to the more elevated position of cardinal.

Almost as useful were appointees serving in the Papal Archives. The Archive recorded all decisions with details of how and why they were made. The records contained the names of everyone who participated in discussions and their position on the issues. It was easy to tell who among their colleagues were gaining favor and who were losing stature.

Since its earliest days, the Church had been accumulating a vast number of documents. Even the words of Saint Paul, written by his own hand, were claimed to be among the fragile scrolls sealed in tight containers and stored in the basement of the archive. No living person was able to view those writings because merely opening the sealed containers would cause the delicate scrolls to crumble into dust. In contrast to the profound teachings of Saint Paul, most of the documents entered into the archive had little significance. Every time a small, obscure church in a distant province restored a painting or installed a statue, they noted the act and sent a record of their accomplishment to the archive in Rome.

Felipe was the first young novice from the Kingdom of Aragon to be honored with an appointment to the Papal Archive. Felipe expected that his assignment would involve combing the depths of the archive to reveal forgotten documents containing undiscovered Church doctrine. He imagined himself discovering long-hidden writings of Saint Peter or even Jesus. His initial enthusiasm faded when he confronted the reality of the job and came to see himself as little more than a file clerk. Documents were added to the archive every day, but few were ever retrieved. Members of the clergy rarely requested any material. The Archive did accept inquiries from scholars, but their requests tended to concern relatively few subjects. The philosophy of Saint Augustine was one of the more popular topics. It took no great skill for Felipe to locate these oft-requested documents in the well-organized archive.

Finally, after several months of performing the same repetitive tasks day upon day, a request was routed to Felipe that challenged his ability. The query asked simply, 'Is Pietra Alta in the Province of Rimini?' The importance of the inquiry was elevated in Felipe's view because the person making the request was the Archbishop of Lucca, the previous administrator of the Papal Archive.

The Papacy employed a small staff of cartographers to update maps of the Papal States. The Archive kept copies of their creations, and Felipe knew precisely where the copies were stored. He retrieved the most recent map that delineated the outline of the Province of Rimini. He usually viewed documents at his workspace using only light from windows high above, but that light was insufficient for deciphering the small text on the map, text that had been faded by the passage of time. Lanterns were prohibited in the archives to avoid any possibility of fire, so Felipe took the map to a well-lit annex. There he unrolled the sheet and studied it carefully using a magnifying lens before concluding that this map did not show a town named Pietra Alta. He returned to the file to pull an older rendering. Again, the small town was not listed. A third, even older, map did designate Pietra Alta, as well as a nearby village called Pietra Bassa. Unfortunately, the older map did not show provincial boundaries.

Felipe's heart beat faster; this was exciting. This task was his first that demanded any research skill. Both maps showed rivers, mountains, and other landmarks. Felipe used these markers to overlay two of the maps and determine that Pietra Alta was not within the Province of Rimini. He composed a brief answer to the request and presented it to the senior archivist for approval.

"How old is the map that shows the provincial border?" the archivist asked.

"It was prepared sixty years past."

"Who was the Lord of Rimini at that time?"

Felipe wore a baffled expression. He had no idea who ruled the Province of Rimini at that time, nor did he understand the reason for the archivist's question.

Seeing Felipe's confusion, the archivist explained, "Generally, when a new ruler is installed in a province, the charter of the province is revised. The revisions can include changes to the provincial boundaries. I suspect that the current Lord of Rimini has not been in office for sixty years. If that is so, the provincial boundaries may have changed when he was appointed."

There was no way Felipe could have known about changes that made maps inaccurate over time; nonetheless, his ego deflated. Back at his workspace, Felipe struggled to accept his shortcoming. He sat with his face buried in his hands and contemplated his failure. What he considered as a proud achievement only moments ago was now testimony to his ignorance. Felipe crumpled the query letter, squeezing it tightly in his fist, smaller and smaller, wishing it to vanish.

In a flash, his commiseration ended. The senior archivist had not admonished him for failure; he had used it as an opportunity for Felipe to learn, to grow. Felipe jumped up from his stool and walked briskly, almost running, down a long corridor to the shelves holding the provincial charters. He lifted the thick, dusty file labeled 'Rimini' and carried it to his workspace.

As the archivist had anticipated, the most recent map that depicted the provincial boundaries was older than the current Lord of Rimini, a man named Sergio Malcranio. An earlier charter revealed that the map even predated the appointment of Malcranio's father. Felipe read both charter documents. The oldest charter revision added highlands extending to the peak of Mount Contarini. Felipe located the mountain on the map and concluded that this revision did not alter the boundary in the vicinity of Pieta Alta. Next, he examined the more recent charter, the one issued at the time of Lord Malcranio's appointment. The report stated that the Papal Court was considering whether to include the diocese of San Martino in the Province of Rimini. The statement demanded Felipe expand his research.

Maps did not show dioceses, so first, Felipe had to find the location and boundaries of the diocese of San Martino. Then, if the diocese did include the town of Pietra Alta, he needed to find the ruling of the Papal Court to learn whether Rimini did gain control of the diocese. This challenging problem was precisely what Felipe had wanted but soon realized that he needed help to address it. He consulted another priest who worked in the archives, a permanent member of the staff, who told Felipe where to find the documents that described dioceses. Felipe's search for those records took him to parts of the archive that were new to him. After sifting through folios that were arranged neither by date nor location, he finally found the information he sought. A single musty sheet told him that Pietra Alta was not part of the San Martino diocese. Knowing that the town was not in the diocese of San Martino, saved him from needing to research outcomes of the Papal Court.

Felipe returned to the senior archivist, confident that his earlier conclusion was correct. "You have done well," the archivist announced. "The evidence is convincing, Pietra Alta is not part of the Province of Rimini. You may send your finding to the bishop if you wish."

Felipe turned to leave, then stopped. What did the archivist mean by the phrase 'if you wish'? he wondered.

Felipe turned back to face the archivist who was smiling in his direction. "I am pleased that you listened carefully to my words," the archivist said, "Your research proves that Pietra Alta is not within Rimini, and that is indeed the question that the archbishop asked; however if you wish to impress him you could give a more enlightening answer to his query."

Felipe's expression changed slowly as he considered what the archivist was suggesting. Finally, Felipe said, as much to himself as to the archivist, "If Pietra Alta is not part of Rimini, it could be an independent commune, or it could be part of another state."

"Very good. The archbishop's query was brief, so we do not know the reason for his question. Perhaps the information you already uncovered is sufficient, but providing a broader response can often be helpful."

Following the same approach he had used researching the boundaries of Rimini, Felipe examined the maps to find other states near Pietra Altra. He saw only the Duchy of Urbino, and he could find no evidence to connect the Duchy of Urbino with Pietra Alta. With the approval of the senior archivist, Felipe dispatched a response to the query: 'Records of the Papal Archives confirm that Pietra Alta is an independent commune and not incorporated into any Province or Duchy.'

15

CASTELLINA, TUSCANY

Nico had no intention of going to Rimini, so the travel warning he had received from the 'connector' was of no concern. However, the 'connector's' caution that magistrates in Rimini were fearful of issuing rulings against Lord Malcranio was significant. For Nico to give any meaningful advice to the priors of Pietra Alta, he needed to know how the Province of Rimini, and more specifically Lord Malcranio, would view a claim of independence by the town. Because Pietra Alta was a small town, Rimini might be willing to dismiss the entire matter. But if the letters at Lucca were correct, a vindictive Malcranio might take an assertion by Pietra Alta as an affront. Nico needed an understanding of the sensitivities in the province. He decided to follow Alessa's suggestion to speak with someone from Rimini. He set out for the town of Castellina to find the new vineyard owners, Gheraldo and Masina, who might provide him with useful insights.

Many folks believed that the rolling hills of the Chianti region were the most beautiful landscape in the Florentine Republic. Legends said that in ancient times the hills were forested, but in all living memories, they have been carpeted with vineyards. Vintners claimed, only partly in jest, that their signature wine consistently achieved excellence because Bacchus, the ancient god of wine, made his home in the Chianti hills. Several roads rose into the highlands from the Arno River valley. The one that the 'connector' had recommended to Nico was flanked on both sides by vineyards as far as his eye could see.

Harvest was at least three weeks in the future, yet vines were already heavily laden with bunches of juicy Sangiovese grapes. In the extensive vineyards, those owned by wealthy Florentines, teams of men were passing through the rows fastening vines to trellises to support the weighty crops. In smaller vineyards, the task of protecting delicate vines fell to the vineyard owners and their wives.

Lower sections of the road, the portion between the Arno River and the town of Panzano, were heavily traveled by farmers in wagons and merchants on horseback. The final section leading to Castellina had very little traffic. Nico met only one rider who was heading down to the Arno valley, from either Castellina or the more distant Republic of Siena.

Then, in a place where the curves in the road lined up just right, he glimpsed a wagon far ahead. Gradually the image of the wagon grew larger, leading him to believe that it was moving toward him. However, when he drew close enough, it became clear that the wagon was actually heading in the same direction as he but doing so at a plodding pace. On the upward sloping road, the vehicle filled with farm produce was a heavy burden for the single donkey pulling it. To ease its effort, the farmer, who usually sat atop the cart, had climbed down and was walking beside the donkey, speaking words of encouragement.

The farmer's chapped lips, cracked skin, and calloused

hands marked him as one who had spent a lifetime working the soil. As Nico drew alongside the wagon, he reached into the sack attached to his saddle and pulled out a flask. He held it out, offering it to the farmer. "Water?"

The farmer answered Nico by accepting the flask and taking two large gulps.

"This is a long way to come from the valley," Nico said. "There are markets in the towns that we passed. Can you not sell your produce to one of them?"

"Many others sell produce to those markets. With so many selling to the same markets, the prices are low. I am the only one who travels to the market in Castellina, where my vegetables fetch better prices." The farmer took one more swig before returning the flask to Nico. Then he added, "And I always return home with a load of grape skins and seeds from one of the vineyards. Vintners are happy to be rid of the remains after they have squeezed out the juice."

"Do you process the skins and seeds into liquor?" Nico asked.

"I do not process them myself. I bring them to a monastery where Jesuit monks make them into grappa. In exchange for the skins, they give me a share of the grappa. The potent liquor keeps me warm throughout the winter." He grinned and pulled a small bottle of the clear liquor from under the wagon seat and held it out toward Nico. "Would you like a taste?"

Nico thanked the farmer but declined the offer.

"I travel this road every week and have never met anyone else traveling to Castellina," declared the farmer, "so I suppose you are traveling to Siena."

Nico responded, "Today the goddess Fortuna must be scampering through these hills for Castellina is also my destination,"

Nico's invoking the name of the mythological goddess of

good fortune amused the farmer because his son, Enzio, occasionally did the same. When Enzio was young, the farmer thought, he knew only two ancient dieties, mighty Zeus and Venus. What red-blooded Florentine youth isn't captivated by sculptures and paintings featuring Venus' bare breasts? It was after Enzio returned from the university as an apothecary that he began inserting the names of mythological beings into otherwise normal conversation. Could it be that students at the universities are taught to speak that way?

Nico interrupted the farmer's thought. "I am seeking a couple from Rimini who recently purchased a vineyard near Castellina. Since you travel to Castellina frequently might you know of them?"

"No," the farmer answered without taking time to reflect on Nico's question. "My only acquaintance in Castellina is the owner of the market. You should ask him about the people you seek. Everyone in town buys from him, so he is sure to know them."

Energized by the brief respite, the farmer grasped the reins and coaxed his donkey to resume its slow plodding along the road. Nico gave the farmer a parting wave and rode on ahead, his horse quickly outdistancing the weary donkey.

The San Salvatore church spire came into view first, then moments later, the fortress tower beyond it became visible as Nico approached the town. He passed through the Castellina city gate and ahead, in a stone building across from the church, stood a toolmaker's shop and a food market, the one that the farmer had described. Nico entered the market and scanned the display of produce. Along one wall, bins contained an assortment of vegetables brought by farmers like the one Nico had passed on the road. Above the bins, a shelf held small containers of honey, fruit preserves, and spices.

A loud cracking sound startled Nico and drew his attention

to the rear of the shop where he saw the flash of a cleaver slamming down and cracking the bone of a lamb being butchered. The butcher's firm biceps suggested that he had long experience at his trade. When he noticed Nico, he set down the blade, wiped his hands, and with a slight limp, came forward to greet the new customer.

A small table off to the side held a collection of fresh citrus fruit, lemons, and kumquats, that must have come from Calabria or Sicily. Citrus fruits are available throughout the summer in the central market at Florence, but it was not common to see them in small town markets.

Nico asked about them, and the shopkeeper replied, "Many wealthy Florentines own vineyards outside the town. They enjoy escaping the noise and heat of the city by spending time at villas in these hills. They all have servants who bring fruit and other comforts relished by the owners. When they return to Florence, the servants sell any remaining goods, such as the fruit, rather than carry them back to Florence. The people of Castellina benefit by having access to the fruit, and the servants benefit from the touch of silver coins."

Although Nico had come to the market solely to obtain information about the couple from Rimini, he felt that courtesy demanded that he repay the shopkeeper for any help by making a purchase. "I have come to Castellina to visit a couple from Rimini who recently purchased a vineyard nearby. Might you know of them?"

"Yes, Gheraldo and Masina, a delightful young couple. They shop here regularly. They bought Gustovino's vineyard. Old Gustovino was sorry to sell, but caring for the plants got to be too much work for him. City people think that vintners sit around and watch the grapes grow, but that is far from the truth. Owning a vineyard means being out in the sun and soil every day. My son works at a small vineyard. The sun stains his skin, and dirt never leaves his hands."

"I would like to bring them a gift to wish them well in their new venture. Is there something you might suggest?"

"Masina was here just yesterday. She looked wistfully at the honey lemons. She asked the price and was disappointed to find that they cost more than she could spend."

"I have never heard of honey lemons," Nico admitted.

The shopkeeper picked a fruit from the bin beside him.

"Honey lemon is her name for these large round lemons. She said they are grown in Calabria and are the sweetest of any variety of lemon. Maybe they are known elsewhere by a different name."

Nico took the lemon that the shopkeeper handed to him. It was larger than most lemons, yellow but with a pinkish cast, and round rather than oval shaped. He purchased four of the attractive fruits, paying twice the amount charged for similar items in the central market at Florence.

As a way of asking for directions without confessing that he didn't know the location of the couple's vineyard, Nico said, "What road is most direct to their vineyard?"

The shopkeeper cracked a smile. "Castellina is not Florence with its city gates and roads leading in all directions. Pass through the gate to the south; there is only one, then follow the first road leading west. Gheraldo's house is about two miles distant. You will see the stone house with a crucifix mounted about the door."

He noticed Nico's surprise at the mention of the crucifix. "Masina is very devout. She attends mass three days every week. On many days she and Father Giuseppe are the only ones."

The shopkeeper's directions made it easy to find the house Nico was seeking. The house was set back far from the road, but the crucifix was easily visible as Nico approached. He followed a dirt pathway to the house, which was set at the top of a slight rise. Listening for any sound, he heard only the chickens scratching in the dirt, as the thick stone walls and a heavy wooden door kept any sounds inside the house from escaping. The was no knocker, so Nico rapped on the door. His first attempt went unanswered. Shortly after his second more vigorous rapping, the door slowly swung inward enough to frame a woman standing in the opening.

She was much shorter than Nico, and thin, although not frail. Her simple smock had fresh smudges of dirt, suggesting that she had been working in the vineyard earlier in the day. Her dark hair was pulled back into a short horse tail that reached only to her shoulders. She wore a thin gold necklace whose pendant was hidden by her smock.

Her deep brown eyes looked up at the stranger; they showed concern over the visit of this tall, well-dressed stranger. Deeper down, her eyes held disappointment and sorrow, and underlying all was fear. Looking at her, at her eyes, Nico suddenly felt that he was about to intrude into a past she wished to forget but could not. Nico introduced himself then, presuming the woman to be Masina, he said, "I would like to speak to you and your husband about Rimini."

At the mention of Rimini, the woman froze. Nico saw a change in her eyes, but he could not know her fear or the horrible memories that she would never be able to forget. She never wanted to speak of Rimini again, not with this stranger, not with anyone. It took a few moments before she was able to respond to Nico.

"Gheraldo is my brother, not my husband. He may be willing to speak with you." Anxiously she added, "He is work-ing. I was about to bring him lunch."

Nico realized that his mention of Rimini was making the

woman uneasy, almost terrified, but it was not possible to retract his words, like a bell having been struck and sounded could not be silenced. His best course now would be to leave her and find Gheraldo. Nico offered, "I could bring the lunch to him."

Masina nodded slowly, turned, and walked into the house, leaving Nico standing alone outside. Moments later, she returned with a basket which she held out to Nico; then she pointed in the direction of a small rise. With clipped speech, she said, "Gheraldo is beyond that hill."

She stepped back into the house and started to close the door when Nico handed her the small bag he had been carrying. He smiled. "For you. Honey lemons."

With a puzzled expression, Masina looked down at the bag, then up at Nico. "Thank you," she said softly as she reached for the sack, then she pushed the door closed.

Nico followed a path between rows of grape vines in the direction Masina had indicated. At the top of the hill, all the vines near him had been fastened to trellis supports. At the bottom of the hill, vines sagged under the weight of dense clusters of grapes. Part way down the backside of the slope, where near met far, Gheraldo bent to secure one of the vines to a trellis with a strip of cloth.

Gheraldo noticed Nico as soon as he crested the hill, but the sighting did not cause Gheraldo to stop or slow his work. He resisted interruptions because many more vines needed tending, and the entire burden of maintaining the vineyard fell upon him and his sister. Walking down the hill, Nico watched as Gheraldo carefully lifted each branch, taking care not to break it by extreme bending. He then held it against a support with one hand while using his other hand to wrap it with a strip of cloth that he tied loosely, so the fabric did not cut into any tender shoots. As soon as one branch was secured, he repeated the process on the next sagging vine.

When Nico reached the place where Gheraldo was working, he held out the lunch basket so Gheraldo could see it. Gheraldo's face brightened because lunch was a valid excuse to pause in his seemingly endless task. "As soon as I finish this row," he declared.

Nico bent down alongside Gheraldo, lifted a vine, and held it in place so Gheraldo could fasten it to the trellis. The two men working together quickly finished the row. After a glance to appraise his work, Gheraldo straightened, wiped his hands with a handkerchief pulled from a pocket, and pointed to a low boulder where he and Nico could sit to eat.

Despite her apprehension caused by the stranger asking about Rimini, Masina had thoughtfully packed enough into the lunch basket for both men. Gheraldo removed items from the basket while Nico reflected on the vineyard that his uncle Nunzio owned in the hills north of Florence. Nunzio's vineyard was larger than this one, and Nunzio was too old to do much of the work himself, so he employed a crew of workmen to assist him. Gheraldo maintained his vineyard with help only from his sister. It was, as the butcher had said, not easy work.

After introducing himself, Nico asked, "Is this what you expected when you bought the vineyard?"

Gheraldo wiped sweat from his forehead before answering. "It is better than I expected. In my hometown...my former hometown, I worked for three years in the autumn, helping a neighbor harvest and process his crop. Here the vines here more bountiful, and they are mine, so I do not mind the work."

Looking at Nico, he said, "Thank you for your help finishing that last row. Plants can be tied in place much more quickly by two people. Masina helps when she is not doing other chores."

His expression became more serious. "I appreciate your

help; however, I doubt that you came here seeking work. You must have another purpose."

After seeing Masina's reaction to his mention of Rimini, Nico was apprehensive about how Gheraldo would react as he said, "I would like to ask you about Rimini."

Gheraldo showed no response whatsoever; he continued eating and waited for Nico to elaborate.

Nico described the Pietra Alta incident, his involvement, and the indictments of the Lord of Rimini that the bishop had shown him in Lucca. Gheraldo listened attentively absorbing all the details.

"It may be sinful for me to doubt declarations made by the Church," Nico said, "but they are so egregious that I feel a need to have them corroborated by someone who lives, or has lived, in Rimini, someone with personal knowledge of life in that Province."

"Some of those accusations are certainly truthful. Lust is but one of the evils that spur Lord Malcranio. I do not know the full extent of his depravity, only that he takes pleasure with Sisters of the Church. Masina was a nun at the convent of Saint Agnes. She heard rumors of Malcranio's behavior from nuns at other convents. Then, one day, two nuns at her convent, friends of hers, were taken by members of the palace guard. The nuns never returned to the convent. Day-upon-day, I saw my sister's suffering grow. She could not forget the fate of her friends and the dread of never knowing if she might become the next victim. That is why we left Rimini. I could not let Masina remain at that convent, knowing what might happen to her."

"How can the Papacy allow this to continue? How can they allow Malcranio to remain as lord of the Province when he is guilty of such inhumanities?" Nico asked.

"Malcranio has been excommunicated. The Holy Father has rescinded Malcranio's power to govern, yet he remains in control. Madonna Isolla, his mistress, now governs by his side. Some say Isolla tries to temper his actions, but his soul is too black ever to be cleansed. I do not understand how his reign continues."

The documents Nico viewed at Lucca did not mention excommunication. Gheraldo's statement meant the denunciations made against Malcranio extended beyond those the bishop had shown him. Nico spoke his thoughts aloud, "So, all the accusations in the bishop's documents must be valid."

"Some of them certainly, but perhaps not all of them," Gheraldo corrected. "Rimini and Urbino have long quarreled over their common border. For that reason, the charges levied by the Duke of Urbino may be suspect. His indictment might be self-serving. There is no way to know."

Gheraldo paused, and Nico could see he was struggling with another thought, unsure how, or whether, to express it. Finally, he divulged the paradox. "Malcranio is a slave to his lust, yet he is favored by many in Rimini who are not victims of his debauchery. He surrounds himself with scholars and artists. That could be an attempt to create an image of himself as an enlightened ruler so people will admire him, as they admire Cosimo de Medici. He assembled a collection of paintings by accomplished artists and exhibits them for viewing by all citizens of the Province. He has engaged skilled architects to construct a building exclusively for those works of art. A neighbor of mine said those actions prove that stories of Lord Malcranio's misdeeds are untrue. But he is mistaken, of that I am certain. Two young nuns were taken when Masina was at the convent. She saw soldiers grab the two women and take them away. The soldiers were members of the palace guard. Some people claim, and I believe them, that it is Isolla who is responsible for any charitable acts done in Rimini."

Gheraldo stopped speaking, unsure of what else he could

tell Nico. Masina had come into the vineyard. She stood behind the two men silently listening to their conversation. "We all harbor good and evil," she said, revealing her presence, "All we can do is nurture the good and ask God's help in suppressing the evil."

After they finished eating, Nico volunteered to help Gheraldo tie the remaining plants in the partially completed rows. The physical labor was refreshing, and Gheraldo was a pleasant person with exciting stories about his time in Rimini. He loved the people and the natural beauty of Rimini; it was only Malcranio that made life there unbearable. Since Gheraldo did not need her help, Masina thanked Nico for the honey lemons and returned to the house.

As he left the farm, Nico thought about Masina's assertion that a single person could harbor extremes of both good and evil. He was a student of law, not human behavior, yet he wondered if there was a different explanation for the humanitarian acts in Rimini. Might Isolla's influence eventually change what was happening in Rimini?

Nico returned from the vineyard to the town of Castellina, and from there he headed south toward Siena. His pulse quickened at the prospect of spending time with Bianca.

16

SIENA

Bianca always engaged with her customers at their homes. She found that familiar surroundings made people comfortable and, therefore, more accepting of new fashion trends. None of her customers ever visited the shop where she designed and created her unique fashions, so she had no reason to rent an expensive storefront in the central business district of Siena. Her modest loft sat above a candle maker's shop on a quiet side street far from the often-hectic center of the city. Having a guardia office nearby guaranteed that the district was free from crime, so Bianca always felt secure walking from the shop to her apartment even late in the evenings when the streets were dark. Bianca's business was a growing and profitable endeavor, yet her father insisted on paying the rent for both the loft and her apartment. It was one of the ways he expressed pride in his daughter's accomplishments.

Nico climbed the steep steps to the second level loft and pushed open the door. Light from the bright work room streamed into the darkened stairwell. Bianca was fortunate to have found a loft with a bright workspace made possible by large windows along two sides of the room. As soon as Nico's eyes adjusted to the light, they locked on Bianca, who was cutting fabric at a table across the room. He barely noticed the other young women at work in the loft, one who was sewing and one who was measuring lengths from a bolt of cloth. Nico stepped softly to a position directly behind Bianca. He placed a hand on each side of her waist, leaned down, and kissed her neck.

Without revealing that his reflection in the window had signaled his approach, Bianca remained motionless and uttered coquettishly, "Is that you, Paolo? No, maybe you are Giulio or Claudio. With so many lovers, it is impossible for me to be sure."

Then, unable to contain herself any longer, she turned and rose in one smooth motion into Nico's embrace. They both stood silent for a long moment, enjoying each other's warmth. A tender kiss on the lips, a nuzzle of her ear, another kiss on the lips, this one longer. While still clasping Bianca's hand, Nico stepped back and held out the package of silk fabric, the gift from Bluffo.

"Oh, this must be from Armando," Bianca said as she unwrapped the package.

She unfolded a length of fabric and held it aloft with outstretched arms. The two young girls ran to where Bianca was standing. "It's beautiful!" one girl exclaimed. "I've never seen anything like it," said the other girl.

Nico hadn't heard anyone use Bluffo's given name in such a long time that it sounded almost unfamiliar to him. Nico waited for the girls' excitement to wane before asking Bianca, "How do you know Armando?"

"All of the silk for the fashions I create comes from his shop," Bianca explained. "We have no silk producers in Siena, and his fabrics are exquisite."

"He said this is a gift that you should use to make something special for a special person."

"Yes, I will use it to make something special. Next month Princess Isabella of Castile will celebrate her thirteenth birthday, one of the most important events of her young life. Members of the Castilian royal court are planning a lavish ball to mark the event. Royalty, nobles, and other dignitaries from many nations will attend. The Florentine ambassador to Castile thinks it would be a triumph for Florence if the princess were to appear at the ball wearing a dress of Florentine silk. The ambassador sought support for his idea from Armando, who enthusiastically agreed with the proposal. I am surprised that Armando did not mention this to you.

"The ambassador was delighted with the fabrics that Armando showed to him, but he was not pleased when Armando suggested that I be the one to design the dress. He wanted the creation to come from a Florentine dress maker, but Armando insisted that I must be the designer. To convince the ambassador, Armando asked that I make a cotta alla catalana for the ambassador's wife."

Perplexed, Nico said, "Cotta alla catalana sounds more like a food preparation than a style of clothing."

"Yes, the term is usually associated with food. It means cooked as they do in Catalonia," Bianca replied, "but in this case, it refers to a style of dresses and blouses that are gaining popularity in Castile. Maybe the term came into use because the dress styling originated in Catalonia, but that is just my guess. I made a blouse in that style using fabric that Armando provided. The blouse was so lovely that I am now making another for one of my customers who enjoys wearing the latest styles. Armando had the blouse delivered to the ambassador's wife, and she loved it. She convinced the ambassador that Armando and I should collaborate."

Nico's visit provided an opportunity for Bianca to take a respite from work. She decided that the best way for Nico and her to share their precious time was to take a relaxing walk in the countryside.

"First, we must stop at the hospital so I can invite my father and mother to dinner later at my apartment."

With their fingers entwined, Bianca and Nico left her loft and headed toward Santa Maria della Scala hospital, where Bianca's father was a surgeon.

Nico said, "Visiting the hospital will give me a chance to see Sandro's paintings. He was commissioned by the hospital directors to create nine paintings. Sandro told me that he had already completed three of them, and they are exhibited in a corridor at the hospital."

When they reached the hospital, the nun who welcomed visitors told them that Dottore Manzio Cellini was with a patient, but she would deliver Bianca's dinner invitation to him. Bianca had seen Sandro's paintings on a previous visit to the hospital when she saw Sandro supervising the installation of his third painting. She led Nico to the corridor where the artwork was displayed. Nico had little knowledge of art, but he had become a fancier of Sandro's works ever since Sandro explained his inspiration for the painting Aphrodite and Adonis, the one in which he modeled Aphrodite on Francesca Pitti. Sandro Botticelli believed that using people he knew as models for his paintings added a dimension of reality.

As they viewed one painting, Bianca said, "These are the three Charities, Aglaea, Euphrosyne, and Thalia."

Nico stepped back in stunned admiration, "Amazing. How could you possibly know that?"

With a mischievous grin on her face, Bianca lifted his hand and kissed it lightly.

"Have I never told you that I am a fancier of Greek mythology?" she teased.

Nico folded his arms across his chest and tilted his head to adopt a skeptical posture. He knew she was teasing.

A broad smile spread across Bianca's face as she confessed, "I spoke with Sandro the last time I was at the hospital. He described all his works to me. You know that I am just a simple country girl who has never studied the Greek legends. Sandro is the expert on Greek mythology. He said the Charities represent beauty, good cheer, and festivities."

Nico recalled hearing of the Greek myth about the Charities, but he did not admit that he knew neither their names nor the qualities they represented.

After viewing the paintings, they walked from the hospital to the nearest city gate. Outside the gate, they stopped to admire the vista. Their hilltop vantage point afforded an unobstructed view of the valley below.

Nico asked in a soft, tentative voice, "Have you ever considered leaving Siena?"

Bianca turned abruptly, taken aback by his unexpected question. What could make him think of leaving all the beauty arrayed before them, she wondered. Seeing her puzzlement, Nico tried to explain the basis for his question.

"The fabric for the clothes you make comes from Florence, and many of your customers are in Florence."

He thought, but did not find the courage to say, if you come to Florence, we can be together.

Although she hadn't expected Nico to broach the subject, she responded quickly. "I have mulled the idea of expanding my business into the Venetian Republic. Women in Venice crave new and unusual fashions even more than the women of Florence. Verona and Padua are other cities that could be promising opportunities as well. Florence does have the advantage of being closer than Siena to all those cities. Maybe some-day..." She let her voice trail off with the statement unfinished.

From the quickness of her response, Nico realized that she had already given thought to the possibility of moving to Florence, although he found her mention of Venice and the other cities disconcerting. His expression brightened until she added, "But my family is in Siena."

He had not rehearsed the conversation in advance. He had not planned where it should lead or what he should say. They both knew that Bianca's business interests were not what prompted Nico's initial question, but neither were they quite ready for a serious discussion about a possible future together.

Their walk followed a route along the perimeter of the city walls, affording them a rare opportunity to be alone in each other's company. At every gate there was a vista where they paused to admire the view. At each stop, Nico stepped behind Bianca and wrapped his arms around her, and she leaned back into his embrace. They set a slow pace. Before they made even a half turn around the city, an old man and his dog, who were also following the city wall, had passed them twice.

They re-entered the city at Porta Tufi, where a nearby market sold the items that Bianca wanted for the dinner with her parents, herbs for a pesto sauce, root vegetables, and a large black grouse prepped for roasting. An enoteca near her apart-ment offered a selection of wines from which they chose a white blend from the Umbrian commune of Orvieto. Having spent much of the past six years at Bologna, Nico had little knowledge of Umbrian wines, but his cousin Donato had intro-duced him to a fruity blend from Orvieto which quickly became his favorite.

Cooking facilities in Bianca's apartment did not include an oven, but the courtyard behind the building had an outdoor oven that the tenants shared. While Nico monitored the grouse roasting in the oven, Bianca worked inside preparing a pasta first course. Her parents had already arrived when Nico returned to the apartment carrying the succulent bird.

Nico had met Bianca's parents, Manzio and Dorena, only once before on a brief visit to Siena. Before that meeting, Bianca had told Nico how her parents met while her father was teaching in the medical school at the University of Salerno. Nico assumed that she had also told her parents about him, and that assumption was proven correct when her mother asked, "Have you received word on when you will be inducted into the guild?"

That led to more questions that Nico answered while Bianca served the first course, pasta with pesto. As they began eating, he described his interest in the plight of Pietra Alta.

"Thinking back to the cases we studied at the University, they all seem simplistic compared with this. We studied basic inheritance cases where two people claimed ownership of the same property. In class, we always assumed that both people were willing participants, and there was never a question as to which tribunal had jurisdiction to hear the case. I am finding that the real world is much more complicated. I am not at all certain whether Pietra Alta has a valid claim, and if they do, who is the defendant, the Lord of Rimini, the Province of Rimini, or the Papal States? Nor is it clear which jurisdiction should hear the claim."

After mentioning all the uncertainties, Nico stopped speaking, worried that Manzio and Dorena might find the subject boring. But that was not the case. Bianca's father leaned forward in his seat, intrigued by the situation that paralleled his own experience.

"Do not be too critical of the university. Medical schools follow a similar approach. When I taught at Salerno, we concentrated on situations that are most likely to be encountered by students, and we did that for a good reason. Young physicians need expertise in diagnosing and treating the most common illnesses. I spent long hours in the classroom, drilling my students on conditions they will face frequently. Very few of them will encounter rare diseases, and those who do can consult with their more experienced colleagues."

Manzio reached up and stroked his chin as another parallel formed in his thoughts.

"To render the best treatment, a physician must gather as much information as possible. We analyze symptoms, and we ask about patient history. I suppose the situation in your profession is the of gathering evidence. Have you begun gathering evidence?"

Before Nico could answer, Bianca stood to clear the dishes of the pasta course. That was Nico's cue to carve the roasted grouse for the second course. The table in Bianca's apartment was not large enough to accommodate four dinner plates plus serving platters, so each person fixed a plate in the kitchen area and carried it to the table. After they returned to the table, Nico did not respond directly to the question asked earlier by Manzio, saying instead, "The evidence I gathered in Lucca may not make the best dinner conversation."

Bianca's parents looked at each other and laughed, then Manzio said, "I am a surgeon. My telling you what I did earlier today would not make proper dinner conversation. Anything short of that is acceptable."

Dorena added, "After years of listening to Manzio's experiences at the hospital, I have a high tolerance for the unseemly."

At their insistence, Nico described his visit to Lucca and the documents shown to him by the bishop. "The Papal edict leaves no doubt regarding the position of the Church, but it is based on hearsay. Although the Holy Father authored the condemnation, he never actually witnessed any of the atrocities himself. I wanted to hear from people with direct knowledge of the situation, and that is why I interviewed the couple in Castellina. They have lived in Rimini, and they painted a picture of the Lord of Rimini as being conflicted. He has done terrible things, of that there is no doubt. Despite his brutalities, the woman leans toward tolerance. She said his actions mean that he has within him both good and evil."

Bianca's father broke into a broad grin and practically bounced out of his chair at the opportunity to share another anecdote from his experience as a medical school professor.

"A colleague of mine at Salerno believed that specific areas of the brain determine behavior. He could never prove his theory, but he did give a convincing lecture using examples of people who changed their behavior after suffering brain injuries. He believed that evil could be eliminated by removing part of the brain."

In a more deliberate voice, he added, "Unfortunately for him, the Church decided that his theory contradicted the teachings of Saint Augustine. Augustine taught that man has the will to choose whether to do good or evil. They could not accept the idea that physical characteristics can force men to sin. Pressure from the Church forced my colleague to be dismissed by the university. He was a creative thinker and an excellent teacher, so his dismissal was a big loss to the school."

Bianca changed the direction of the conversation by asking, "Does the Papacy have a military to enforce laws and discipline in its territories?"

Nico answered, "There is a Papal Army, but its primary mission is the defense of Rome. The Papal Army is not large enough to adequately control the vast territory of the Papal States. In outlying areas, the provinces and duchies employ mercenaries for security and to enforce their laws. The use of mercenaries is effective when the ruler of the territory has integrity, but not where the ruler is a tyrant."

Manzio said, "One month past, an officer of the Papal Army was brought to the hospital here in Siena for treatment of a serious injury. He was thrown from a horse during a maneuver, and Santa Maria della Scala was the closest hospital. We spoke often during his recovery. He is part of a contingent under the command of Captain Malvezzi stationed at Perugia. He was careful not to speak of their mission, but their presence in Perugia means the Papal Army does have at least a small force outside Rome. Malvezzi has an outstanding record of victories and a reputation for sound judgement."

The conversation continued after dinner on a range of topics while they drained the three bottles of wine. Bianca's parents listened intently, hoping to detect clues about her relationship with Nico, although neither of them broached the subject directly. Nico also listened to discern whether Manzio already had a plan for his daughter's future. Most women of Bianca's age were married. As a surgeon, Manzio's substantial compensation would enable him to offer a generous dowry. His position at the hospital let him associate with young doctors. Nico wondered whether Manzio had selected a promising young doctor as a suitor for Bianca. But Nico reminded himself that Bianca rejected many traditions that society imposed on women. She lived in her own apartment rather than with her parents, and she had established her own business. Both of her parents supported and encouraged her independence. Would they also grant her the freedom to select her mate? By the end of the evening, Nico had answers to none of these questions.

17

FLORENCE

Nico tried not to think of Bianca during his return to Florence. He diverted his mind by admiring patches of wildflowers alongside the road, he watched hawks circling above, and he cast enthusiastic greetings to every traveler he passed.

If he thought about her, he would miss her.

He thought about her, and he missed her.

While they were together, he should have asked when she would be making her next delivery to a client in Florence. He should have invited her to the upcoming birthday celebration for Uncle Nunzio, but it didn't occur to him to do so. Fortunately, the peace treaty between Florence and Siena had provided for an efficient courier service between the two cities, so it was possible to remedy his lapse and extend the invitation by letter. Couriers would not know how to deliver a message to Signorina Bianca Cellini, but they could deliver messages to her father, Dottore Manzio Cellini, at Santa Maria della Scala hospital.

During the remainder of the journey, Nico replayed in his mind the previous evening's dinner with Bianca's parents. His thoughts did not return to the present until he arrived at casa Argenti. He went directly to the dining salon for a glass of lemon water to relieve his parched throat. An elaborate gold-trimmed envelope addressed to him had been placed prominently on the dining table. Nico took a generous swig of lemon water before reading the letter. The parchment carried the seal of the Archbishop of Lucca. The short note read, 'Enclosed is the finding of the Papal Archive.' The archbishop had signed the note and stamped the signature with his personal seal.

The enclosure was plain paper, not official Papal stationery. It was not signed, and it had no official seal. It too was brief and stated simply 'The records of the Papal Archive show Pietra Alta to be an independent jurisdiction and not part of the Province of Rimini.'

That finding was exactly what Nico needed to begin formulating advice for Pietra Alta. Nico refilled his glass and sat back to consider the legal alternatives. Laymen might conclude that the determination of the Papal Archive would be enough to ensure a ruling by a tribunal in favor of Pietra Alta, but six years of law school had taught Nico that legal matters were never that straightforward. Any competent lawyer would explore every eventuality, and Nico was determined to be more than just competent.

He closed his eyes to visualize cases he had studied at the university. Without looking, he reached for the glass of lemon water, and instead his fingers closed on the archbishop's note. Touching the wax impression made by the archbishop's seal brought forth a vision of the archbishop's ring, the silver and gold ring bearing the Cross of Constantine.

Accompanying the vision was the echo of the archbishop's parting words, 'Malcranio's vile behavior has persisted or too long. His domain cannot be allowed to expand any further.'

What did those words mean? Were the Priors of Constantine planning to take action against Malcranio? Did they have the resources to do so? In the past two weeks, Nico had encountered two members of the clergy who displayed the symbol of the Priors of Constantine. Nico felt that he needed to understand the mysterious Priors, and if anyone could help him do so, it would be Chancellor Scala. Scala always took lunch at an osteria near the Palazzo dei Signoria. Nico decided to meet the Chancellor for an informal lunch so he could ask about the Priors without interrupting the Chancellor at his office.

The osteria was similar to the one owned by his friend Stephano. Tempting aromas greeted Nico as soon as he entered. He spotted Scala sitting alone at a table in one corner of the room.

"The soup today is chilled cucumber," Scala announced as Nico approached his table. "The soup changes every day and every day it is delicious. The soups are what brings me here whenever I am in the city."

"I apologize for interrupting your meal, Chancellor, but I am hoping you can help me to understand something."

Scala held his soup-filled spoon motionless, waiting for Nico to finish his request.

"The Priors of Constantine," Nico said, completing his request.

Scala emptied the spoon. "The only thing that can make your visit here worthwhile is the soup because I regret to say, my knowledge of the Priors is limited."

Nico, who had been standing, settled into a chair across from Scala. He was sure that modesty was the motivation for Scala's statement. He mouthed the word soup to a server. The server nodded to acknowledge Nico's bid and headed to the kitchen.

"You already know the Priors are a secretive sect of priests committed to defending the Church. They employ means that are not always in keeping with civil and canon law."

"How do they determine when to act? Who makes those decisions?" Nico asked.

"Rather than having me answer those questions, I suggest that you seek the answers in the archive at the Chancery Annex. You will find it more satisfying to do the research yourself, but do not expect to find much even in the archive. The Priors have always been careful to hide their activities."

Nico gave a dismissive shrug. "A notary at the archive made it clear that I am not permitted to access the archive until I am inducted into the Magistrates Guild."

"That obstruction is easily eliminated," Scala said.

Scala had the server bring him a writing pad. He penned a short directive: Grant Signor Nico Argenti unfettered access to the archive. He signed the note, B. Scala.

Nico enjoyed the soup and his conversation with Scala, then he headed directly to the Chancery Annex.

Galetto, the notary who assisted Nico on his previous visit to the Chancery Annex, greeted Nico when he stepped from the entry vestibule to the workroom. A team of notaries was busily cataloging new documents and entering them into the archive just as they had been doing the last time Nico was in the room. Nico held out the note from the Chancellor. Galetto unfolded the paper and registered surprise upon reading it. Chancellor Scala had the ultimate authority for all aspects of the archive, so his directive preempted Galetto's regular work. Galetto signaled to a colleague that he would be occupied with a high priority assignment, then he turned to Nico.

"What records are you seeking?"

"I would like to see documents that mention the Priors of Constantine."

Galetto nodded and said, "Follow me."

He led Nico through a corridor to a room at the rear of the building. Floor to ceiling shelves containing identical folders arranged in alphabetical order lined the four walls of the room.

"These are the indexes of all documents in the archive," Galetto announced.

He scanned the shelves to locate the relevant folder.

"Recall on your previous visit clerks were organizing data by topic. This folder should contain the index for the Priors of Constantine. All documents in the archive that mention the Priors should be listed."

Nico peered over Galetto's shoulder as he examined the listings. Finally, a bewildered Galetto announced, "Most unusual. The folder has no index for the Priors of Constantine."

Disappointment showed on Nico's face. He spread his arms in an all-encompassing gesture and said, "In this entire collection there is not a single document that refers to The Priors? The brotherhood has existed for more than a century. Stories about them are legendary. How is it possible that throughout its entire history, the Priors have managed to escape official notice?"

Galetto suddenly became animated. He snapped the folder back in place and dashed to the corridor.

"Follow me," he called to Nico who hurried behind.

As they climbed a stone staircase to the third level, Galetto explained, "The central archive contains documents for all subjects added since the year 1293, when our constitution, the Ordinances of Justice, was adopted. There is a separate collection of documents about topics that predate the formation of our constitutional republic. As you said, the Priors of Constantine has existed since Roman times, so all documents mentioning the Priors will be filed in this collection. Even recent information concerning the Priors will be here."

The two men stepped into a room like the one below, but

here the shelves and furnishings were covered with a thin layer of dust. Galetto flicked a dead insect from one of the shelves. Most of the folders were similar to those in the central archive, but some had additional protection. To Nico's eye, they appeared to be wrapped in a specially treated leather covering and sealed with wax.

"This room holds our Republic's most revered documents, but we rarely come here. Everyone either takes our history for granted, or they have no interest in it. I'm not sure of the reason, but in any case, we hardly ever get requests for these records."

He pointed to one of the specially packaged folders.

"This folder contains the bequest by Contessa Matilda in 1115 that granted autonomy to the city of Florence."

From his study of history, Nico knew it was the courageous act of Countess Matilda that had granted Florentines the unprecedented freedom to create a self-governing republic. He never dreamed he would be in the presence of the time-honored document. While Nico looked in awe at the folder, Galetto moved on and opened one of the index folios.

He muttered to himself, "Pope, Pope, Pope. Ah, here it is."

Galetto held up the sheet titled Priors of Constantine. Both men were surprised how few documents were listed. Chancellor Scala was correct when he said that the Priors conceal their activities.

"Is there something specific that interests you?" Galetto asked.

"I would like to understand the organization of the brotherhood. How they make decisions."

Galetto pointed to the first item on the list. "This is the oldest document. It mentions Emperor Constantine."

They moved to the aisle labeled 'C-D', where Galetto retrieved the folder that held document C744. It was an old parchment, thin enough to be nearly transparent. Despite its age, the inked writing had not faded. A note fastened to the page named the person who submitted the document and the date it was entered into the archive. The note named Magnus of Milan as the author of the paper. It was a name Nico did not know. The note did not give his purpose for recording the information. The note was written in modern Italian, but Magnus had penned the text of his document in elegant Latin script. Galetto waited until Nico donned a pair of silk gloves before handing him the paper. Nico carried the page to a chair at the end of the row where he sat and began reading.

In the early days of the Empire, Christians were tolerated as a small, although troublesome, sect. As their numbers grew over time, so did religious intolerance. Their persecution began with Emperor Nero and culminated in The Great Persecution that rescinded all rights of Christians to hold meetings or otherwise practice their religion. Emperor Diocletian confiscated their property and some he had put to death. He banished Popes, leaving them to die in exile.

The future brightened for the faithful when Constantine the Great, spurred by a vision from the Christian God, led his army to victory in Rome and positioned himself as the new Emperor. He restored the rights of Christians to assemble and practice their religion. His actions were praised throughout the Empire by all except one sect of the clergy, who claimed that Constantine had been forced to compromise. They argued that Constantine's edicts were insufficient because they did not provide restitution for past suffering, and they did not set Christianity as the official religion of the Empire. They decided that more was needed to secure the faith. They joined together as The Priors of Constantine.

The Priors committed to preserving the Church by silencing heretics, evildoers, and all who would oppose their cause. Initially, Church officials welcomed the Priors and let them establish a presence at the basilica in Rome that Constantine founded to serve as the Papal residence. From there, The Priors scrutinized everyone in public office. They uncovered and eliminated all whom they judged as threats to the faith.

As the Priors expanded outward from the heart of Rome to the far reaches of the Empire, their activities became increasingly bold. They used every means available to eliminate all who they claimed to be in Satan's grasp. Then in the sixth century, the sect made an unforgivable error . . .

A dark brown stain obscured several lines of the writing. In the stained portion of the page, the phrase 'crown prince of the Kingdom of Seuvi' was the only part still legible. Nico had never heard of the Kingdom of Seuvi, but he was confident that no kingdom with that name ever existed on the Italian peninsula.

Below the stain, the message continued.

. . . Church leaders demanded that the Priors disband, but the wily leadership of the Priors avoided dissolution by transforming themselves into a semi-secret cult. From that transformation, the Priors adopted a mode of operating unlike any other, a structure for which there is no name. From what little I know, membership consists of decision-makers and implementers. Whenever any three decision-makers join in sponsoring an objective, the implementers act to achieve the desired outcome.

Every law school course emphasized the importance of substantiating evidence. To that end, Nico studied the remaining documents listed on the index. They described historical events in which the Priors had a role, events so significant that the Priors could not conceal their involvement. None of those reports discussed the formation or operation of the brotherhood.

Nico concluded that if the Priors continued to operate as

the document described, then the acting Archbishop of Lucca must have been one of its decision-makers. The archbishop spoke with confidence that steps should be taken to defend Pietra Alta, and he implied that he had authority to initiate the necessary measures. According to the document, before the Priors could act, the archbishop would need to persuade two additional decision-makers to share his view. Neither the material in the archive nor the archbishop's words gave any clue as to how the archbishop might do that or what action the Priors would take if he were successful. Nico came away from the archive with more questions than answers.

18

UNIVERSITY OF FLORENCE

Legions of monks in monasteries throughout the Christian world spent their days copying the scriptures. Despite their dedication, manuscripts were too expensive for people of modest means to possess more than their treasured family Bible. Pretenders to wealth displayed their collection of classic works, Dante, Cicero, Petrarch, and the like, where visitors to their homes were sure to notice. Only true aristocrats, the Medici and their kin, amassed collections large enough to be considered libraries. For many, their motivation was to preserve rare and valuable works. Very few read the volumes themselves.

Professionals in need of information relied on documents collected and maintained by their guilds. For many years, the Magistrates and Notaries Guild, mainly through donations from its members, accumulated manuscripts on legal matters. Initially, the collection was kept in a room on the third floor of the guild office building. Two decades past, the University of Florence entertained the thought of forming a law college, and, to encourage the idea, the guild transferred its collection to the university where a dedicated room served as the law library. There were no restrictions imposed on access to the materials. The only constraint was that they not be removed from the room. Although everyone was allowed to use the materials, in practice, the only people who used the law library were magistrates, notaries, and law clerks.

Nico believed that prior legal proceedings might have precedents that he could use to guide Pietra Alta in taking legal action against Rimini, and he hoped to find those in documents at the law library. He was not familiar with the law library, but he was acquainted with the university's philosophy library, and he was confident that a student or staff person could explain to him the organization of materials in the law library.

Late summer was a quiet time at the university. Whenever possible, students arranged to escape the heat of the city by visiting relatives at villas in the countryside. Only three tables in the philosophy library were occupied when Nico entered. To his right, a small group of students was engaged in animated discussion and pointing to a map spread across the table. At the far end of the room, two students sat side-by-side peering into a single book. They appeared to take turns reading passages to each other.

Near the center of the room, at a table by himself, sat Professor Marsuppini. Chancellor Scala had recently introduced Nico to the professor. Scala called Marsuppini a world champion puzzle master, and in Nico's experience, the accolade was well deserved. The professor had completely covered the table in front of him with an assortment of books and manuscripts. His eyes flitted from one document to another as he analyzed the writings. Periodically he stopped reading to make a notation on a paper resting on his lap – there was no space for his notepad on the crowded table - then he flipped pages in some of the books and resumed reading.

As Nico drew close, he noticed the pronounced tremor of the professor's hands. How sad. His mind is as keen as ever, but his body is failing.

Marsuppini looked up when Nico's shadow crossed the table. With a flash of recognition, he said, "Ah, the young friend of Chancellor Scala. Have you come seeking my help with another puzzle?"

Nico pulled out a chair and sat across the table from the professor. He enjoyed talking with this old man, a font of knowledge and wisdom. Nico's uncle Nunzio had taught him to appreciate wisdom.

"Today, my interest is a legal matter. The information I need is probably somewhere in the law library. One problem will be in finding the data among the shelves filled with documents." Reflecting on the problem, Nico added, "I suppose that can be considered a puzzle."

"Students have the same problem finding information in this library," Marsuppini said, gesturing to the books lining the walls around them. "In class, the philosophy students are given a quote and told to read a treatise by its author. They come here and stand in the middle of the room, bewildered with no idea where to find works by the author of the quote. I am happy to help the poor souls whenever I can. Professors generally give the same assignments every year so I can usually point students to the appropriate shelf before they even tell me the quote."

The professor paraphrased himself, "If it is mid-October, the subject must be Cicero," and without looking, he pointed to a shelf behind him. "All Roman era works, Cicero, Plutarch, Julius Caesar, are grouped in that area."

Nico raised an eyebrow; "Are there philosophical works by Julius Ceasar? I only know of the writings about his military campaigns."

"As you know, the university has one room dedicated to the

law library. Another room holds all religious materials. Our collection of science books is kept in one of the offices because it is too small to merit a room of its own. The university suffers from limited resources, so all other books are in this room. Calling it the Philosophy Library is a misnomer."

"When I was a young professor, there were disagreements every year as to where to place the works of Aristotle. Some said his treatise on biology belonged with the sciences; the opposition argued that all of Aristotle's works should be kept together in the philosophy collection."

"Where is Aristotle kept now?" Nico asked.

Marsuppini erupted in laughter loud enough to distract everyone in the room. Through the fit of laughter, he managed to answer, "He is buried in Sicily . . . at least that is what the Sicilians claim."

Nico joined the laughter, knowing he had laid the opening for the professor's humor.

Finally, Marsuppini calmed enough to say, "Eventually, we acquired a Latin translation of his writings on biology and botany. That manuscript is with the sciences. The original Greek volume is in this room."

"Everyone must be pleased with that arrangement," Nico guessed.

Marsuppini shook his head. "Exactly the opposite."

As he looked around at the collection of documents lining the walls around him, Nico recalled how much effort was needed to index documents at the Chancery archives.

"It will never be possible to index an entire collection of books as large as the one in this room. Do the students realize how fortunate they are to have professor Marsuppini's assistance in helping them find the materials they need?" Nico thought.

Returning to Nico's concern, Marsuppini said, "I am not

acquainted with the law library, but I can point refer you to someone who knows it better than anyone else. Messer Viviani was an esteemed law professor at this university, that was before your time. Twice he was elected as proconsul of the guild. When the guild donated its reference collection to the university, Viviani had responsibility for arranging the transfer. Lately, he spends his time at the Brancacci chapel studying the Masaccio frescoes. Viviani is the best person to consult regarding the law library. Also, he has extensive experience with complicated legal issues."

Rather than wander aimlessly through the law library, Nico opted to follow Marsuppini's advice. He bid farewell to Marsuppini, departed from the university, and crossed the Arno River to the Santa Maria del Carmine church. Nico entered and walked the length of the long central aisle to Brancacci Chapel. He found Professor Viviani sitting on a wooden pew facing Brancacci's striking depiction of Adam and Eve. Nico recognized Viviani immediately by the narrow band of white hair encircling his bald pate, his ample paunch, and the heavyweight mantello that he wore even in the heat of summer.

Not wanting to interrupt the man's concentration, Nico watched Viviani stare at the fresco for several minutes without moving. Finally, the old professor leaned heavily with both hands onto his cane and struggled to push himself to a standing position.

Nico moved forward to offer assistance. He walked with Viviani toward the exit, introduced himself, and explained his reason for being there. He asked if Viviani would join him for a pastry so they could discuss legal recourse for Pietra Alta.

The mention of pastry caught the professor's interest. He took Nico by the arm and led him to a small shop on a narrow street at the rear of the church. They selected a table outside, and as soon as they were seated, a young boy bounded out of the shop to serve them. The friendly greeting that Viviani exchanged with the boy signaled that Viviani was a frequent patron. "Are there crostata alla susina?" Vivana asked.

"Yes, and they are fresh from the oven," the boy replied cheerfully.

To Nico, Viviani said, "Giusto, the owner of this shop, makes the best plum tarts in the city."

Nico accepted the recommendation and added for himself a glass of the house red wine.

To the professor, the boy said, "And for you, vino magro?"

The professor nodded his acceptance, which prompted Nico to ask, "What is vino magro? I have never heard that term."

"I have always enjoyed good wine, but in recent years my old body has been raising objections, but it still tolerates wine mixed with a splash of mineral water. When I first ordered the mixture at this shop, Giusto asked if the water was to make me magro."

Viviani patted his robust stomach. "As you can see, becoming thin was not my goal. Giusto is the one who began calling the drink thin wine."

The boy returned carrying a tray with their drinks and the plum pastries, drizzled with honey. Between nibbles of the delicacy, they discussed the Pietra Alta situation.

"Although the soldiers from Rimini said that the citizens of Pietra Alta would be taxed, they did not demand payment at that time, so there can be no allegation of criminality thus far."

"Yes, that is correct," agreed Viviani.

"At the university, we studied a case involving two individuals where the court issued a ruling that enjoined one of the parties from taking action. The court said that if the action were taken, it would injure one of the parties, so the court issued its ruling in advance of any action. I believe that ruling can be used as a precedent. If it can, then Pietra Alta should be able to petition a court before any crime is committed."

Again, Viviani agreed. "Pietra Alta can certainly ask the court for a ruling. Of course, no one can predict what ruling might be forthcoming. On what basis can Pietra Alta argue that it should not be taxed?"

"There is evidence to support its claim of independence. I have a letter from the Papal Archive stating that Pietra Alta is not within the Province of Rimini."

"That should help. Is the letter notarized?"

"No"

Viviani shrugged, "Too bad. Next time have the statement authenticated by a notary."

Viviani's statement stung. Nico felt that he was still at the university being rebuked by his professor. In practice cases at the law school, students in the roles of prosecuting and defending lawyers were given materials to use in making their case. The purpose of the mock trials was for them to learn how to use available evidence. Students always assumed that the evidence was authentic. Student lawyers were never in the position of having to procure or validate proof. The need to collect and validate evidence struck Nico as yet another difference between the academic and real worlds.

"Because the Lord of Rimini initiated the tax program, I cannot be sure whether Pietra Alta should name the Lord of Rimini or the Province of Rimini as the defendant," Nico said.

"That is a good question . . . an excellent question. There was a seminal case ten years past in the Duchy of Mantua that may provide the answer. That proceeding concerned the Duke of Mantua's order to change the course of a road. An affected town petitioned the court to halt the work. My old memory cannot recall whether the Duke or the Duchy was named as the defendant, but the law library does have a record of that case."

Duchy of Mantua. Ten years past. Nico would review that case at the library.

Viviani raised another issue. "Have you decided where to file the case?"

"Since Pietra Alta is in the Papal States, Rome seems to be the appropriate venue. However, I am worried that traveling to Rome and filing with a tribunal in Rome will take time. Pietra Alta needs to obtain a ruling before soldiers from Rimini return to the town."

"Rome is certainly an appropriate choice," Viviani affirmed, "but the laws of the Papal States grant the flexibility to file in any of their courts. Conceivably the filing could be made to a court in Rimini, although considering the circumstances, I do not recommend doing that. I suggest Perugia. Perugia is closer than Rome, and I am certain the magistrates in Perugia will give the petition a fair hearing."

The mention of Perugia reminded Nico of what Bianca's father had told him: 'Captain Ludovico Malvezzi commands a contingent of Papal military troops at Perugia.' Nico reasoned that there could be an advantage to filing the case in a city where the Papal States had a military presence.

Viviani regretted being too old to continue teaching and practicing law. He was invigorated by the discussion and delighted to find that his knowledge still held value. After they consumed the last of their wine, he offered to meet again if Nico thought it would be helpful.

Nico returned to the university and found a student to guide him to the law library. Four men worked silently and independently at the two tables in the small room. As Viviani had said, documents in the library were arranged chronologically. Even with that knowledge, Nico had to leaf through twelve volumes before finding the case he was seeking.

With the thick folder in hand, Nico joined the other researchers at one of the tables. Perusing the information reassured him that the prosecutors in Mantua had faced a dilemma similar to his. They were unsure whether their filing should cite the Duke of Mantua or the Duchy itself as the defendant. They opted to avoid the issue by naming both the Duke and the Duchy as co-defendants and letting the court decide where to place blame. Nico would advise Pietra Alta to do the same.

The document listed the names of all the lawyers involved in the case and the names of all witnesses who had testified. The folder did not contain a verbatim transcript of the arguments, but it did give a lengthy summary of the legal points presented by each side. When Nico finished reading the summary, he found to his dismay that the document did not include the final ruling. The magistrates hearing the case must have taken a long time deliberating before they reached a decision, and the summary must have been written before the tribunal made its decision. Surely an archive in the Duchy of Mantua recoded the ruling, but the law library at the University of Florence had not received a copy.

The only additional information that Nico gleaned from reading the document was the name of one of the lawyers, Michele Cetti. That name was familiar to Nico as one of the most highly regarded lawyers in Florence. Cetti established his reputation with a nearly spotless record of winning cases where the defendant was the City of Florence or the Florentine Republic. His clients were businesses or wealthy aristocrats, and he always had more clients seeking his services than he could accommodate. With his consistently heavy caseload in Florence, it was indeed strange for him to have taken a case in the Duchy of Mantua. There must have been an aspect of the case that he found intriguing.

Nico closed the folder and glanced around the room. He had found the information that he sought in a brief time. In contrast, all the other men in the room were still anguishing over documents and making extensive notes in the hot, stuffy room. Nico wondered how often in his career he would be returning to the law library to anguish over piles of documents.

19

THE RIMINI-URBINO BORDER

In recent weeks, knight Scalari had led a cavalry troop through the Province escorting a tax collector. Escort duty was an easy assignment for the troopers because they returned to their barracks at the end of each day and spent each night in their own comfortable beds. For Scalari, it was hell. Being nursemaid to a low-level bureaucrat was an insult to his aristocratic heritage.

Scalari sat alone contemplating his revenge. People usually consent to pay their taxes because they know the alternative is a prison cell. Fear of imprisonment is generally enough intimidation. Additional coercion by soldiers is rarely necessary. Only once did we encounter resistance, and that was not from an individual but from the entire town of Pietra Alta. It is a mystery to me that Lord Malcranio does not punish the people of Pietra Alta for their defiance. It is humiliating. Humiliating to Rimini, humiliating to Malcranio, and humiliating to me. If he does not punish them, then I will deal with them myself. Deal with them severely.

Without explanation, the ministry had suspended the tax

collection operations. New orders said, 'the focus will be on more lucrative opportunities.' The soldiers' new assignment took them away from Pietra Alta to an encampment along the border with the Duchy of Urbino. The purpose of their mission was to identify poorly defended towns across the border that would make worthwhile additions to the territory of Rimini.

In a makeshift shelter at the center of the encampment, the cavalry captain and two scouts stood examining a map displayed on an easel. The scouts had returned to camp earlier in the day before the rain started. What began as a light shower steadily increased in intensity to the downpour that hammered against the fabric canopy.

The scout they called Fantasma, earned for his ability to move around as a ghost without being detected, raised his voice to be heard over the pelting rain.

"The map is wrong," he said. Pointing to a location on the map, he continued, "This town is farther from the border than the map shows, at least twice as far."

Both scouts had proven themselves on previous missions, so the captain had no reason to question their report. A drip fell from the covering about their heads, spotting the shoulder of the captain's uniform. Looking up, he saw another drip forming. He stepped to the side to an area where the fabric above appeared dry. He tried to concentrate on his mission despite the weather.

"Are there any fortifications? Walls?" he asked.

"There is no wall," the second scout replied. "There are woods on the north side of town. We could approach from the woods without being seen until we reach the town center."

The captain evinced disappointment, which confused the two men. Seeing their expressions, he explained, "In peacetime towns with walls keep their gates open to allow everyone easy entry. An attacking force can infiltrate one of those towns without incurring any opposition. Then, after seizing the town, they can close the gates to control the townspeople and defend against any possible counterattack. Walls would be an advantage to the conquerors."

Soldiers sought the opportunity to serve with this captain because he was always willing to share knowledge and experience with his men.

Brushing aside his concern, the captain added, "The absence of walls is not surprising since very few small towns have defensive walls. More important is what things of value are in the town."

Both scouts threw up their hands. "The houses and shops are meager. There is a market, and a physician, but the only business of value is a wainwright shop."

The captain recorded their findings in a logbook.

Fantasma pointed to a different location on the map. "Here, near this small river are a group of houses and a gristmill powered by a large waterwheel, large enough to mill many moggii of grain. In the short time we were watching, we saw two wagons loaded with flour leave the mill."

The second scout added, "The houses and the mill are on the near bank of the river. A wooden bridge connects to the road on the far bank."

Following their inference, the captain reasoned, "So, if we remove the bridge, the houses and the mill would be isolated from the town. The mill is a valuable target we can occupy without difficulty."

"Yes, exactly. We rode along the river at least two miles in each direction. There is no other bridge. The river is not deep, but it is littered with snags from fallen trees that could catch the leg of any horse trying to cross. Not even a fool would take the risk. No aid will come to the mill from the far side of the river."

The captain noted their findings in the log. They were not authorized to seize any territory. Their mission was to identify possible acquisitions and report them to the military headquarters whose staff would then choose the most promising targets. The following day, if the rain cleared, another pair of scouts would be sent to investigate a different section of the border. They sent only two scouts on patrol at any time because the appearance of many strangers might raise concern among the locals in Urbino. Soldiers who were not on patrol, and that included most members of the troop, spent their days doing little other than playing cards.

In a nearby shelter, knight Scalari stood with arms folded across his chest and looked out at the muddy campground. He watched the water flowing through two depressions in the mud that had been made by the passage of wagon wheels. The soldier he had sent on a special mission shook water droplets from his oilskin cloak. The rain was so intense that even the heavy cloak had not prevented his tunic from becoming soaked. He had just returned from a reconnaissance visit to Pietra Alta, and he had to make his report to the knight before he could deal with his wet clothes and soggy boots.

"There is no sign that the people of Pietra Alta are preparing any resistance. They have not blocked any roads nor constructed any barriers, and no outsiders have come to their aid. They behave as though they do not believe you will return. Of course, our soldiers are not in contact with the people of the town, so we cannot be certain what they are thinking or planning."

Scalari reviewed his planned revenge. "The town has about thirty men, but they are farmers, not soldiers. I can send six more men from this troop. Six, plus the six observers already there, should be more than enough to defeat thirty farmers. Do you have anything else to report?"

"A young recruit named Soli is becoming a problem. He fights with the others and needs discipline constantly."

"Soli. I know that name. He was a pain in the ass when he was here. Anything else?"

"The men are becoming impatient."

"They will not be waiting much longer. As soon as the rain clears, the peasants in that town will get what they deserve."

20

CASA ARGENTI, FLORENCE

Nico's favorite place for problem-solving was the table in the dining salon. He claimed that having snacks within easy reach boosted his mental processes. There was also the comfort of being in the place where the family gathered at mealtimes to share their thoughts, concerns, and joys, although Nico may not have been consciously aware of that advantage. When he was younger, uncle Nunzio's late wife welcomed Nico's presence in the dining salon as she prepared dinner and he worked on problems assigned by his tutors. Later it was Joanna who welcomed his companionship as she prepared dinner.

Currently, Nico was alone in the salon. He sipped a glass of wine while organizing the papers spread out across the table. The papers were notes he had taken in his classes at the university, notes he hoped would give him an insight to formulating advice for Pietra Alta.

Alessa entered the room trailed by a young man who padded in behind her like a puppy following its mistress. She had that effect on men. His gaze locked onto her wavy black hair as it bounced rhythmically from her shoulders with every step.

Upon hearing them enter, Nico looked up. "Welcome, Filippo. I see you have met Alessa."

At the sound of his name, the spellbound Filippo managed to pull his focus from Alessa, but the incoherent phrase he muttered proved that her spell was not yet entirely broken.

"We almost met," Alessa interjected. "I told him my name, but he gave no indication that he actually heard it. And he seems to have some difficulty in telling me his name."

"Filippo was my roommate at the university. He is usually more lucid," Nico explained.

Addressing Filippo, Alessa said, "It is a pleasure to meet you." Then she turned and swept out of the room.

Filippo watched her depart, and when she was finally out of view, he asked doubtfully, "Is she one of the servants?"

His uncertainty arose because her stylish tunic, well-coiffed hair, and the ruby tint of her smooth brown cheeks were not the characteristics of a servant.

"She is my sister," Nico replied.

Nico knew that Alessa's dark skin and dark, deep-set eyes belied his answer, but it usually silenced people and let him avoid the long explanation of her origin.

Replaying Alessa's presence in his memory, Filippo said to himself but out loud, "She smells nice, like a kind of cookie that my nonna used to make."

Nico responded to Filippo's bizarre statement with a matter-of-fact comment. "She creates her own perfumes with flowers and oils from North Africa."

Nico waited until Filippo finished processing whatever fantasy might be passing through his thoughts. Filippo's return to normalcy was signaled by brushing back his unkempt hair and lifting the wine bottle from the table in front of Nico and holding it aloft expectantly.

"There is a glass on the sideboard," Nico said.

Filippo picked the largest available glass and filled it to the brim. He leaned down to inhale the scent of the purple bougainvillea that had been arranged in a nearby vase by Joanna or Alessa.

Nico called out, "Have one of the muffins if you wish."

Other than the glasses and vase of flowers, the only other object on the sideboard was a plate containing scattered crumbs.

Filippo tilted the plate so Nico could see its condition.

"Someone must have eaten them," Nico confirmed, knowing full well that he was the someone.

With a full glass in hand, Filippo sat next to Nico and scanned the papers covering the tabletop. "This reminds me of our days at the university, with good wine and a challenging legal problem. But what is all this? You cannot be working on a real case because we haven't been inducted into the guild yet. I hope you remember that if you want to work in private practice, my father would be delighted to have you join his firm."

"I don't intend to be a lawyer of record for this case if indeed there is a case. I promised to help an acquaintance of my cousin who needs advice with a legal problem. I agreed to give advice, but if he decides to proceed with legal action, he will need to retain a qualified member of a guild to serve as his lawyer. But the lawyer will not be a Florentine because the case does not involve anyone in Florence. Both parties are in the Papal States."

"They must be desperate if they're asking for help from you, a foreigner who has not yet been inducted into the guild," Filippo teased. "So tell me, what is the issue?"

Nico decided not to mention his interaction with the bishop

of Lucca, nor his visit to Castellina. His reason for meeting with Filippo was solely to refresh his memory regarding two cases they had studied at the university concerning jurisdictions.

"Do you remember the case we studied where the plaintiff claimed ownership of a parcel of land through inheritance?"

Filippo answered proudly, "Yes, of course. That was one of the finest moments in my six years at Bologna. I had the role of magistrate."

"The defendant had an official map that showed him as the landowner," Nico began.

"Yes," Filippo continued, "then the plaintiff presented a will that was left to him by the previous owner. He thought the existence of the will was all he needed to win until I asked him to demonstrate the will's authenticity. The document he presented was a simple handwritten paper. He was completely bewildered by my question. Authentication had never occurred to him.

"I could have ruled against him, but instead I granted him a one-day recess. The following day he called a witness, a student in the persona of the notary who claimed he had drafted the will. He testified that the original, duly notarized will was secured in his office. That totally changed the outcome, and I ruled in his favor. The professor congratulated me for not rushing to judgement. He said that magistrates must realize that it often takes time for justice to be served."

Filippo's account spurred warnings in Nico's memory. He heard professor Viviani saying 'too bad the statement of the Papal Architect is not notarized.' And he recalled the caution of an irritating, squirrelly-looking professor at Bologna who repeatedly told his students 'Always pursue every possibility. Never leave anything to chance.' Nico wrote a note for himself: the lawyer for Pietra Alta must be told to obtain a notarized statement from the Papal Archive.

"There was another case," Nico began. "A town in the Duchy of Milan claimed jurisdiction over a prosperous farm so they could levy town taxes. The farmer claimed his farm was not within the boundary of the town."

"I do remember that case, though I did not have a role in its reenactment. Although the court ruled in favor of the farmer, the town ignored the court ruling and sent agents to collect the tax. The Duchy of Milan should have used its military to enforce the court ruling, but the army was occupied elsewhere, so the farmer had no recourse but to pay the tax."

Nico added to his notes two questions highlighted with dark underlines: Will Rimini honor the rule of law? What action can be taken if it does not? Knowing how to deal with those uncertainties would take some thought.

"Do you recall any other cases we studied that dealt with jurisdictional disputes?" asked Nico.

"A few," Filippo responded, "but they were simple contests between neighboring landowners. I don't remember other cases as consequential as the two you just cited."

Since they had no additional legal accounts to discuss, their conversation shifted to rehashing their experiences at the university, some sad, most happy. Sporadically, Filippo's gaze went to the doorway where he wished for Alessa to reappear. To his dismay, she did not.

UNCLE NUNZIO'S VINEYARD, NEAR FLORENCE

Before retiring to his vineyard in the hills between Florence and Fiesole, Nunzio Argenti owned the Uccello restaurant. Nunzio passed the Uccello to his son Donato who converted it to a private dining club and the finest eating establishment in the city. Uncle Nunzio, as Nico addressed him, cared for Nico as a son when Nico's parents died.

Nico, Donato, and all other members of the Argenti family were looking forward to celebrating Nunzio's fiftieth birthday. Donato, Joanna, Giorgio, and Alessa traveled to the vineyard a day earlier with a butchered hog ready for roasting. Two workers at the vineyard had dug a pit and set a fire so the coals would be hot when the hog arrived.

The two workers took shifts through the night, rotating the spit to ensure that the animal cooked evenly. Giorgio tried his best to sit with them during the night. During the first hours of darkness, Giorgio was in high spirits. Slowly his energy faded, leaving him sitting quietly, watching sparks dance from the fire into the black sky. He was asleep by midnight when Donato carried his sleeping son to a waiting bed inside the villa.

4

560

KEN TENTARELLI

To Nico, the celebration had an additional significance. Bianca, who was in Florence meeting with a client, happily accepted an invitation, extended by Joanna, to join the family celebration. Bianca had never met Nunzio. Nico rode to Palazzo Spinelli where Bianca was delivering one of her designs.

Bianca sprang out from the palazzo with a spirited step. Nico helped her climb aboard and settle onto the horse cart. When he climbed back onto the seat, she kissed him lightly on the cheek and held his hand as they rode from the city to the vineyard.

"Your exuberance suggests that Signorina Spinelli was pleased with your creation," Nico said.

Bianca's eyes sparkled. She wrapped her arms around Nico, leaned toward him until their foreheads touched, and said softly, "More than pleased, she loved it!

"Most of my designs are what Parisians refer to as avant-garde. Signorina Spinelli has conservative tastes. It was a challenge for me to apply my design concepts to her conservative style. Her reaction upon seeing the dress told me instantly that I had succeeded. Her fiancé, Signor Soderini, was at the palazzo. He too, was impressed by my creativity."

"Ah, Paolo Soderini, son of a Captain of the Guardia. I have heard that he is easily impressed," Nico teased.

Bianca accompanied her words, "Nico, don't be wicked," with a playful poke to Nico's ribs.

"Signor Soderini asked if I could design a shirt for him. He described in detail the style he wants. He said that he had already posed the request to a member of the Florentine tailors' guild only to be met by a blank stare. I am certain that I can create the shirt he envisions."

"Might that cause a problem? The tailors' guild tolerates your selling to women because you are not directly competing with members of the guild. They are likely to object if you start designing for men. The guild will not relish competition from a woman, even though you are a foreigner."

"The tailors' guild does have women, but only as apprentices, not as full members," Bianca explained. "So yes, it will be interesting to see how the guild reacts. You will soon be a member of a guild, the magistrates guild. How would you react if a woman lawyer applied for membership?"

"That could not happen because there are no women lawyers." Nico's thoughts flashed back to Bologna, "A century past, two women legal scholars, sisters, taught at the university law school. The law school has expanded dramatically since then, yet it still has no women students."

Nico turned off the main road onto the dirt path that led to the villa at Nunzio's vineyard. As his wagon crested a slight rise, they saw the haphazard collection of carts parked in a clearing to their left and directly ahead a large gathering of people on the terrace of the villa. Among those who had come to celebrate Nunzio's birthday were friends Nunzio had made over the years, former employees who worked at the Uccello when Nunzio owned it, and men who were the initial members of the Uccello when it became a private dining club.

On the near side of the terrace, groups of women engaged in fast-paced conversations encircled Nunzio's special friend Lexia. She barely had a chance to join in one of the discussions before being drawn into a different one a few seconds later. She felt like a ball in constant motion from one player to another.

Lexia had lived on a small Greek island until the previous year when she came to Florence with her grown son, who had found work as an apprentice goldsmith. She had not even settled into a house in the city when Nunzio heard of her skill in caring for olive trees. He sought her help in tending his small olive grove of ailing trees. She welcomed the invitation to move from the bustling city to the serenity of Nunzio's villa, where she worked magic with the trees, and as she did so, her relationship with Nunzio deepened.

At the far end of the terrace, men even more boisterous and animated than the women surrounded Nunzio. His stiff posture showed a certain unease over the size of the celebration and the attention he was receiving. In his younger days, as the owner of the Uccello, Nunzio enjoyed late-night partying with friends, but as he grew older, his preference shifted to one-on-one and small group settings where he could have more meaningful interactions.

As Nico surveyed the group, he found that he knew very few of the guests at the birthday celebration. Perhaps his lack of familiarity was due to his being away at the university for six years, or maybe it was because the men were of an older generation known to Nunzio from years past. Bianca followed close behind Nico as they skirted the crowd of women and then weaved a path through the cluster of men to reach Nunzio. Nico leaned close so Nunzio could hear him through the cacophony of words swirling around them. Nico introduced Bianca to Nunzio, who reached out, wrapped an arm around each of them, and pulled them into a tight embrace.

"I have been eager to meet you, my dear. Nico's eyes always brighten when he speaks of you. I am honored that my friends have journeyed here to remind this old man of his age, but with so many people here I cannot. . ." He let his words trail off.

"Later, when everyone is well-fed, there will be time for us to talk," Nico said. "For now, you should enjoy the company of your friends."

Nunzio shrugged and aimed a gentle smile at Bianca. "Later," he agreed.

Nico assumed that Donato and Joanna were inside the villa since they were not among those on the terrace. He started to escort Bianca to the villa when one of the women took her by the arm. "Look. It is her, Bianca Cellini," the woman squealed.

Nico stopped abruptly, motionless. He watched helplessly as the swarm of women enveloped Bianca. Before he lost sight of her, Nico heard another woman exclaim, "She is the person who is creating the gown for Princess Isabella's birthday."

He resigned himself to the situation and continued to the villa, leaving Bianca to cope with her newly found admirers. Inside, Donato was supervising workers from the Uccello as they prepared the trays of food they would soon serve to the guests.

Seeing that Nico was alone, Donato asked, "Where is Bianca?"

"A horde of women spirited her away," Nico explained.

"How could you let them take her so easily? We Argenti men have a reputation to uphold." Donato chided.

"You know I would fight dragons alongside San Giorgio to protect her, but rescuing her from those women was beyond my ability." Nico held out his hands, palms up, in a defenseless gesture that drove both men to laughter and brought forth chuckles from the nearby workers who overheard the exchange.

When they calmed enough to resume speaking, Donato said, "Joanna is out there somewhere in their midst. I'm sure she will rescue Bianca eventually."

Changing the subject, Nico said, "I noticed Alessa walking down by the vineyard with someone whom I don't recognize."

"I don't know his name," Donato responded, "but his father is a banker whom Nunzio has known for many years. As the owner of the Uccello, Nunzio came to know people in a wide variety of occupations. There is even a member of your vocation among the men on the terrace."

"A lawyer?"

"He was a lawyer, he is retired now, although he is still a sought after consultant."

"Do you recall his name?"

"Michele Cetti."

Nico immediately recognized the name. He was the Florentine lawyer mentioned in the case involving the Duchy of Mantua that Nico had studied at the law library.

"How well do you know Signor Cetti? I would very much like to meet him. He was involved in a legal proceeding that has similarities to the Pietra Alta situation."

"I have known Michele for many years. He is a long-standing member of the Uccello. His outstanding reputation as a lawyer earned him clients from the entire length of the Italian peninsula. A number of them were nobles, dukes and counts. Cities and states sought him to represent them in disputes with their neighbors. Once he represented the Kingdom of Naples in a charge against the Kingdom of France. That case extended his reputation far beyond Italy. Michele never formed relationships with his clients. Shortly after winning a favorable judgement for Naples, he filed a complaint against them on a different matter for another client. His only loyalty was to legal principles.

"When he was practicing law, Michele frequently brought clients to the Uccello as his guests. He always told me that the food and service at the Uccello let him attract his important clients, but everyone knew it was his skill in persuading magistrates that accounted for his success."

Donato walked with Nico to the doorway that opened onto the terrace and pointed to a man in the distance. "He is the one with the dark blue tunic."

Cetti was shorter than average with thick white hair that hung to his shoulders. His tunic was stretched tight across his ample stomach. Lawyer folklore said that the stress endured by

hard-working lawyers kept them lean even if they did no physical exercise. The corollary said one should never hire an over-
weight lawyer because the excess weight meant that he wasn't a
hard worker. But all lawyers, even the most conscientious ones,
added pounds after they retired and no longer had stress.

Cetti and one other man stood apart from the others. Nico
did not wish to interrupt their discussion, so he moved slowly
in their general direction, intending to wait for a break in the
conversation before introducing himself. However, Nico was
still a distance away when the two men acknowledged his presence by suspending their conversation and turning to watch
him approach.

"I'm sorry for intruding. My name is Nico Argenti. I was
hoping to speak with Signor Cetti when it is convenient."

"You are Nunzio's nephew, a recent product of Bologna's law
school," Cetti responded, "I wanted to meet you as well."

The second man introduced himself as a retired member of
the guardia and then excused himself to refill his wine glass.

"I am also a graduate of the University of Bologna. Of
course, that was many years past. The University has changed
since I was a student there. In my time, a council of students
determined the stipends for the professors. That wasn't an ideal
arrangement. I served on the council for two years. Most of us
believed in rewarding the most talented and knowledgeable
professors, but there were always some slackers on the council
who favored rewarding those professors who demanded the
least from students. Fortunately, during my years at Bologna,
the slackers were in the minority."

"That situation has changed," Nico explained. "The University itself now has a greater role in determining payments to the
faculty. Do you miss practicing law now that you are retired?"

"I still consult on some cases, but as you can see," Cetti
laughed and patted his stomach as he continued, "consulting

does not bring enough anxiety to tame this bulge. My physician argues that I should do more walking, but I think it will be easier to have my tailor-fit me with a larger tunic.

"You said that you wish to speak with me. If you are bringing me an issue that will cause me to fret, then I might be able to postpone the next appointment with my tailor."

Cetti was in such a jolly mood that Nico felt a pang of guilt by raising a serious topic.

"Do you recall the details of all the cases you prosecuted? I have been reading of a case of yours in Mantua filed against the Duke and the Duchy."

"I don't remember all my cases, there were so many, but I do recall that one. None of the plaintiff's lawyers had ever brought a case against the Duchy, so they asked me to join their team because I had recently obtained a ruling against the Duchy of Savoy. Actually, they did more than ask me; they offered a generous fee for my services."

"The document in the University of Florence law library has some information about the case, but it does not tell the outcome. Did your team prevail?"

"The lead lawyer on our team decided to name both the Duke and the Duchy as co-defendants. Normally, covering both possibilities is a sound approach, but I found one earlier case in the archive where the Duke had been named as a defendant. The plaintiff in that case presented solid evidence, and there was little doubt in my mind that the ruling should have gone against the Duke, but instead, the magistrates dismissed the case. They were afraid of retribution by the Duke if they had issued a ruling against him. I know the Duke. He is a man of integrity who would have accepted a fair ruling. By dismissing the case, those magistrates distorted the law. They were the same magistrates assigned to preside over our case, so I urged our team leader not to name the

Duke in the suit, but he did not take my advice. The result was that the magistrates, again fearing retribution, dismissed our case."

Nico saw a clear relationship between Cetti's experience in Mantua and the Pietra Alta situation. He spoke his conclusion aloud as it formed in his thoughts. "So, it is best to avoid naming a royal as a defendant whenever possible."

"Not necessarily," Cetti replied. "The important lesson to be learned is that it is not possible to obtain justice from magistrates who feel intimidated. Intimidation can stem from many causes, fear of offending a royal is but one. Often problems of this kind can be resolved by a change of venue. Unfortunately, in Mantua that was not a possibility. There was no other tribunal in Mantua with jurisdiction in the matter."

Cetti's advice supported the recommendation of professor Viviani that Pietra Alta should not bring charges before a tribunal in Rimini. Viviani had suggested the city of Perugia as an appropriate venue. Nico wished to continue the discussion with Cetti, but servers were setting out the food trays. Guests lured by tempting aromas spread across the terrace, and Signor Cetti was eager to join them in the queue. As Cetti sauntered away, he pressed both hands against his stomach as if wondering how much food he could pile onto his plate before the buttons would pop from his strained tunic.

After guests plucked the last morsel of food from the table and showered Nunzio with toasts to his continued good health, one guest departed. Like lemmings, others quickly followed his lead. Travelers on the road could only wonder at the reason for the parade of carts and wagons streaming toward the city. Family members and their closest friends remained at the villa. The quiet evening allowed Nico and Bianca to have an unhurried conversation with Nunzio. As a dutiful surrogate father, Nunzio embarrassed Nico by regaling Bianca with tales from

Nico's youth. Bianca impressed Nico and Nunzio with the names of women who wished to join her list of clients.

The following morning, Nico and Donato enjoyed a filling country breakfast before leaving for an early meeting with Vittorio, the carpenter whose brother-in-law was a prior of Pietra Alta.

21

Vittorio's shop, Florence

Donato guided Nico along one of the main roads in the city to the far end of the Chiavi district where Vittorio's carpentry shop was located. In years past, farms dotted that quarter of the city. Growth eventually drove the farms to the countryside, leaving the farm buildings that enterprising businessmen soon adapted to other purposes. Vittorio acquired an old barn lined with goat pens. He had the pens in the central area removed to create an open workspace and used the remaining pens as storage bins to hold lumber of various sizes and projects under construction.

To expand his business, Vittorio also took on two apprentices. Laborers were always eager to place their sons as apprentices to successful artisans. They dreamed that one day their youngsters would gain the skills needed to become a guild member with a business of their own. When Nico and Donato arrived at the shop, one young man was rubbing oil onto a newly built piece of furniture. The oil imparted a lustrous honey-colored patina to the wood and emphasized its tight grain. The other apprentice was using an adz to round the edge of a long plank.

Donato watched the man pull several long curls of shavings from the plank before asking, "What are you making?"

"This will be a serving counter in a tavern. The owner

wants to upgrade all the furnishings. We will also be making tables and chairs for him."

Nico and Donato watched the apprentice transform the square edge of the plank into a gentle curve.

"We are here to meet with Vittorio," Nico said. "Can you tell us where to find him?"

The apprentice pointed to a corner of the building where one of the goat pens had been altered to form an enclosed area. "He uses that space as an office. You will find him there."

Vittorio and his wife Teresa were seated around a table. He motioned for Donato and Nico to join them.

Teresa's downcast expression reflected concern for her brother, one of the priors of Pietra Alta. She raised her head to acknowledge Nico and Donato when Vittorio introduced them, but she said nothing beyond thanking them for their willingness to help.

Vittorio lifted two sheets of paper from the table. "These are from Fapane, my brother-in-law. Six soldiers are stationed at Pietra Alta as monitors. Mostly the soldiers stay in a camp that they established at the edge of town. Their mission is to unnerve the people of the town by watching them. The soldiers have been ordered not to go into the town, but some of them defy the order. Fapane is the town baker. One of the soldiers approached him to buy bread. While doing so, he warned Fapane that not only will the town be made to pay taxes; it will be made to suffer for its earlier refusal. The soldiers do not always buy what they need; sometimes they take what they want. One family reported that two chickens disappeared from their chicken house during the night. Another family said one of its trees was stripped of fruit on the same night. Girls and women are afraid to go out alone."

"Have there been any more demands for tax payments?"

"Not yet. The soldiers were dispatched to the town by the

knight. They expect him to return with a full cavalry contingent soon."

Vittorio had been referring to one of the notes as he spoke. Nico asked, "What does the other note say?"

"This one came today at first light. I had told Fapane that I would meet with him. This note names the place in Arezzo where I will meet with him later today."

Vittorio looked at Nico with an expectant expression. "I hope there is something . . . that you found something, I can tell him."

Nico clasped his hands together on the table in front of him. He opened his mouth but held back momentarily before speaking. "I have uncovered information that might be helpful."

Nico paused again. "Will you be returning to Florence tonight following the meeting in Arezzo?"

"Yes. There is enough time for me to travel to Arezzo and return tonight."

"The matter is complicated. There are options to consider. It will be better if I travel to Arezzo with you to meet with your brother-in-law."

For the first time, Teresa looked hopeful. Vittorio waited for Nico to continue.

"The Papal Archives have confirmed that Pieta Alta is not part of the Province of Rimini, so the Province has no basis for imposing a tax on the town. I can describe to Fapane the ways that the town can seek a ruling in its favor. That is one aspect of the problem for us to discuss. The other aspect, the more problematic one, is how to ensure that the ruling is carried out."

Nico was interrupted by the appearance of a young man standing at the entrance to the office area.

"I am Mauro. I have a message from the Guild for Signor Argenti."

To the newcomer, Nico said, "Thank you for joining us," and to the others, he explained, "Pietra Alta will need to engage a lawyer in the Papal States who has relevant experience. The Magistrates and Notaries Guild here in Florence maintains lists of lawyers in other states."

Mauro handed a sheet to Nico. "Here is the list you requested of lawyers in the Papal States."

As he scanned the list, Nico said, "Most of these are in Rome, but there are three in Perugia. They might be candidates to represent Pietra Alta."

"Our lists are not always complete," Mauro said. "There may be more than three lawyers in Perugia."

Pointing to the names of those in Perugia, Nico asked Mauro, "Do any of these have experience filing cases against sovereign?"

"The Guild records the specialties of lawyers in the Florentine Republic, but not for lawyers elsewhere. I did confer with two of the Guild consuls who believed that those lawyers in Perugia only dealt with cases involving local disputes, although the consuls' opinions were little more than speculation."

Nico thanked Mauro for this help, then turned to Vittorio. "This is the last piece of information I was expecting. We can leave for Arezzo whenever you are ready."

Within the hour, Nico and Vittorio were en route. To cover the distance as quickly as possible, they rented two speedy horses from a nearby stable rather than using Vittorio's wagon. Dark clouds covered the hills to the east as they departed from Florence. By the mid-point of their journey, a light rain had begun to fall, and soon afterward, channels of water from the heavier rain in the mountains were streaming down the hillsides and washing across the road. By the time they neared Arezzo, a steady downpour had drenched their oilskin cloaks. The coats kept their bodies dry, but their faces were pelted constantly by cold drops. The rain did not hamper the horses. Even without the benefit of oilskin coverings, they continued along the increasingly muddy road. The men carried a sack of food for a mid-day meal, but they found no shelter along the road, so they opted to forego eating. Nico was thankful for the bountiful breakfast he enjoyed at Nunzio's villa.

22

AREZZO

Fapane had provided detailed instructions to the tavern where they would meet, but reduced visibility made it impossible to find all the landmarks he had listed. Vittorio decided that they needed to seek help when they realized that they had failed to locate the church of San Domenico. The owner of a nearby butcher shop agreed they had missed a turn and needed to turn back. At least now, the driving rain was at their backs. Following the new instructions, they found the tavern midway down a small street at the point where the narrow vicolo constricted further into a small alley that vanished around a tight curve behind the tavern.

The building was strangely shaped for a tavern. The long narrow room gave the impression of being a corridor, except it led nowhere. It was closed at the far end and had no side rooms. Nico and Vittorio shook the water from their cloaks and stepped to the bar hoping it offered warm drinks to dispel their chill. Behind the counter, a bored tavern keeper was sitting with his feet propped on an old crate, head down, and eyes closed. The bartender must have been a hired hand because no tavern owner would have shown such little interest in customers. Grudgingly, the barman rose. He stood facing them without any greeting, waiting for one of them to speak.

"Something warm?" Vittorio queried.

"Fasani," the barman countered.

The name meant nothing to Vittorio or Nico. "What is Fasani?"

"The warm drink. The only warm drink."

"What is in it?" Nico asked.

"I don't know. I don't make it."

The barkeep jerked his head to the side to indicate a vessel on a shelf behind him. "I just scoop it from that crock."

Having no alternative, they ordered two mugs of Fasani. The barman upended two mugs and shook them to dislodge particles that floated slowly to the floor. Into each mug he ladled the unknown liquid. Its tawny color gave no clue as to its original components. When he set the drinks on the serving counter, Nico and Vittorio looked at each other wondering which of them would be brave enough, or foolish enough, to take the first sample. Nico shrugged, lifted a mug to his lips, and sipped.

"It is warm," Nico informed his companion before taking a full swallow.

The tavern was practically empty. Dim daylight entering through a single window made it possible for Vittorio to recognize Fapane who sat alone at the far end of the room. The only other patrons were two men sitting at a table close to the door. With drinks in hand, Vittorio and Nico walked the length of the room, leaving a trail of wet boot prints on the floor behind them. As Fapane rose to greet them, Nico was struck by his appearance. The prior was younger than he had imagined. Nearly all members of the Florentine Signoria had at least some grey hair, and for many, it was their only color. On that basis, Nico had the impression that all men in their position were elderly. Fapane's hair had only a slight trace of grey at his temples. His brown hair was the shade of walnuts, an uncommon hair color among Italians. Fapane had other uncommon characteristics as well; his face was round with puffy cheeks, and his nose was small, or maybe his puffy cheeks merely made his nose appear small.

The only other person Nico had known with those characteristics was a student at the university who was said to be from Genoa. Nico was never close with that student, so he never asked whether all those in Genoa shared the same characteristics. How unusual it would be for a prior of Pietra Alta, a small town in the Apennine mountains, to have roots in Genoa. Maybe someday Nico would have the opportunity to discuss the topic with Fapane, but this was not the time.

As Fapane rose to greet them, he radiated a hopeful optimism. Nico felt a twinge of guilt for imagining that Fapane's buoyancy might be due to the arrival of a Florentine lawyer who had graciously researched Fapane's dilemma and traveled fifty miles through driving rain to offer advice. After the briefest of introductions, they turned to the topic that brought them together. When Nico mentioned the report of the Papal Archive, Fapane's tension melted away.

"A statement by the Papal Archive will be strong evidence to a tribunal," Nico stated.

"Will it be enough to win?" Fapane asked.

Nico didn't want Fapane to become overconfident, so he said only, "It's a good start."

Fapane thought for a moment then expressed his concern, "There is one problem. Pietra Alta is a small town. We have no tribunal. We do not have even a single lawyer in Pietra Alta."

"It is not necessary for the tribunal to be in Pietra Alta," Nico replied. "You can bring your case to a tribunal elsewhere. I discussed this matter with two lawyers experienced with the legal practices of the Papal States, and they believe it would be advantageous for you to file your case with a tribunal in the town of Perugia."

Nico handed Fapane a sheet of paper. "These are the names of lawyers in Perugia. I have no information about the nature of their practice or their experience. You will need to interview them to determine which are willing and capable of prosecuting a case against the Province of Rimini."

Fapane nodded his head slowly as he studied the list. While he did so, Vittorio stepped from the table to order another round of drinks. No one else had entered the establishment, and the two men who were previously seated near the entrance were gone. The barkeeper was again slumped in a chair with his eyes closed. His heavy breathing and his lip quivering when he exhaled meant that this time he was sleeping soundly. Vittorio dropped the three mugs onto the counter from a sufficient height to cause a resounding thud that echoed throughout the room. The startled bartender pitched forward and slid from his chair to the floor before controlling his senses. Looking up, he saw three mugs still dancing across the counter. Behind them, Vittorio grinned, obviously pleased with the reaction he provoked. Without speaking, he again ladled Frasani into the mugs. This time instead of being tawny-colored, the liquid was the color of prunes. Vittorio didn't ask what accounted for the changed appearance; he just accepted the drinks and carried them to his companions at the rear of the corridor-room. They drank the unknown brews and shared the food they had brought with them from Florence while Nico considered the best way to tell Fapane the additional uncertainties Pietra Alta would face.

"Whenever charges are filed, the tribunals inform the accused of the charges and request them to present their defense. At that point, if the Province fears that the tribunal will rule against them, they might act immediately and dispatch soldiers to collect taxes before the tribunal can reach a verdict. To prevent that from happening, your lawyer should ask for a temporary injunction, that is, a ruling to suspend any action by the Province until the tribunal can conduct a full hearing. Temporary injunctions are common, so the tribunal will honor such a request unless the Province could demonstrate that a delay would cause it irreparable harm, and I do not see any possibility of them making that claim."

"Unfair taxes would have a big impact on us, on my neighbors, but any taxes from the people of Pietra Alta couldn't possibly cause significant harm to the Province of Rimini."

Nico nodded. "Yes, I feel certain the tribunal will share that view."

After listening to the exchange between Nico and Fapane, Vittorio asked, "What evidence could the Province present to make its case? How could they counter the statement of the Papal Archive?"

"That is an excellent question," Nico replied, "and one I cannot answer. I did not uncover any information that could support Rimini's position, but that doesn't mean the lawyers representing the Province won't find something. There is always uncertainty in any legal proceeding."

Nico paused to frame his next statement. He did not wish to worry Fapane unnecessarily, but the prior deserved a complete understanding of the risks.

"Even if the tribunal issues a ruling in favor of Pieta Alta, the Province may decide to ignore the ruling."

Fapane's eyes opened wide as Nico continued. "Legal rulings have been defied in other jurisdictions. I am not aware of that happening in the Papal States, but my knowledge of cases in the Papal States is limited."

"What happens if the Province does defy the ruling?" Fapane asked.

"In Florence, magistrates would order the guardia to enforce the ruling. I am not familiar with the procedures in the Papal States, and that is why you need a lawyer who practices in that jurisdiction."

Nico regretted that he was not able to answer Fapane's difficult questions. Thinking about his lack of knowledge gave him an even greater appreciation for the skills of Michele Cetti, who argued and won cases in different jurisdictions throughout the Italian peninsula. Having no more to discuss, the three men prepared to leave. Nico and Vittorio were eager to return to Florence before nightfall.

"I had planned to return to Pietra Alta to share the information you gave me with my fellow priors, but I have decided instead to travel directly to Perugia to find a lawyer who can represent us. Before I came to Arezzo, my colleagues empowered me to take whatever action I deem appropriate on behalf of our town. I feel that I should act expeditiously because the soldiers from Rimini might return at any time."

The three exited the tavern, first Vittorio, then Nico, and finally Fapane. Each man pulled his cloak tight as he stepped out into the rain. The door had barely closed behind Fapane when the three were startled by the loud thwack of an arrow embedding itself in the door jamb only inches from Fapane's shoulder. At the far end of the vicolo, a lone archer was already cocking his bow with another arrow. The sound of a second arrow embedding itself in the center of the door dashed any thought of returning to the tavern.

"This way!" Vittorio shouted.

He sprinted down the alley with his two companions close at his heels. At the rear of the tavern, they turned to follow the curving path. Two men jumped out from hiding, and each swung a wooden club; one slammed into the back of Nico's head, the other hammered Fapane. Both men collided, then slumped down as a single unmoving tangle onto the muddy road.

Vittorio turned to face the attackers. He recognized them as the two men that had been in the tavern earlier. He raised his hands to deflect their next blows. It was a futile attempt. One attacker swung low, striking Vittorio's leg with bone-breaking force that twisted his knee to an inhuman angle. Vittorio pitched forward, a move that put him in range of the second attacker, who smashed his club into Vittorio's forehead. The attackers jumped clear as the impact of Vittorio's inert form striking the road lofted a spray of muddy water into the air.

23

THE APENNINES

It was the cold that brought Nico awake. He was lying on something hard, and his head hurt. He was sure that his eyes were open, but he saw only darkness. He flattened his hand against the ground and pressed down, expecting to leverage himself upright to a sitting position. Instead of being raised upward, he screamed as stinging pain shot up his arm. The terrifying scream sent a flock of birds racing into the black sky. He fell onto his back and shuddered uncontrollably until the pain gradually subsided. Tears filled his eyes.

Nico knew that pain. When he was seven years old and learning to ride, his horse had stumbled in a rabbit hole. Nico was launched into the air and landed with his arm twisted beneath him. His panicked mother ran to him and comforted him by pulling him close and stroking his hair. From medical training received in the military, his father knew immediately that the arm was broken. He splinted his crying son's arm and fashioned a sling to immobilize the limb. This time there were no parents to soothe the suffering and tend the injury.

Gently, Nico flexed the fingers on his other hand; slowly he rotated the wrist, then he raised the arm slightly by bending it at the elbow. There was no pain. With great care, he pressed his hand against the moist ground, lightly at first, then with increasing pressure until he was sitting upright. At least one arm functioned properly.

Sticky resin-coated pine needles clung to his palm when he lifted the hand. Again, he lowered his hand to the ground and swept it in a wide arc. Pine needles carpeted the entire area within his reach. There were no groves of pine trees in the city of Florence, and it seemed equally unlikely that there would be a stand of pine trees in the city of Arezzo. He must be in a wooded area outside the city. Where? And how did he get there?

Nico tried to remember what had happened and how he got there. He recalled that he and Vittorio met with Prior Fapane. Arrows! As the three were leaving the tavern, someone was shooting at them. They ran and then. . . His memory offered nothing further.

Nico turned his head to the left and then to the right, eager to spot something, anything, in the darkness. There was no sign of his companions. Over his right shoulder, a sliver of pink shown in the sky. Nico stared at the light for several minutes. Instead of fading from a rose color to a deep red as it does at dusk, the sliver of light expanded and brightened. Morning. He had been asleep or unconscious throughout the night.

Squinting in the dim light, Nico observed that he was not in a small pine grove. The trees that surrounded him extended to the limit of his vision. In all directions, distant trees towered above those nearby. He was sitting at the bottom of a ravine or hollow. The land rising from the depression was steep, so climbing out would not be easy, but Nico knew he had no alternative.

Before attempting a climb, he needed to deal with his

injured arm. From a pocket in his torn tunic, he withdrew a handkerchief, which he wrapped around his hand and wrist to secure the wrist in a fixed position. Using his working hand and his teeth, he pulled the ends of the cloth tight and tied them. Nico's money pouch was missing. Whoever pulled it free had torn his tunic. Loss of the bag was of little consequence because Nico kept only small value coins in the pouch. His silver coins and gold florins he secreted in a wallet affixed to a cord around his waist hidden under the tunic.

Nico unbuttoned the tunic and removed the cord. He looped one end around his neck, and the other end around his battered arm to create a makeshift sling. It was a crude device that would keep his arm in place only if he moved slowly and carefully. He leaned to the side and grabbed the trunk of a small tree, which he used to pull himself to a standing position. He scanned the sloping ground, searching for the most suitable route for climbing. He also listened for any sounds that might suggest a promising direction.

Almost masked by the rustle of breezes through the trees, he heard a faint groan. At first, he attributed it to tree branches rubbing together, but a cough soon followed. Clearly, the sound was being made by a person. Nico picked his way around rocks and over fallen branches to where he found Fapane lying on the ground. He was on his side with his knees pulled up to his chest. Even in the dim light, Nico could see that dried blood covered the side of Fapane's head.

"Fapane, it's Nico. Can you hear me? Can you speak?"

Another groan, this time followed by a series of coughs, and then faintly, "Nico?"

"Yes, it's Nico. How badly are you hurt?"

In a weak voice, Fapane pushed out his reply, "My head is throbbing, and my ankle is twisted. It hurts, but I don't think it is broken."

Nico studied the surroundings for any sign of Vittorio. If Vittorio was unable to move or speak, then a disturbed patch of foliage or even a broken tree branch might be a clue to his location. Nico found no clue that Vittorio had been left in the forest with them. At length, he announced to Fapane, "There is no sign of Vittorio."

Fapane merely grunted in response.

"My arm may be broken, so I can't help you stand or walk. I must leave to find someone who can help us. Then I will return. Do you understand?"

Fapane grunted again, followed by one feeble word, "Go."

A break in the tree line mid-way up the hillside indicated a stretch of flat ground that Nico assumed might be a woodland path. Nico began climbing the steep slope toward the break. He paused several times during the climb to reassess his route and alter it to avoid fallen tree limbs and other obstacles. Despite taking care to protect his injured arm, he could not prevent it from brushing against branches and saplings in the dense forest. Each strike caused him to stop moving until the pain subsided.

When Nico reached the flat ground, he saw that it was indeed a woodland path. Wagon tracks suggested that the road was used by wood cutters to carry their logs from the forest. The road extended into the forest, disappearing from view in both directions and giving Nico no clue as to which direction he should favor.

A snuffling sound accompanied by the rustling of a small bush a short distance from the edge of the road suggested the presence of a small animal. Nico's first glimpse wasn't one of the forest creatures he anticipated; it was a curly pink tail. Pigs with their sensitive noses were a favored way of locating truffles, the valuable fungus that grows from the roots of hazel and oak trees. If the tail belonged to a truffle-hunting pig, then its owner had to be near. Moments later, a man still hidden in the forest levied praise on his truffle-hunting pig, saying, "Bene porcino."

Nico called out to the hidden figure, and upon hearing Nico's plea for help, a short man wearing a leather cape stepped into the road. Relying on a cane for balance, he hobbled along the path to where Nico was standing. Nico described his predicament, at least to the extent he understood it himself.

"My wagon is on the road around the bend," the man said. "Come with me."

Nico pointed to the hollow. "My friend is down there. He is hurt, unable to walk. I don't want to leave him."

The man did not feel physically able to assist Fapane himself but said he would fetch his son who could do so. He headed off down the road toward his wagon with his trained pig at his heels. Nico sat at the edge of the road, waiting for the man to return and listening for any sounds of Vittorio, but hearing nothing. From the sitting position, he could look downward into the hollow, but he was not able to see Fapane through the dense foliage.

Sunlight was streaming through the treetops by the time Nico heard the wagon approaching. When it came into view, the short man was riding as a passenger, and a younger man, his son, was driving. The younger man helped Nico into the wagon before he climbed down into the hollow to assist Fapane. Even with the young man supporting him, Fapane struggled to make the climb. It required Nico and the young man working together to lift Fapane into the wagon. They positioned Fapane on his side, leaning against a hay bale with his knees bent so his legs and injured ankle fit in the short bed of the wagon. With the assistance of the young man, Nico pulled himself into the vehicle. He sat upright leaning against another bale and let his legs dangle from the rear deck.

Snatches of conversation from the two men driving the wagon drifted back to Nico and Fapane, but the sound of the wheels bouncing over the rough road masked their words and prevented Nico from learning their destination. Pain and the aftershock of their experience dissuaded Nico and Fapane from speaking. Nico became mesmerized, staring at the road receding behind and the parade of trees flanking it on each side. His daze broke when the noise and motion of the wagon ended.

From a nearby low stone building, two strapping monks wearing the black robes of the Order of Saint Benedict strode to the wagon. They quickly assessed the condition of its passengers, then one of the monks supported Nico's shoulder and eased him from the wagon to the ground. Nico remembered Bianca telling him that her father had once traveled to a small hospital in Arezzo. He tried to recall the name.

"Is this Saint Jerome hospital?" he asked.

"No, it is San Benedetto monastery."

Nico may have misremembered the name, but he knew there were several hospitals in Arezzo, so why had they been taken to a monastery? He repeated the name quizzically. "San Benedetto?"

The monk, who was by then helping his companion to lift Fapane from the wagon, replied, "Yes, this is the San Benedetto monastery in Monterchi."

Monterchi was not a place known to Nico; however, before he could ask about the location, the monks positioned themselves on either side of Fapane and carried him toward a courtyard alongside the monastery. Nico followed them to a row of small buildings at the far end of the yard. The monks maneuvered Fapane into one of the buildings. Inside, they passed through a short hallway and into a sparsely furnished room where they lowered Fapane onto a cot. Other than the cot, the room contained only two chairs and a table set against one wall. A crucifix hung high on the wall above the table. A cabinet mounted on the wall across the room held a variety of medical supplies. Fapane chose to sit at the edge of the bed rather than to lie down. Nico lowered himself into one of the chairs.

As the monks moved toward the doorway preparing to leave, one of them said, "Friar Giovanni will be..." He stopped speaking when a large burly man appeared in the doorway.

"I am Friar Giovanni. I am not a physician, but I do have medical training, and with God's help I tend to the medical needs of the monks at the monastery, the nuns at the convent, and to travelers such as yourselves."

The friar knelt near Fapane. With care, he slid his hands over Fapane's leg and ankle. Satisfied that he understood the extend of the injury, he rose to examine Fapane's head wound. After his examination, he announced, "Your ankle is twisted, but not broken. We can treat the damage to help the ankle mend. Blows to the head can cause hidden damage that only makes itself known in time. To heal that wound, my brothers will offer their prayers."

Friar Giovanni moved to Nico and unwrapped the handkerchief, revealing a reddened hand and a purple wrist swollen to nearly double its normal size. Nico braced for the pain to come as the friar played his fingers along Nico's forearm toward the wrist. To Nico's surprise, there was no pain. The friar's muscled hands looked to be those of a metal smith, but their touch felt like the toes of a butterfly.

"God has favored you with sturdy bones. You can tell from your pain that the sprain is severe, but it is only a sprain. There are no broken bones."

The friar rose to address both of his patients. "You were traveling with another. One called Vittorio. He was brought here earlier and has been fearful for his companions. He has suffered a severe injury that is much worse than yours. As soon as your wounds are dressed, you may see him.

"He said you were attacked on a street in Arezzo. Arezzo is a peaceful city. Never before have I heard of anyone preying on travelers in that way."

Friar Giovanni paused before saying anything further in the hope that one of the two men might provide details of the incident. When they did not, he said, "When you return to Arezzo, you must report the episode to the authorities so the assailants are stopped before they can harm others. We prefer that travelers who visit us do so in good health."

"Do many travelers visit here?" Fapane asked.

"Travelers have passed through this monastery for more than four hundred years. Two hundred years past, it was visited by the beloved Saint Francis. He said mass in our church," the monk said proudly. "Since then, the church and the monastery have been favorite stopping points for pilgrims who walk in the footsteps of that holy man."

"One of the monks mentioned that the monastery is in the town of Monterchi," Nico said. "I do not know of the town. Is it far from Arezzo?"

"Monterchi is about fifteen miles from Arezzo. You may not know of the town, but it has become a popular destination since the artist Piero della Francesca painted his magnificent Madonna del Prato at the church of Santa Maria. The painting is known as the pregnant Madonna. Many who love beautiful art and the Holy Mother come to Monterchi to view the masterpiece." Giovanni beamed with pride as he spoke.

"These may not be the right circumstances for you to visit the church, but you must return in the future. I assure you that the beauty of Piero's work will make the journey worthwhile."

Friar Giovanni blessed both men before he turned to leave.

He had barely stepped from the room when two nuns entered. One of the nuns set a bucket on the floor near Fapane, dipped a cloth into the foaming liquid, and used the wet cloth to clean his head wound. The other nun withdrew a handful of a gray paste-like substance from the bucket that she carried. The potent astringent fumes caused Nico's nostrils to tighten and his eyes to tear. The nun, obviously accustomed to the salve, did not react to the smell. She slathered the paste on Nico's wrist and hand; then she wrapped them with a clean linen cloth.

Nico knew his question was foolish, but he asked nonetheless. "Does this salve work well?"

His question caused the other nun, the one ministering to Fapane, to begin chuckling. A smile crept across the face of the nun who was bandaging his hand, and she responded, "The ones we treat always recover quickly. All of them receive this creation of Friar Giovanni, and he believes that it is responsible for their rapid healing. Sister Agata and I offer prayers for everyone we treat. We have faith that our prayers do more to promote the healing than this paste, although we do agree that God also guides the hands of Friar Giovanni."

As the two nuns finished their work, a third nun entered. She carried a tray holding two bowls of broth and bread for dipping. The restorative power of the soup made Nico and Fapane talkative. They speculated on why they were attacked and then taken to a forest. They wondered why they were at a monastery rather than a hospital in Arezzo, and how far was Monterchi from Arezzo. They regretted that they had not learned the names of their benefactors, the truffle hunter and his son.

A young man wearing a plain gray tunic, not the black robe of Benedictine monks, stepped into the room. He waited politely without speaking until Nico and Fapane stopped speaking, then he handed Fapane a crutch and said, "I can take you to see your friend if you wish."

Vittorio lay on a bed in a room at the end of the hall. Wooden planks on both sides of his injured leg were wrapped tightly with wide cloth strips to hold the leg firmly in a fixed position. Upon seeing his fellow travelers, Vittorio's lips curled up in a weak smile.

"My leg twisted, and my knee was displaced."

Speaking of the injury let him recall his pain and made him wince.

"The big one, the friar. . ." He paused, trying to recall the friar's name.

"Giovanni," Fapane said, completing the thought.

"Yes, Friar Giovanni. He put the knee back in place."

Vittorio winced again, this time remembering the pain when the friar reset the dislocated knee.

"The friar said he had fixed a displaced knee once before. That time it was the knee of a cow, but the friar said that after a long recovery, the cow was able to walk again, so he believes there will be no permanent damage to my knee. He said that all I need now is rest and prayer."

After Nico and Fapane described the extent of their injuries, Vittorio said, "I saw the men who attacked us. They were the same men who were sitting in the tavern when we arrived. They left the tavern before we did. The archer wasn't trying to strike us; his mission was to force us to flee into the dark alley where the others were waiting."

"If robbery was their motive, why did they beat us?" Fapane asked.

"And why bring us to a forest?" Nico added. "Were you also abandoned in a forest?"

"Yes, a farmer found me at the side of a road and brought me to this monastery. But the ones who attacked us were not thieves. Before they hit me, they said, 'You should have stayed in Florence. Pietra Alta is not your business.'"

Fapane sank into a chair, bent forward, and held his head in his hands. "They must have been soldiers from the encampment near Pietra Alta. They must have followed me. God forgive me; I brought this misery to you."

"They did not follow you," Nico declared.

Fapane and Vittorio looked at Nico and waited for him to explain the meaning of his statement.

"They could not have followed you because they arrived at the tavern before us. Someone must have informed them about our meeting. Who else knew of the meeting?"

"Only the priors, Albizzo, Pandolfo and I. We planned the meeting. I trust Albizzo and Pandolfo with my life. I cannot believe they would disclose our plan to the soldiers. It is not possible."

"Then someone else must have overheard your planning," Vittorio reasoned.

The room fell silent while the three men wondered what would make someone betray his friends and neighbors.

"I can only imagine that the soldiers forced someone to reveal our plan for the meeting," Fapane said.

Vittorio looked to Fapane and said, "The monks offered to transport us to Arezzo. From there, Nico and I can make our way to Florence, and you can return to Pietra Alta."

In a firm voice, Fapane stated, "I will not be going to Pietra Alta. The information Nico provided has convinced me that I must go to Perugia to find a lawyer who can represent Pietra Alta."

"But you are injured. You can hardly walk," Vittorio protested.

Fapane dismissed Vittorio's concern. "It is my ankle that is injured. I promise I will not walk to Perugia. Anyway, the healing power of Friar Giovanni's concoction will be as strong in Perugia as it is here, and I do not doubt that the prayers of the nuns will follow me."

Seeing that Vittorio remained skeptical, Fapane added, "The vicious attack on us shows what the soldiers are capable of doing. I cannot let them loose their vile behavior on my entire town."

Vittorio nodded his understanding. Then Nico spoke, directing his words to Fapane.

"I will accompany you to Perugia. The original tax dispute is a civil matter, but the assault is a criminal matter. It should be addressed as well, especially if the soldiers acted at the direction of the Lord of Rimini. As one of the crime victims, I can help to make the case."

24

FLORENCE

Joanna set a bowl of figs on the table and sat facing her husband. At mealtimes, she usually sat next to Donato, so that both of them faced their son Giorgio. Breaking with their customary arrangement told Donato that she had an important matter to discuss.

"Nico's bed is unused. Didn't he expect to return last evening?" she asked.

"That was his plan," Donato replied. "He and Vittorio were to meet with Vittorio's brother-in-law in Arezzo and then return directly to Florence. They would spend most of their time on the journey to Arezzo and the return. They expected the meeting itself to be brief. Nico planned to return by dark."

"I am worried."

"There are many reasons why he could have been delayed."

"And most of the reasons are not for a good cause," Joanna countered.

"Oh, I can think of one or two enticements that might have kept him in Arezzo."

Donato's playful suggestion did not calm Joanna as he

intended. It had the opposite effect, causing her demeanor to harden. She pressed both palms down firmly against the table, and her posture stiffened.

"Don't trifle with me, dear husband. You know Nico's spirit has settled since he met Bianca. Like all you men, his eyes are attracted by large breasts, but he no longer lingers over every woman with generous curves. He did not remain in Arezzo to play."

Donato leaned back in his chair to increase the distance between himself and his wife's intensity. He decided to put forth more plausible rationales.

"The road between Florence and Arezzo is well-traveled. There have been no reports of highwaymen on that road. Perhaps one of the horses went lame. Nico managed to care for himself for six years at Bologna; he should be able to survive one night in Arezzo."

Joanna liked events to proceed in an orderly fashion precisely as planned. The fact that Nico had intended to return the previous evening and he did not was upsetting to her. Alessa came into the room while Donato and Joanna were speaking. She was still wearing her night clothes and had her hair tied back as it was when she slept. She waited until Donato and Joanna finished their exchange before making her presence known.

"I did not sleep well. I kept waking from a dream. In the dream, I was wandering through a forest. Trees kept falling all around me. They always fell toward me as though they were intentionally trying to strike me. I awoke with a strong feeling that something is not right with Nico, as though he is lost or injured."

As she spoke, she rubbed one wrist with her other hand. The subconscious gesture went unnoticed by her and the others. Even though Joanna and Donato did not understand the special connection between Nico and Alessa that let them share thoughts and feelings, her foreknowledge had been proven correct many times in the past. Alessa's premonition enhanced the anxiety that already troubled Joanna, and it gave Donato reason for concern.

Donato palmed another fig as he rose from the table. He said, "I'll visit Vittorio's shop to ask him about Nico. If Vittorio has not returned, the apprentices may have received word from him."

Joanna pushed her chair back. "I'll go with you."

"Is today your day to bring Giorgio to his tutor?" Donato asked.

Joanna's hand touched the grammar book resting on the table near her. Joanna and a neighbor escorted their sons to the boys' tutor on alternate days, and Donato was correct, this was her day. Although Giorgio was old enough to venture through most areas of the city on his own, the tutor, a well-respected scholar himself, lived in a shabby area of the Santa Maria Novella district. Neither Joanna nor her neighbor felt comfortable having the boys venture through that part of the city alone. Donato and the other boy's father believed the women were overly protective, but the men had the good sense to keep their opinions to themselves.

Alessa slid the book from under Joanna's fingers. "I'll take Giorgio today."

A commonly held view of Florentines is that their city was at its best in the early morning. The air was clean and fresh, city workers had removed the previous day's litter from city streets, and early risers were optimistic that the day would bring them good fortune. All those positive signs that Joanna and Donato encountered on their way to Vittorio's shop did not lessen their anxiety.

Both apprentices were outside the shop, loading a tall

display cabinet into a wagon when Joanna and Donato arrived at the shop. They tipped the piece back and sat it down carefully on a thick pad spread across the wagon's bed. Donato helped them surround the item with other pads that would protect it during travel.

When the cabinet was secured, Donato asked, "Is Vittorio in the shop?"

"Signor Ciampelli should be here, but he is not. We came here early this morning to get this shipment ready for him. The cabinet must be delivered to the hospital in Caldine today because the padrone of the Cresci family, the one who commissioned the piece, will be there for the dedication of the hospital. This piece is being featured at the dedication."

Joanna leaned over the wagon to study the intricate carvings on the doors that enclosed the lower portion of the cabinet. "The scene is lovely. Is the woman in the scene Santa Maria di Maddelena?"

"Yes, it is she. Signor Cresci's mother always admired the work of the artist Michelozzo who included the saint in many of his works. In honor of his mother, Signor Cresci requested that we create several pieces of furniture in Michelozzo's style. Signor Ciampelli has worked many weeks doing the carvings."

"I am not familiar with the work of Michelozzo," Joanna said, "but this design is exquisite. Vittorio must be very pleased with his creation."

"He is pleased and is eager to see the reaction of Signor Cresci. That is why he planned to be here this morning so he could deliver the piece himself."

"Have you received any word from him?" Donato asked.

"No. We have heard nothing since he departed for Arezzo yesterday."

"Is his wife Teresa in the shop?"

"No, she has not come here yet this morning."

Donato had never been to Vittorio's home, so he obtained directions from the apprentices. Vittorio and Teresa lived in the Campo di Marte district in an apartment on the third level of an old building above a leather shop. The farm building that he purchased as his new shop and the equipment he bought to expand his business had strained Vittorio's finances. Until those investments proved profitable, Vittorio and his wife resigned themselves to living in a modest rental space. Small windows covered with a gritty film filtered the light and made the stairwell appear dark and dingy. Lack of ventilation contributed to a slightly sour smell on the third level landing outside Vittorio's apartment.

When Teresa opened the door, Donato and Joanna were pleased to see that the interior of the apartment, in contrast to the stairway, was bright and cheerful. Windows in the open space were large and clean. The air was as fresh as outdoors. The presence of Donato and Joanna did not surprise Teresa. Her appearance showed that she too was worried about Vittorio and Nico. Her face was reddened and puffy, her hair uncombed, and her dress wrinkled as though she had slept in it.

Before Donato could say a word, Teresa said, "Vittorio is not here. He has not returned from Arezzo. He must make an important delivery today for a ceremony at a hospital in Caldine. Something is wrong. I know something is wrong."

Tears filled her eyes. Joanna pulled her close, and the two stood silently wrapped in each other's arms until Teresa shuddering stopped and her breathing slow to a smooth even rate.

"Nico has not returned either," Joanna said.

Only after she spoke did Joanna consider whether knowing of Nico's absence would make Teresa feel better or worse.

"Do you know where they were to meet with your brother?" Donato asked.

"No. No. Only that it was somewhere in Arezzo. That is all he told me."

Donato had not been troubled when he first learned that Nico had not returned. As he told Joanna, many reasons might cause the men to change their plans. He first became anxious when Alessa voiced her premonition; her instincts were rarely proven wrong. The added news that Vittorio's absence was jeopardizing a crucial business commitment convinced Donato that the men were not delayed by choice.

At length Donato announced, "I will go to Arezzo."

He did not say what he planned to do when he reached Arezzo because he had not thought that far ahead.

Joanna's hand shot out and grasped Donato's wrist. Two men were missing. She believed Alessa's vision that at least one of them, Nico, was lost or injured. As much as she cared for Nico and wanted him to return, Joanna feared that if her husband went to Arezzo, he might be exposed to the same danger. Donato looked down and saw the worry in her eyes. To ease his wife's anguish, he said, "Orsino will go with me."

Orsino was as much a bear of a man as his name implied. Orsino had recently begun working for Donato at the Uccello. He had developed his bear-like muscles in his previous job at a leather tanning shop where he moved large bundles of animal hides. At the Uccello, he single-handedly loaded and unloaded wine barrels from wagons, barrels that ordinarily required two men to lift. Joanna had been clenching Donato's wrist so tightly that his flesh had gone white. Upon hearing Orsino's name, her grip relaxed enough for color to return.

To Teresa, Donato said, "I'll go to the shop and tell the apprentices that they should deliver the display cabinet to Caldine."

Teresa nodded appreciatively as Donato and Joanna prepared to leave. When they reached the street, Donato kissed

Joanna on the cheek and said, "Orsino will be at the Uccello. Tell him to meet me at Vittorio's shop." Then laughing, he added, "And do not worry, I will keep Orsino safe."

At the carpentry shop, Donato instructed the apprentices to deliver the display cabinet themselves; he informed them that he would be going to Arezzo to search for Vittorio and Nico. The taller of the two apprentices, the one with the scar on his chin, led Donato to the rear of the shop.

"We have two small horse carts. They were badly damaged when Signor Ciampelli acquired them. One is restored. You can use that one to go to Arezzo."

The shorter of the two apprentices said, "I am going to the stable to fetch a donkey for the delivery wagon. I will also bring a horse to pull the cart."

While they waited for the animals, Orsino arrived at the shop. Donato explained the situation and his intention to search in Arezzo for the missing men. Alessa's misgiving did not dissuade the always-optimistic Orsino. He responded to Donato's summary by saying, "Signor Nico Argenti is smart. He will think himself out of difficulty."

The Arno River valley, known as Valdarno, extended southeast from Florence to Arezzo. Via Aretina, the principal road between the two cities, followed the course of the river through the middle of the valley. Some sections of the Valdarno were narrow with steep hillsides rising not far from the road. Other parts of the valley widened enough that farms spread over the fertile soil.

Donato and Orsino were traveling Via Aretina one day after a drenching rain. Mud caused by the rain made travel difficult in low lying stretches of the road. Wagon drivers with experience lightened their loads to keep their vehicles from becoming stuck. Other travelers did not fare as well. One wagon carrying a heavy load of timber toward Florence had become bogged in the mud. Despite its most vigorous effort, the single horse could not extricate the wagon from the thick mud that held it fast. The fuming wagon driver had no choice but to discard part of his load by the side of the road. The small cart carrying Donato and Orsino was light enough that the horse did not strain even when pulling the cart through the deepest of the muddy patches.

Although Donato had never traveled the full length of the Valdarno, he had visited farms along the route that grew grains that the chef at the Uccello used in various recipes. Farro was an ingredient in many different soups. It, along with barley and spelt, were milled into flour to make bread. Donato passed the time pointing out to Orsino the farms and other sights they passed.

Approximately one third of the distance from Florence to Arezzo, Via Aretina passed directly through the walled town of Figline. Donato had pleasant memories of the town where he once spent a week as a guest in the palazzo of a wealthy landowner. Donato regaled Orsino with obscure facts about the town's history that he had learned during his stay.

"Figline is one of the towns mentioned in Dante Alighieri's Commedia. Many years before Dante wrote Commedia, a lawyer from Figline had opposed Dante's political views. Dante chose to include their feud in his writing. Imagine, he wrote Commedia two hundred years past and people still read it today."

Orsino listened politely. He had heard the name Dante, but it held no meaning for him. Both men were so involved in Donato's recounting the history of Figline that they paid no notice to a wagon coming toward them until it was practically abreast of their cart. Like the wagon that had become mired in mud, this wagon also carried lumber, but only a modest load.

As Donato raised his arm to wave a greeting to the passing vehicle, he noticed a passenger alongside the driver.

"Vittorio!" he shouted. His outburst startled the horses as well as the other men.

"Madre di Dio," exclaimed the wagon driver, who pulled back sharply on the reins to keep his horse from bolting.

Donato turned his cart and pulled alongside the lumber wagon. It was then that he saw Vittorio's leg splinted and strapped to a support affixed to the wagon. Orsino lifted Vittorio from the lumber wagon and moved him to the bed of the cart. On their way back to Florence, Vittorio gave Donato a summary of the Arezzo adventure. As he listened, Donato tried to imagine how Joanna would react to Vittorio's story: She will understand why Nico chose to accompany Fapane to Perugia, and, at the same time, she will call it an ill-considered decision. She will be thankful that Nico's injury was minor. She will remind Donato repeatedly that Alessa's vision was flawless, Nico was both lost and injured. She will be delighted that her husband returned home safely.

25

SOMEWHERE IN TUSCANY

The Pietra Alta situation haunted the acting Archbishop of Lucca. He possessed copies of documents that detailed the many vile deeds of Sergio Malcranio, the Lord of Rimini. Among those documents were Papal orders that deposed and excommunicated Malcranio, but the Papal verdicts accomplished nothing. Malcranio had learned from his father the importance of maintaining a large well-trained army, and the power of his army let him ignore the deposition order and laugh at the excommunication censure.

The Holy Father realized that the only way to unseat Malcranio was war. The primary mission of the Papal Army was to safeguard the Papal States against incursions by foreign forces; however, too often in the past century, it had been called upon to tame rogue elements inside the Papal States. Bishops commanding the Papal troops stood ready, even eager, to rid the Italian peninsula of Malcranio and his followers by driving them into the Adriatic Sea. More conservative counselors to the Papal Secretary cautioned that a contest pitting the Papal Army against Malcranio's forces would result in unacceptable carnage on both sides. They asserted that the only way to avoid excessive bloodshed would be to act with overwhelming force, and doing that meant enlisting support from the Duchy of Milan, the Republic of Venice, and the Kingdom of Naples. Unfortunately, the Holy Father was already pressing those states to join him in mounting a crusade against the Turks, so he could not ask for their help against Malcranio. The Papacy was stymied.

The archbishop concluded that only the Priors of Constantine could prevent Malcranio from pillaging Pietra Alta. Malcranio's army was large and powerful, but it was not unlimited. Border disputes with Urbino, and occasionally with Venice, demanded that most of Malcranio's forces remain in Rimini. He could spare only a small contingent of soldiers to harass Pietra Alta, so there might be an opportunity for the Priors of Constantine to deliver a sting.

The archbishop sipped a glass of the local wine on the deck of a villa belonging to one of the Priors' wealthy benefactors. The villa, perched on a cliff near one of Tuscany's picturesque hilltop towns, afforded its guests a commanding panorama of the vineyards and villages in the valley below. The view let the decision-maker from Lucca watch the approach of the two carriages that held his colleagues. For this meeting the archbishop did not wear clerical vestments. He wore the plain black robe worn by monks of his Benedictine order. When decision-makers met to conduct the business of the Priors, all views and opinions were valued equally, even though one attendee might be a Cardinal and another only a parish priest. The long-standing tradition of wearing simple monk robes helped to foster equality.

The Benedictine did not know who would be joining him. Whenever a decision-maker proposed a call to action, the organizing council, identified within the Priors as the Abilitori, arranged for a judgment session. None of those appointed to participate in the meeting learned of the other participants until they arrived at the designated place and time.

The Benedictine descended from the deck to great the first guest as his carriage came to a stop in the courtyard. The passenger was not visible until the carriage door opened. The Benedictine was pleased to see the white-robed Dominican who emerged. Like many members of his order, the Dominican was a teacher, in his case a highly respected instructor at the University of Siena. Although the two men had met at the Council of Mantua five years past, neither man remembered the other's name, but the lapse was of no consequence because at this session they would only call each other brother. Judgment sessions had a singular purpose; to determine whether the Priors should take action. Past familiarities had no relevance.

After the two men exchanged blessings, the Benedictine said, "Rooms are available for you and your driver to freshen. Please meet us on the deck when you are comfortable."

The second carriage was near, so the Benedictine remained in the courtyard to await the third decision-maker. A flash of brown cloth, the color of the Franciscan order, shown through the carriage window when the vehicle turned into the courtyard. The Franciscan who stepped out was unknown to the Benedictine. On a chain around his neck was the Tau cross worn by many Franciscan friars from Sardinia. He may have lived in Sardinia when he joined the order, but it was unlikely that he still resided there. The Abilitori who arranged the session would not require anyone to travel such a great distance. When offered the opportunity to freshen after his journey, the Franciscan declined, which confirmed that his posting was not far, probably in Tuscany or nearby Umbria. After their customary exchange of blessings, the brothers said nothing as they moved from the courtyard to the deck.

The villa's owner always kept a full staff available even though business commitments prevented him from spending as much time at the villa as he wished. The staff had graciously prepared an antipasto, a platter of fruit, several bottles of wine from a local vineyard, and a selection of pastries for the guests.

To ensure that the decision-makers reached their conclusions objectively, the Priors discouraged informal socializing, so as soon as the three brothers had filled their plates, the Benedictine began explaining the purpose of their meeting. Unlike himself and the Dominican, whose touches of gray hair testified to their age and experience, the Franciscan's dark hair and unlined face spoke to his youth. For his benefit, the Benedictine began by giving his colleagues copies of documents that described the full range of allegations made against the Lord of Rimini over many years.

"These are assertions by the Duke of Urbino and others attesting to Malcranio's unholy behavior. As you can see, the oldest of them was sent to the Holy Father more than two decades past."

He paused to give the others time to read the pages. The Dominican scanned the papers quickly. He had seen them before. In contrast, the Franciscan digested the writing slowly. He looked up when he had finished reading and said, "How has this conduct been allowed to continue?"

The Benedictine did his best to answer the question.

"I have been following Malcranio's transgressions closely since he allied with the Prince of Taranto and the French Duke of Anjou five years past. With their support, he began a campaign of conquering territories to expand his realm. The strength of the alliance prevented his neighbors from resisting him. The Holy Father demanded that Malcranio relinquish the appropriated holdings, and he commanded that Lord Malcranio pay his outstanding debts, but Malcranio ignored both demands. For his refusal and his continuing inhuman acts, the Holy Father excommunicated him."

"If I recall, he was excommunicated twice," the Dominican interjected.

"Yes, that is correct, although I fail to understand the additional consequences to his eternal soul brought forth by a second condemnation. Malcranio persisted until he suffered a string of defeats at the hand of the Duke of Montefeltro, whose army liberated much of the conquered territory. Malcranio was quiet for a time, but now he seems to be reverting to his old ways and again claiming territories that are unequipped to defend themselves."

"Is there any indication that Montefeltro will intercede again?" the Dominican asked.

"Thus far, Malcranio is being careful to avoid confronting the Duke."

"Is it not the duty of the Papal Army to protect the integrity of boundaries within the Papal States?" the Franciscan asked.

"It is indeed," the Benedictine answered. "Through the years, opponents have likened Malcranio to many animals: dog, snake, and vulture are some of the references I have heard. Now, he is acting with the cunning of a fox. He formed a coalition with Venice by promising to lead an expedition to drive the Ottomans from one of the Venetian colonies in the Mediterranean. The Papal States link to Venice through another treaty, the Peace of Lodi. That treaty precludes any signatory from acting against allies of another signatory. By allying with Venice, Rimini enjoys the protection of the treaty. Malcranio is cleverly exploiting a treaty loophole to escape pressure from Papal forces. Now with that background, let me explain the reason I requested this session."

His brothers listened attentively as the Benedictine recounted his meeting with Nico Argenti. He finished the story by holding aloft with a flourish a single sheet.

"This is a copy of the finding by the Papal Archive stating that the Province of Rimini has no rightful claim to the town of Pietra Alta."

The Franciscan rose and refilled his wine glass before speaking.

"Your knowledge of this matter comes from one person, a young lawyer from Florence. Are there brothers in Rimini who know the details of the situation?"

"Malcranio admits to his court only priests who pledge loyalty to him, so we are not privy to his private scheming, but we do know from our brothers in the Province that Malcranio has not changed his behavior. Also, brothers in Urbino say that troops from Rimini have made scouting incursions into Urbino. They fear that Malcranio is readying a military action, but thus far, there have been no attempts to seize land."

"Where exactly is Pietra Alta?" asked the Dominican.

"An archivist at the Papal Archives claims there is only a single map that shows the location of Pietra Alta. It is on a ridge in the Apennines near Mount Freccia. At the base of the mountain is a village called Pietra Bassa, and that village is known to be at the extreme limit of Rimini territory. By map measure, the two towns are not far apart, but the rugged terrain makes them more than an hour distant by horseback."

The Franciscan wrinkled his brow. "I do not understand. If Rimini forces are spread thin with some deployed along the border with Urbino and others preparing for the expedition with the Venetians, why is Malcranio concerned with a small town that is difficult to reach? It seems foolish."

The Benedictine had no explanation to offer. He merely shrugged and spread his hands in a submissive gesture. The

Dominican, deep in contemplation, paced the deck from one end to the other before summarizing his thoughts.

"In the past, Lord Malcranio has responded only to overwhelming military force, which is not an option available to a small town like Pietra Alta, so they are following the only recourse open to them, a legal proceeding. Signor Argenti has consented to help them. What do we know of his plans?"

"He traveled to Arezzo to meet with one of the priors of Pietra Alta. One of our brothers in Florence learned that Signor Argenti intends to advise the town to file a legal case in Perugia. He believes that the tribunals in Perugia render fair judgments and that there are competent lawyers in Perugia who can prosecute the case."

The Dominican said, "Filings and actions by tribunals in Perugia will be in the public record, so our brothers in Perugia will be able to monitor the proceedings. We can task Implementers in Perugia to support the town's position by whatever means possible."

The Dominican watched as the others nodded their consent to his proposal.

Turning to the Benedictine, the Franciscan asked, "What will happen if Lord Malcranio rejects the finding of the tribunal? Would the Papal Army be called upon to enforce the tribunal's decision? Would it not violate the Peace of Lodi if the Papal Army moves against Rimini?"

"Since Pietra Alta is not part of Rimini," the Benedictine answered. "The Papal Army has every right to defend the town. Indeed, if Rimini were to send forces to the town after a tribunal forbids them from doing so, then Rimini would become the aggressor. However, treaty violation by the Papal Army is not the major concern. Papal forces are preparing to act against the Ottomans, so it is unlikely that the Papal Army would be in a position to protect Pietra Alta if Rimini rejects a court ruling."

From the Dominican, "I agree. I believe we should task Implementers to intercede if necessary."

From the Franciscan, "Intercede? Against skilled soldiers?"

"Implementers have different skills from those of soldiers. They achieve results through subterfuge and covert means. If Malcranio is likened to a snake, then Implementers are owls, vigilant and fierce but unseen until they strike against their prey," the Benedictine explained.

"They should be positioned at a monastery close to Pietra Alta. The Implementers will know how to choose the optimum location. Is there more for us to consider?"

"The papers you showed us contained grave accusations against Lord Malcranio. Neither of our two proposals will depose him or controvert his vile behavior. He continues his tyranny within the Province, and he is pressing outward on several fronts. As we have said, Pietra Alta is of little consequence to his overall plan. I believe that the brotherhood should support Pietra Alta, but is there nothing else we can do?" the Franciscan asked.

It was the Dominican who responded.

"Others have asked your question for more than a decade, and the answer, unfortunately, is that until the Papal Army is prepared to move against him, his reign of terror will continue. Preventing his acquisition of Pietra Alta may indeed be of little consequence to him, but it is crucial to the people of the town."

There were no other responses to Benedictine's query, which meant it was time to consecrate their decisions. When the Abilitori arranged decision-making sessions, they designated one participant as the vote collector. The Franciscan stepped forward and handed each of the others a medal bearing the image of Constantine. On the table, he set a small wooden bowl and a candle that he lit. It was the key for each man to pray for divine guidance before rendering his final decision. If the Holy Spirit led them to favor the proposals, they would place their medals into the bowl. The measure before them would be approved only if three medals were in the container when the candle extinguished.

The Benedictine had already spent many hours praying for guidance; he rose quickly and dropped his coin into the wooden bowl. Without speaking, his companions walked down the steps from the deck to the broad field surrounding the villa where they could listen to their God. The Dominican heard the Holy Spirit from birds who chirped to each other and to him from the top of a towering chestnut tree. The Franciscan connected with God through grass still wet with morning dew that touched him between the straps of his sandals. By the time the candle had melted to half of its length, the bowl contained three images of Constantine.

26

TIBER RIVER, UMBRIA

Nico and Fapane were not familiar with roads in Umbria. The friar who had helped them when they arrived at San Benedetto monastery explained the route they would travel from Monterchi to Perugia.

"Monterchi sits in a pass through the low mountains. Not far to the East, the pass drops to the floor of the Tiber River valley."

Nico started at hearing the name Tiber. "Is it the same Tiber River that flows through Rome?"

"Yes, the river's source is in the high mountains. From there it follows a long curving course before it reaches Rome. At least that is what I have been told. I have never been to Rome myself.

"An ancient Roman road, the Via Aretina follows the river, and that is the road you will take to Perugia. The friars here at San Benedetto do not travel far from our monastery, so we do not have horses. Mules are what we use for transport, and the stable boy who tends our animals is readying mules for you. Mules are slow, but they can take you to Citta di Castello, a town along the river, where you should be able to find horses.

The boy will accompany you to Citta di Castello and return with the mules."

From the rear of the monastery, a young boy walked toward them, leading three mules. The animals had bridles, but instead of saddles, they had only wool blankets across their backs. The friar demonstrated a method of mounting the mule by leaning across the animal's back and then pivoting while thrusting one leg up and over the mule. It was an awkward move, but Nico was able to execute the maneuver after watching the friar's example. Due to his injured ankle, Fapane required assistance from the friar.

With the stable boy in the lead, the procession departed the small town of Montrechi on a narrow path nestled between two ridges. Gradually the trail descended, and they were soon able to see the dark ribbon of the Tiber River cutting through a wide valley and farms dotting the landscape alongside the river. When they reached the valley floor, the town of Citta di Castello was visible as soon as they turned onto the Via Aretina. Recent heavy rains swelled the river over its banks, flooding broad swaths of low-lying land and inundating the adjacent farms.

Nico's mule followed its leader without needing guidance, so Nico fixed his attention on the town ahead. A flag atop the city wall flapped in the brisk breeze channeling through the valley from the north. The sturdy walls told Nico that Citta di Castello was not a simple farming community. He eased his mule forward until he was abreast of the stable boy.

"Is this road the Via Aretina?" Nico asked.

"That is what the Romans called it. Some people still use that name; others call it the way of Saint Francis."

The boy's answer made Nico laugh. "Apparently Saint Francis left footprints throughout the Italian peninsula because many roads claim that honorific."

The boy shrugged. "The Romans were not the ones who created this road. People speak of an ancient tribe called the Umbri who used this path many centuries before the Romans arrived."

"Where did you learn so much history?"

"I have a cousin who lived in Citta di Castello. His is very proud of his city's history and would be sad if I did not share at least some of his enthusiasm. He is the one who can help us find horses for your journey to Perugia."

Nico was studying two tall towers that loomed above the city wall. "Are those towers part of a fortress?" he asked.

"The round tower is the bell tower of the cathedral. The square tower is called Torre Civico. I do not know its purpose, but my cousin surely does, and he will be delighted to feed your interest," the boy said smiling.

Moorings of the bridge across the Tiber River were visible, but fast-moving water completely covered the bridge deck. Fapane and Nico stopped beside the boy while the three speculated on whether to risk a crossing. As they watched the churning water, a horse cart emerged from the city through the Santa Maria gate and proceeded directly onto the submerged bridge. The sight took on the aspect of a miracle as the horse and cart seemed to be supported on the surface of the water. Only the horse's hooves were hidden from view. Once the cart cleared the bridge, the three riders realized it was safe for them to make their traverse.

Seeing debris being propelled along in the swift current and having one arm immobile, convinced Nico that falling into the rapid flow could be fatal. He pressed his legs tightly against the sides of his mule and leaned forward to grip the animal's neck with his elbows. His injury prevented him from securing a better hold. With his head tilted downward, Nico saw the only turbulent water rushing past. Adding to his anxiety, the gushing flow sounded like a roaring beast.

The mule hesitated only briefly as Nico coaxed it forward onto the submerged bridge. Tree branches carried in the current brushed against the animal's legs without disturbing its forward progress. Finally, back on solid ground, Nico released his grip, rose slowly to a fully upright position, and resumed normal breathing. A quick glace assured him that Fapane and the stable boy also had made the crossing successfully.

In a short distance, they entered the town through an elaborate stone gateway. Following the customary practice, Nico and the boy dismounted to walk their animals through the town. Fapane's injured ankle made it acceptable for him to continue riding. Nico surveyed the small, compact town. It was much smaller than Florence and smaller even than Arezzo, yet it had several substantial buildings that projected an air of elegance and prosperity. The towers that Nico had seen earlier were the dominant structures, but striking palazzos sited along the main road also confirmed that Citta di Castello was home to wealthy families. Wealth explained the reason for the protective wall that encircled the town. Few towns of modest size needed such protection, but any town showing evident prosperity, as this town did, was sure to become a target for bandit gangs and rogue mercenaries.

The boy pointed to the right toward a gray stone church. "That church is San Dominico. Behind the church is a convent where some rooms are used as a school. That is where my cousin is teaching." The three turned onto a side road alongside a multi-story palazzo bearing a distinctive coat of arms. They proceeded to the church and then followed the boy to a clearing behind the church. The boy secured the mules to a fence rail.

"Wait here. I will return soon," he said as he dashed into the rear entrance of the convent.

Fapane listened for the sound of squealing children. Hearing nothing, he exclaimed, "It is quiet."

Nico looked up and waited for Fapane to explain his comment.

The prior smiled and continued, "In Pietra Alta, children and silence are never in the same place. If there is a group of children being schooled here, I am eager to learn how they became so disciplined."

Moments later, the boy emerged from the convent carrying a crutch. "The sisters of this convent not only teach the children of the town, they also serve the infirm," he announced.

With Nico and the boy supporting him, Fapane slid down slowly from the mule's back. He leaned onto the crutch and took a few cautious steps, then nodded enthusiastically to confirm that he could move about without putting weight on his sprained ankle. The stable boy led them into the convent and through a hallway where they paused at an open doorway to watch a nun engaging a group of young children. The children sat on the floor in a circle, and the nun walked around the outside of the group like a planet circling the sun. She would ask a question in an assertive voice that contrasted with her diminutive figure; then she would take a few steps and raise a hand which signaled the children to answer in unison. Fapane muttered an approving comment to himself when he observed that every child had responded to the question.

Farther on, the men came to a room where older children sat in an informal grouping on the floor facing a young man who was seated on a low bench. The children, all boys except for two girls who were sitting off to the side, listened attentively to their teacher. They had neither books nor materials for taking notes. The extent of their learning depended solely on their memories.

"That is my cousin Giulio," the boy whispered to avoid interrupting the class.

Like his cousin, the teacher was thin, with a boyish face. He lacked facial hair except for thick eyebrows that almost met directly above his nose. Nico made a quick sideways glance to confirm his recollection that the stable boy did not share his cousin's bushy brows.

Giulio's teaching style differed from that of the nun. He would ask a question and then, rather than listening for a unanimous response, he would point to an individual student who was expected to provide the answer. The confident students responded with loud voices while uncertainty was betrayed by those who responded with soft wavering voices. One of the girls beamed proudly after she answered a question that had stumped an older boy.

When the class ended, the boy introduced Giulio to Nico and Fapane. Nico explained their mission and their need for horses that could take them to Perugia. Giulio's face brightened when he learned that Nico lived in Florence. He volunteered to take the Florentine lawyer and his companion to Perugia himself and dispatched a student to fetch a horse cart. The seat of the small cart could accommodate only two people. They decided that Fapane should sit in front next to Giulio. A nun fashioned a sling to hold Fapane's leg suspended from the harness that connected the horse to the wagon. The nun made the sling loose and flexible enough to keep his ankle from bouncing during the journey. Nico sat behind on a crate in the wagon bed.

Within an hour of arriving in town, they were underway to Perugia. Again, they crossed the submerged bridge, but Nico found this crossing less traumatic than his earlier experience.

He felt more secure riding in the cart than on the back of a mule. Near Citta di Castello they passed through patches where standing water covered the road. Gradually the character of the land changed, and the roadbed rose above river level. Wet and muddy spans gave way to firmer ground. The horse, oblivious to the changing conditions, kept the cart moving forward at a steady pace.

Fapane, too, paid no attention to the road conditions as he peppered Giulio with questions about the school and the classes Giulio was teaching.

"In Pietra Alta we have no school. Children are taught at the church by a friar. He is a good man who does his best, but age is making him forgetful. We need a better way to educate our children. Either we must bring a teacher to the town, or we must send the children to a school elsewhere. I am very impressed with the discipline of the children at the school in Citta di Castello. Do you think the convent school might be willing to accept children from another town? Of course, we would be willing to pay fair compensation."

"Yours is a question for the mother superior at the convent. The school does accept children from farms outside the town, but whether the school would take children from a distant town I cannot say."

Fapane continued by complimenting Giulio on the decorum of even the youngest children.

"I cannot take credit for that since I am not one of the regular teachers," Giulio responded. "The friar who normally teaches the older children was injured when he was thrown from a horse. My father, who lives in the town, asked if I could help at the school until the friar recovers. I have a fondness for the school because I was born in Citta di Castell and lived there until my twelfth year when my father sent me to study with a tutor in Siena. "

"Are there no tutors in Citta di Castello?" Fapane asked.

"Indeed there are, but my father wanted to expose me to the wider world. For five years I lived with the tutor, his wife, and three other boys who were also there as students. They became like a second family to me. I excelled at mathematics, so the tutor arranged an apprenticeship for me with a master architect, and I have been learning the trade from that master for two years. The master is a kind person who readily agreed to let me return home to aid the school."

Giulio's own words made him laugh. "Is it strange that I still regard Citta di Castello as home even though I have not lived there for seven years?"

"People are not like plants," Fapane answered. "When a plant is moved its roots move with it, but when people move their roots remain behind. Will you return to Citta de Castello when your apprenticeship is complete?"

Before answering, Giulio turned his head to be sure that Nico could hear his words.

"During the summer, a physician came from Florence to Siena for special work at the Santa Maria della Scala hospital. He brought his daughter with him to show her the sights of the city. Siena is a beautiful city with an excellent university, a cathedral older than the one in Florence, and a tower that affords outstanding views of the city and the surrounding countryside."

"Surely you have traveled to Siena," he added, directing this comment to Nico.

Nico detected increased enthusiasm in Giulio's speech and suspected it was not prompted by Giulio's keenness for Siena. Giulio's next words confirmed Nico's suspicion.

"Business kept the girl's father constantly occupied, so I became her escort. We spent the entire summer, many weeks, together. We became very close until she returned with her father to Florence."

Here Giulio's speech transitioned from enthusiastic to mournful. "I miss her . . . more than I would have thought possible."

Giulio's reverie triggered in Nico's thoughts an image of Bianca and the realization that Giulio's situation paralleled his own. Giulio lived in Siena and longed for a Florentine woman while Nico was a Florentine who dreamt of a woman from Siena. It was truly unfair for Cupid to play such games with human hearts. Nico knew he could not ask Bianca to leave her family until he was admitted to the magistrates' guild and established himself as a lawyer. Before Nico could speculate further on Giulio's situation, the apprentice revealed his intention.

"Nico, are there opportunities for apprentice architects in Florence?"

Giulio had not considered asking his heart's desire to leave her home and her family. Instead, he was considering moving himself to Florence. Nico had never entertained the prospect of relocating to Siena to be with Bianca. He had only imagined the possibility of Bianca moving to his city.

Am I thoughtless and inconsiderate? If I truly care for her .. . Nico knew he had to finish that thought, but this was not the time. He forced himself to refocus on Giulio's question.

Nico had no insight into the architecture profession, but everyone in Florence watched as the master architects competed with each other to gain acclaim, ever since Brunelleschi had created his magnificent dome atop the cathedral.

"Florence is a fast-growing city. Constructions are underway everywhere. There is certainly work for architects, and every architect welcomes competent apprentices. Have you ever visited Florence?"

"No, I have not," Giulio answered.

"Then you must go there. Everyone should visit Florence, and for you, it is only a short distance away, a few hours on horseback. There is an architects' guild. They can tell you which masters need apprentices."

Conversation ebbed as each man receded into his own thoughts. Giulio contemplated a visit to Florence. Fapane wondered whether the people of Pietra Alta would willingly send their children to school in a distant town. And Nico called up memories of Bianca. The air held only the sounds of rushing water and the creaking wagon.

Along its course, the Tiber River valley varied in character. In some sections, large farms filled wide expanses of flat bottom land on the far bank. In other sections, the Apennine foothills drew close to the river. In contrast, on the near bank, there were no expanses of flat land. Parallel ridges of hills extended down from the mountains like fingers clawing toward the river. At the tip of each finger, land dropped steeply to the road. In narrow swales between the fingers, the ground sloped more gently. Woodsmen cut wagon roads up the swales to reach virgin timber at the higher elevations.

As they passed each swale, Fapane let his eyes follow the woodmen's road into the hills, wondering if the way might lead to a town like Pietra Alta nestled in the high mountains. Ahead, two widely spaced fingers bordered a broad swale. Giulio pointed to a road snaking its way up the swale. "That is the road to Perugia," he announced.

As they drew closer, Giulio pulled the cart to the side of the road. "It's a long uphill trek to Perugia," he said. "I want to water the horse before we begin the climb."

Giulio released the straps fastened to the horse's harness

and led the animal across a narrow grass strip alongside the riverbank, where a large boulder extended into the rapidly flowing water. Sheltered below the boulder was an eddy of nearly still water where the horse could drink safely. After the horse took its fill, Giulio ran his hand along the animal's flank. The absence of sweat told Giulio that the journey from Citta di Castello was not unduly taxing, so there was no need to rest the animal before starting the ascent to the hilltop town.

From river level, trees blocked any view of the city that was their destination. They proceeded only a short distance when the steepness of the track increased enough that the horse began to slow. To ease its burden, Nico and Giulio climbed down to walk alongside the cart, leaving Fapane as the sole rider. At the crest of one steep section of road, the swale widened and presented them with their first view of the city wall still far above them and off to the left of the road.

Nico became intrigued by a grayish-white patch of ground in the distance to the right of the road. It appeared as a field covered with dirty snow, but Nico knew there could not be snow in the hills at that time of year. When they climbed higher, he discerned that the area was not a single white patch, but distinct clusters of whitish objects. Closer still, the mystery objects resolved into the linen tents of a military encampment. Banners waved in the light breeze on tall poles near the center of the camp. A silver dragon with its claws thrust high above its head filled one banner. Others were emblazoned with intricate red and white designs. Nico, who was unfamiliar with military insignias, could only guess that the flags identified units of the Papal Army.

A short distance beyond the camp the road turned sharply to the left where the Porta Sant'Antonio entrance to the city of Perugia loomed directly ahead.

27

PERUGIA

Fapane stopped the cart beside the portal and slid down from the wagon seat. He slowly shifted some of his weight onto his injured ankle and was pleased to feel only moderate discomfort. He offered a short prayer of thanks to the friar and nuns at the Monterchi monastery who had treated his injury. Nico and Giulio were still a distance from the city and moving uphill at a slow pace. The combination of summer heat and the long climb had sapped their energy.

While Fapane waited for his colleagues to join him, he walked to the wall and rested a hand on a stone block more than half his height. Fapane had seen other towns with protective walls, but none built of such massive blocks and no walls that towered above him many times his height as that wall did. He could not fathom how the Etruscans had constructed such a wall when they founded the city more than two thousand years past.

When Nico and Giulio finally joined Fapane, the short-of-breath apprentice said, "I must return to Citta di Castello. The road directly ahead beyond the wall will bring you to il corso, the main road of the city." Giulio rested a hand on Fapane's shoulder and said, "I hope a tribunal here in Perugia grants you the justice that you seek." Turning to Nico he added with a smile, "Perhaps one day we will meet in your city."

Perugia was at peace with its neighbors and the nearby army encampment discouraged any predatory gangs from causing trouble, so there were no guards at Porta Sant'Antonio. After thanking Giulio for his generosity, Nico and Fapane passed through the portal and proceeded slowly toward the city center. Walking on cobblestones can be trying for anyone, but for Fapane who relied on a crutch it was especially tricky. His challenge was made even greater by a rain shower earlier in the day that had made the stones slippery. After Nico's arduous uphill trek, he did not object to strolling at a leisurely pace as it gave him a chance to regain his vigor.

Neither man was familiar with the city of Perugia, but Nico was confident that someone at the city government offices could direct him to the magistrates' guild where they could inquire about engaging a lawyer. They reached il corso where the road terminated at a piazza that fronted the cathedral. In the center of the piazza, women were drawing water from a large circular fountain. One woman had dipped a large pail into the fountain and was struggling to lift the heavy vessel over the fountain lip. Nico approached the woman, grasped the pail handle, raised it to clear the fountain edge, and set it down beside the woman. She uttered her appreciation, although she did so in a local dialect that Nico could not understand.

"Excuse me, but can you direct me to the city government offices?" Nico asked. He hoped her reply, even if in dialect, would be recognizable. The woman stepped back, a puzzled look on her face. Without a word, she raised an arm and pointed to the building directly behind her, the one that was casting them both in shadow. For a moment, Nico considered explaining his unfamiliarity by saying that he had just arrived in the city, but instead, he just thanked the woman. Then he and Fapane headed to the building entrance.

In one corner of the building lobby stood a larger than life-size statue of a military officer in a commanding pose with one hand resting on his sword. Nico did not recognize the figure, whom he assumed to be a hero of local fame. Against one wall was a small desk where a clerk might be stationed to direct visitors, but the chair was vacant. Running a finger through the thin layer of dust covering the desk told Nico that it would be fruitless to wait for a clerk to return.

Directly across the lobby was a large set of ornate double doors. Nico pulled open one of the doors and stepped into a large salon, an assembly hall, that appeared to be the meeting place of the city's Signoria, or whatever Perugia called its governing body. Light streaming in from upper level windows in the high-ceilinged room illuminated portraits hung in rows on the side walls of the salon. Each portrait showed an elderly man clad in a dark robe whose expression suggested that he was contemplating a serious issue vital to the well-being of the community. None of the portraits bore an inscription naming its honoree. Unlike the lobby with its dusty desk, the assembly hall was maintained in pristine condition.

As Nico and Fapane scanned the picture gallery, voices reached them from a corridor that extended from the far end of the lobby. They followed the sounds to an office where two men were seated behind desks and a third man paced in a narrow space beside one of the desks as he verbally accosted one of the seated occupants. In rapid-fire speech, accompanied by vigorous arm waving, he vented a complaint and demanded that the city take action to remedy the condition. Nico heard only snatches of the ranting that mentioned a neighbor and the killing of chickens. Whether the victimized chickens belonged to the complainant or the neighbor, Nico could not tell.

Taking care to avoid the protestor's wild gestures, Nico made his way across the room to the idle clerk, the one who was both sympathetic and bemused by the verbal abuse being hurled at his colleague. The two clerks were employed by the city to accept constructive petitions from its citizens; however, most of their time was spent hearing about problems that neither they nor the city could fix.

The silent clerk was so enthralled by the protestor that he failed to notice Nico's presence until Nico stepped directly between the clerk and the complainer. Startled by the sudden appearance of a person looking down at him, the clerk only managed to mutter two words. "Who? What?"

Rather than enter a lengthy dialogue, Nico asked directly, "Can you direct me to the magistrates and notaries guild?"

It took a moment for the clerk to compose his thoughts before he sputtered an answer. "Palazzetto dei Notari." Realizing the name alone meant nothing to Nico, he added, "The building directly across il corso."

Nico spun around and strode to the doorway where Fapane was still enjoying the fascinating spectacle. As Nico passed, Fapane commented, "Again, I thank The Lord for letting me live in a small town away from such behavior."

The Palazzetto had no sign with the name or function of the building, but an insignia depicting a griffin on an ink bottle was prominently displayed above the entry door. Each guild designed its insignia from elements of local and historic significance so little, if any, similarity existed among guilds in different cities. Nico's familiarity with the symbol of the Magistrates and Notaries Guild in Florence did not help him to identify the insignia of the guild's counterpart in Perugia.

Gothic styling and construction details marked the

palazzetto as being newer than many of the neighboring buildings along il corso. In keeping with the latest architectural practices, the palazzetto featured a cavernous lobby occupied only by a sandy-haired young man sitting behind a small desk. Nico recognized the book being studied by the young man as the same contract law text he had used at the University of Bologna. The man became aware of his visitors when a shaft of light from the open door fell across his desk. He greeted the arrivals with a cheerful, "Welcome."

"I am Ser Nico Argenti of Florence" – that was the first time Nico had referred to himself using Ser, the honorific enjoyed by lawyers – "and this is Prior Fapane Rizzo of Pietra Alta. We wish to engage a lawyer in Perugia to represent the town of Pietra Alta."

"We have many excellent lawyers in Perugia. If you can tell me the nature of the matter, I can suggest the names of lawyers who specialize in that area."

This time it was Fapane who spoke; "It concerns taxes."

Without asking for further detail, the young man assumed that the town of Pietra Alta intended to file a tax claim against a citizen of Perugia. It was a reasonable, although incorrect assumption.

"Ser Braccio works exclusively on tax matters. The tribunal that decides tax cases is not in session today, so Ser Braccio should be in his office, which is on il sopramuro."

Upon seeing Fapane's blank expression the young man added, "il sopramuro and il corso are the two main streets of Perugia." He then gave detailed directions to the law office.

A simple sign on an unremarkable building identified the law office of Ser Sergio Braccio. Fapane pushed the door open, stepped in, and was struck by the elegance of the décor before him. A couch and two chairs were clustered together to form a seating area at the center of the room. The three pieces had luminous bronze leather covering the thickest cushions Fapane had ever seen. Beyond the seating area, a vase of freshly cut flowers sat on one end of a carved wooden desk. Tiny figures spiraled around the desk legs reminiscent of those on Trajan's column in Rome that depict ancient military victories. Nico's vision locked onto a fresco that filled the wall to his left. The pastoral scene reminded him of paintings done by his friend Sandro Botticelli, except Sandro's works were of modest size compared to this gigantic rendering.

Across the room, Ser Braccio stood leaning against the wall. The dignity of his dress matched the grace of the room's furnishings. He wore an emerald green tunic trimmed with white piping at the cuffs and a double row of silver buttons extending from the collar to the hem. He had been studying a sheaf of papers held in his hand, but when the visitors entered, he set the papers on the desk and gestured for the guests to be seated. His bright eyes projected confidence and warmth. Lowering himself into one on the chairs, he said, "I am Sergio Braccio. How may I be of service?"

Braccio did not use a title when introducing himself, so Nico followed Braccio's lead and also dispensed with titles. Braccio listened attentively as Nico explained the problem faced by Pietra Alta and their intent to seek relief through legal means.

When he finished, Braccio said, "I have represented clients in tax matters longer than three decades. All cases have involved either a citizen filing a complaint against the city of Perugia, or a citizen defending himself against action being taken by the city. I have never participated in a case where both the plaintiff and the defendant are remote government entities, as in this matter between the town of Pietra Alta and the Province of Rimini. The case is certainly intriguing, and, as you said, we magistrates of Perugia take great pride in our reputations for rendering fair and just verdicts. However, there is one serious obstacle. All the tribunals in Perugia have jurisdictions limited to the people and government of the commune of Perugia. There is no tribunal chartered by the Papal States to hear cases on its behalf. For that reason, I believe that none of the fine lawyers in Perugia can help you. You must take your case to Rome."

Two discouraged travelers exited from the law office to the wide il supramuro roadway. Their plan to secure a favorable legal ruling, a plan that had seemed flawless, was now in shambles due to the lack of a tribunal in Perugia with the judicial scope to hear their plea. A favorable verdict enforced by the nearby Papal Army unit could have provided security for Pietra Alta, protecting it from Rufio Scalari, the Rimini knight who swore vengeance against the mountaintop town. Both Nico and Fapane dismissed Braccio's suggestion that they seek help from a tribunal in Rome. Excommunication of Lord Malcranio, the despicable ruler of Rimini, did not persuade him to change his behavior, so surely minor officials in Rimini would only scoff at any ruling by a tribunal in distant Rome.

A gaggle of voices from a throng of passersby pulled Nico from his funk. Students. Nico pivoted to face Fapane and exclaimed, "The law school," then he spun to face the students and repeated the same words as a question, "The law school?"

Without breaking stride, a member of the group pointed over his shoulder to a building behind him and grunted, "Second level."

Nico jogged toward the building and reached the middle of the road before he stopped to wait for Fapane, whose speed was hampered by his reliance on a crutch. Fapane spoke no words when he joined Nico, but his expression called loudly for an explanation.

"Braccio told us he has represented clients in tax cases for decades. Sometimes he speaks for plaintiffs, and at other times he serves defendants, but always his cases are similar. I know of lawyers like him in Florence who build their reputations through expertise in a narrow field. They are like rivers always flowing in the same course. We need to find a lawyer who has not yet carved himself a riverbed.

"At Bologna, there is one professor who prides himself on knowing arcane Florentine laws, laws that remain valid despite not being cited in trials during the past century. On more than one occasion, I witnessed him flummox an opponent by invoking a little-known statute. If the goddess Fortuna supports our purpose, she may lead us to a professor at the University of Perugia who is similarly versed in obscure laws and procedures of the Papal States. Perhaps there is an ancient law that confers broad powers on a tribunal in Perugia."

In deference to his injured companion, Nico climbed slowly up the slick steps to the second level of the building that housed the law school. Midway along the second-level corridor, two men were engaged in a quiet conversation. One man appeared young enough to be a student. The other was much older and wore a tunic in the long loose style favored by professors. Nico waited until the conversation ended and the young man departed before approaching the older one who confirmed that he was indeed a professor of civil law.

With little preamble, Nico explained the predicament: Pietra Alta wished to obtain a judgement against the Province of Rimini, but Ser Braccio claimed that no tribunal in Perugia was authorized to hear the plea. At the mention of Braccio's name, a broad grin spread across the professor's face.

"Sergio Braccio is an excellent lawyer," the professor remarked, "but even he will admit that his skill is narrow."

The professor held up a finger to pause the discussion and ambled to a nearby window. Below, walking across a courtyard, was the young man that the professor had been speaking with. Through the open window, the professor called down to him, "Marco, please rejoin me here."

Then to Nico, he said, "Marco is a recent graduate of the law school and one of my finest students. His thoughts are not restricted by years of narrow experience. Let us see whether he can offer a solution to your dilemma."

Marco, slightly out of breath from running up the staircase, listened attentively as Nico again described the problem. Without hesitation, Marco began, "It is true that civil tribunals in Perugia have narrowly defined jurisdictions. However, military tribunals are permitted to rule on all legal issues."

The professor beamed proudly at his former student's response. The implication was immediately clear to Nico, who said, "We passed an army encampment outside the city. Might that unit include a tribunal?"

It was the professor who answered. "It is customary for civil tribunals to have panels of three or more magistrates, but the number is arbitrary. At the army encampment a single magistrate, Captain Paolo Vanucci, decides all legal matters. I have known Captain Vanucci for many years. He, too, was once a student of mine. He delivers justice as fair and swift as any judicial panel."

"Is there a lawyer in Perugia who could represent Pietra Alta before a military tribunal?" Fapane asked.

The professor's beaming smile broadened further as he answered Fapane's query. "The person standing next to you, Marco Bellini, is a guild member and well qualified to represent your claim."

Nico turned to assess the young lawyer. Marco graduated from law school only recently. Had he even entered a case before a real tribunal? Nico had expected they would find an experienced lawyer in Perugia who could give Pietra Alta its best chance of prevailing. Then suddenly young Marco became a mirror. Nico realized his apprehension toward the young untested lawyer was the same uncertainty that others would feel about him. At least Marco had the benefit of an esteemed professor vouching for his capabilities. In Florence, Nico would have no such advantage. His professors were in Bologna, too far from Florence to testify to his competence.

A more understanding Nico asked, "Ser Bellini, are you available to plead the case for Pietra Alta?"

Later, when Fapane, Nico, and Ser Marco Bellini presented themselves at the army encampment, they were detained at the entrance while a messenger took their request for an audience to Captain Vanucci.

Rigorous procedures were followed when submitting cases to civil tribunals. First, a written accounting of the complaint was filed with an admitting notary. If that notary deemed the filing to be proper and within the jurisdiction of the tribunal, he would then send the filing to a scheduling notary, who would set a date for the complaint to be read by the panel of magistrates. Then they would determine whether they wished to act on the complaint or not. If the magistrates accepted the case, only then would the defendant be advised of the complaint, and the scheduling notary set a date for the actual trial to begin.

Captain Vanucci dispensed with those complex procedures. He had no need for a staff of notaries. He reviewed all petitions personally and decided immediately whether any complaint warranted a hearing. For those cases demanding action, the Captain established a trial date and dispatched a courier to summon the defendant. As the professor had said, Captain Vanucci believed in swift justice.

Barely a minute after Bellini had requested an audience, the messenger returned and beckoned the three visitors to follow him to an area near the center of the camp where smartly dressed military officers huddled at tables under a large canopy. Behind one table, Captain Vanucci leaned back in a chair with his arms folded across his chest as he watched a heated discussion between two junior officers at a nearby table. The table in front of Vanucci was void of any materials, and across the table, opposite the Captain, there were no chairs for visitors.

When the three approached, Vanucci looked to Marco suggesting that he knew the young lawyer either personally or by reputation. Again, Nico saw his reflection in Marco and wondered whether he had a reputation among Florentine magistrates. It hardly seemed possible.

Vanucci unfolded his arms and spread his hands as a signal for Marco to begin. Although Marco had heard Pietra Alta's complaint only once, he recounted it perfectly. Nico and Fapane stood ready to elaborate, clarify, or correct Marco's presentation, but he needed no assistance. When Marco began, Vanucci showed only intrigue that two foreign civilians had traveled to Perugia to seek justice from a military tribunal. Vanucci's interest grew as Marco continued speaking, and when Marco finished, the Captain again leaned back in his chair, refolded his arms, and announced, "Tomorrow. I will hear the pleadings tomorrow."

Both Marco and Nico opened their mouths to speak, but Vanucci anticipated their concerns. "A trial can be held tomorrow because it is not necessary to wait for a representative of the defendant to travel from Rimini. The Province of Rimini has an emissary permanently assigned to Perugia. He returned from the Province two days past, so he should be versed in all matters of the Province and fully capable of speaking for the defendant."

28

TRIBUNALE SUPERIORE, PERUGIA

Nico expected that the trial would be conducted at the army encampment, but the following morning he and Fapane were notified that they should proceed to the salon of the Tribunale Superiore, Perugia's supreme tribunal. Inside the salon, seven high-backed cushioned seats were positioned on a raised platform that spanned one wall of the room. Captain Vanucci occupied one of the seats; the others were vacant. At floor level in front of the seats were two tables. At one of the tables, Marco reviewed a folder containing his notes and the letter that Nico had obtained from the Papal Archives declaring that Pietra Alta was not within the Province of Rimini. Nico and Fapane approached Marco, intending to join him at the plaintiff's table. Before they could reach for chairs, Marco advised them of the protocol followed at the military tribunal.

"Only legal representatives are permitted at the tables. Plaintiffs, defendants, witnesses, and observers must sit in the gallery at the rear of the room. The magistrate will allow us to confer if that becomes necessary."

As Nico began moving away, he asked Marco, "Will other magistrates be joining Captain Vanucci?"

"No, the Captain will be the presiding magistrate. He requested the use of this salon because this is a civil trial, so he feels this venue is more appropriate than the army camp. The city government accommodates requests from the army whenever they can do so. Magistrate Vanucci is punctual. The trial will begin when the cathedral bell strikes the hour, whether a legate from Rimini is present or not."

The central section of gallery seats was filled with law students who seized the rare opportunity to observe a military tribunal. They were also eager to watch the performance of their former classmate, Marco Bellini. Even though the trial had not yet begun, the students sat silent and still. Either they were extremely well disciplined, or they had been warned that magistrate Vanucci insisted on absolute decorum.

A Franciscan monk occupied the seat at the far end of the gallery. Tribunals in the Republic of Florence did not include religious elements, but Nico supposed that invocations might be delivered to open tribunals in the Papal States. The monk's eyes were downcast, and his hands were clasped together and resting on his lap. Nico did not notice the Cross of Constantine hung on a cord around the priest's neck.

Footfalls from heavy boots of two men dressed in Rimini army uniforms broke the silence as they escorted the Rimini emissary into the salon. The emissary in his official dress, a full-length green robe overlaid with a silk sash in the colors of the Malatesta family coat of arms and bearing the silver insignia of his office, strutted proudly to the defendants' table. He had barely seated himself when the sound of the cathedral bell echoed throughout the room.

"Ser Bellini, state your complaint," Vanucci instructed as soon as the echoes died.

Marco recapped how a fierce Rimini army detachment invaded the independent territory of Pietra Alta, intending to levy taxes and other penalties on the defenseless citizens of the town. Marco chose eloquent words to make his case crisp and brief. He was certain the Captain expected brevity. He concluded by presenting the magistrate with a single sheet.

"This document, issued by the Papal Archives, affirms that Pietra Alta is not within the Province of Rimini and therefore not subject to taxation by the Province."

While Vanucci read the document, Marco added, "At your pleasure I can obtain a notarized copy of the letter."

"I am sure the Papal Archives could have someone on their generous staff of functionaries create a notarized letter. Civilian tribunals may insist on that formality, but I do not. This letter is sufficient."

When Vanucci finished reading, he set the letter on a table and indicated that the document was available for inspection by the emissary. The emissary made no move to take the letter. Still addressing Marco, the magistrate asked, "What remedy does your client seek?"

"Rufio Scalari, the knight who commanded the Rimini military unit, boasted that he will return to the town with a more substantial force to extract payment. The priors of the town fear he will unleash vengeance against citizens of the town. They ask that knight Scalari and the unit under his command be recalled to Rimini. Further, they ask that the Province of Rimini acknowledge that Pietra Alta is an independent commune not subject to taxation or control by the Province of Rimini."

"Is that all?" Vanucci asked.

Marco hesitated, fearful that he had overlooked an important condition. A thin bead of sweat formed along his hairline.

At length, he responded in a less confident voice, "Yes, that is all."

Vanucci turned to face the emissary. "What is the response of the Province of Rimini to this complaint?"

The emissary rose and started pacing slowly from one end of the table to the other. "Most honorable magistrate," he began.

He reached out, he took hold of the Archive letter and raised it aloft for all to see. "The Province of Rimini has no basis to dispute this finding of the Papal Archive."

With a dramatic flare he waved the document in the air, lowered it to the table, and resumed pacing.

"However, as is well known, the Archive is staffed by novice priests who receive only minimal training in the methods needed to research that vast storehouse. In the past, well-meaning but meagerly trained novices have made erroneous declarations by failing to locate relevant materials. We contend that in the future another archivist might uncover contrary evidence to this. Therefore, we ask that the tribunal allow for this possibility."

The emissary gave a quick sideways glance to see Marco's reaction to his opening words. It pleased him that Marco appeared unsettled by his attempt to discredit the Archive letter. The emissary ceased pacing, faced the magistrate, and adopted a somber voice.

"I am authorized to reveal to this tribunal our knowledge of confidential reports suggesting that the Province of Rimini may become the target of hostile actions perpetrated by the Duchy of Urbino."

A chorus of murmured voices swept through the salon. Urbino had a well-established reputation as a peaceful and generous member of the Papal States. No one in the salon, save the Rimini emissary, could conceive that the Duchy of Urbino

would mount a hostile act against a neighboring state. Speculation passing through the gallery held it more likely that the
emissary's contention was yet another fabrication to serve a
nefarious purpose of the Lord of Rimini. The undertone ceased
as soon as the emissary resumed speaking. No one wanted to
miss a single word.

"To safeguard our territory, Lord Malcranio has
commanded that all army units be ordered to positions along
the Urbino border."

Vanucci, who had a skill for detecting speech contrived for
deception, asked, "Have the orders been acted upon?"

"As a military man you understand there are protocols to be
followed. It can take time for orders to reach units in the field."

That response was exactly the equivocation that the magistrate expected, so he continued pressing.

"Have knight Scalari and his unit moved to their new
position?"

The emissary's shoulders slumped, and his expression
turned sheepish. In a quivering voice, he answered, "The
ministry is awaiting confirmation that Sir Scalari is complying
with the new orders."

Vanucci shifted in his seat. He understood the meaning
behind those words. Scalari was a rogue knight commanding a
rogue force, a dangerous situation, Vanucci realized. "Anything
more, excellency?" he asked.

The emissary merely shook his head and returned to his
seat. The magistrate turned his glance to Marco, who also indicated that he had nothing else to contribute. With neither
lawyer having additional testimony to present, the magistrate
announced his ruling.

"The document from the Papal Archive affirms that Pietra
Alta is independent of the Province of Rimini; therefore, the
Province shall not levy any claims against the town or its citi-

zens. The Province of Rimini is directed to dispatch couriers in sufficient number to ensure that all of its military units are informed of this ruling expeditiously. If evidence is found in the future that contravenes the finding of the Papal Archive, this tribunal will entertain a motion to reconsider its ruling."

Fapane's neck and shoulder muscles loosened. Nico's breathing slowed. The magistrate's verdict melted their anxiety and justified the painful difficulties they had endured. Tension fled the salon almost instantly. Fapane barely had a chance to thank Marco before the cadre of students paraded their new champion to a nearby tavern to celebrate his victory. Fapane already had directions to a stable where horses were available for lease. In five hours, his town would learn the good news and he would be home with his family. Despite Nico's eagerness to return to Florence, he had accepted Fapane's invitation to visit Pietra Alta. Nico estimated it would add only one day to his journey.

As the two men descended the stone steps exiting the Palazzo dei Priori, a voice called from behind.

"Signor Argenti."

Nico turned to face a Franciscan monk wearing a silver Cross of Constantine medallion. Having gained Nico's attention, the monk continued speaking.

"The young lawyer gave a respectable account of himself in his first appearance before a tribunal. He is justified to feel proud, but he fell short of perfection. The magistrate gave young Bellini an opportunity to request additional action, but he failed to seize that opportunity."

Nico puzzled over the monk's assertion. He flashed through the proceedings, and his mind froze on the image of Vanucci, asking, 'Is that all?'. He, too, had remained silent when Vanucci asked 'Is that all?' Nico saw his own inexperience reflected in Marco's failure to seek additional action.

The monk continued without interruption. "The mandate that Rimini hasten distribution of new military orders is without teeth. Lord Malcranio will see that 'expeditiously' is made into a meaningless concept. Of even greater concern is knight Scalari. His pride is wounded, and he will mete out revenge to heal his wound regardless of any new orders."

Fapane began to speak. "The magistrate has not yet moved from the salon. We can ..."

The monk raised a hand to silence Fapane. "That opening has passed. The magistrate will not recast the proceedings."

Fapane shivered, struck by the monk's words like an icy wind that carried off the joy he had felt moments ago.

Nico had brought Fapane to Perugia for a fair verdict enforceable by the Papal Army. They had achieved a favorable verdict, but military action could come only after a violation of the tribunal's judgement, too late to help Pietra Alta. Marco—and Nico, if not Marco—should have asked that the magistrate send an army detail to protect Pietra Altra.

As if reading Nico's thoughts, the monk said, "There is no guarantee that the magistrate would have authorized pre-emptive protection. Such measures are rarely sanctioned."

"We cannot know because I did not ask. An experienced lawyer would have asked," Nico said quietly.

"Do not dwell in regret, my son. Experience comes from climbing over a wall built of errors and flawed actions. Everyone must create his own wall before he can vault over it."

"It is difficult for me to find comfort in that philosophy, Father, if my errors cause the people of Pietra Alta to suffer."

The monk placed a hand on Nico's shoulder. "God usually provides more than one way to safeguard His innocent children. In the hills above Arezzo is the village of Palazzo del Pero. In that village at the church of San Donnino a Maiano you can enlist my brothers to your cause."

"Monks?" asked a dubious Nico.

"Why do you hold doubt? You have researched our brotherhood, the Priors of Constantine, at the Chancery Archive in Florence. You sought guidance from my brother at the cathedral in Lucca. You learned of our pursuits for justice ever since God anointed Saint Constantine with the vision in the sky over Milvan Bridge. You know our commitment and our resolve."

Still uncertain, Nico said, "I may know of them, but they will not know me."

"The brotherhood achieves success by preparing for many possibilities. This outcome was anticipated. Nico Argenti and the danger to Pietra Alta are already known at San Donnino."

29

CHIANA VALLEY, TUSCANY

Fapane paid generously at the Cavallo Potente stable. His gold florins and the recommendation of a Franciscan monk let him secure the finest steeds available. While stable hands readied the two mounts, Nico watched a man carefully wrap a lute with a soft cloth and fasten it securely to the saddle of his horse. The man introduced himself as Suonatore, a singer and musician who had come to Perugia to perform at a wedding. He was preparing to return home to Cortona and said he would welcome the company of fellow travelers. His familiarity with the roads of Umbria suggested he would be a valuable guide for Nico and Fapane.

The ancient Etruscan road leading northwest from the city descended slowly through stands of pine and oak forest. Gradually the slope flattened, and woodlands gave way to green pastures and golden fields of sunflowers. Fascinated by the sight, Fapane declared, "All the bright color... I feel that I am riding through an orange and yellow sea."

"Or that the Sun has joined to the Earth," Nico added.

Conversation passed between the riders in fragments.

Suonatore learned from Nico the latest Florentine news. He regaled Nico and Fapane with an amusing tale of the visit to Florence when he entertained at a festa hosted by the Medici family.

"Among Cosimo's grandchildren," Suonatore said, "only one impressed me. Lorenzo was only twelve years of age at the time, but I could already detect that he will have a prominent future."

They stopped once near the village of Magione when Suonatore spotted a pretty farm girl walking along the road. He eased his mount to the roadside, straightened in the saddle to full height, and serenaded her with a love ballad. When he rode on, leaving the girl delighted and breathless, he turned to Fapane and said, "Of what purpose are love songs if not to charm beautiful women?"

Roads encircled Lake Trasimeno, the largest lake in central Italy. Suonatore chose a road that followed the eastern shore. When they reached the northern end of the lake, they stopped for a second time in a grassy field.

"If you are a student of history, you may know this place," Suonatore said. "It is here where Hannibal, with an overwhelming force of Carthaginian soldiers, defeated the Romans. Fifteen thousand Romans perished in that battle."

"We all share in that loss," Nico said. "In Roman times, everyone was Roman. All Italians were brothers. Now we struggle to maintain peace between cities and states. Foolish differences often turn brothers into enemies. We can only hope that one day unity may return to the Italian peninsula."

"Unity will remain only a dream while Malcranio and other despots rule," Fapane said.

The three men held still in silent reflection before moving on.

Beyond Lake Trasimeno, they entered the fertile Chiana

Valley. In ancient times, marshes and swamps dotted the valley, but now farms filled the wide expanse that stretched ahead to the distant horizon. Nico could almost imagine seeing all the way to Arezzo. Within the hour, they reached the road that branched off to Cortona.

Gesturing to the hilltop town, Suonatore said, "Up there is my home, so here I must leave you."

His words seemed to be the trigger for a flock of birds that lifted from somewhere in town and circled overhead as if to welcome a returning member of their community.

Suonatore embraced Fapane. "The road to Arezzo is straight and true. I will pray that justice serves the people of your town."

Embracing Nico, he said, "In one hour you will reach the fortress at the town of Castiglion Fiorentino. There you will find a road leading into the hills to Palazzo del Pero. I traveled that road only once. It is like a snake always bending and twisting, but it is not difficult to follow."

Nico found the Cassero fortress and the road immediately beyond exactly as Suonatore had described them. Fapane would continue north toward Pietra Alta, and Nico would head east into the mountains to find the Priors. He and Fapane parted at the fortress with only a few words exchanged between them because each man knew the other's thoughts. Nico said only, "I will rejoin you soon."

From the open valley, the road to Palazzo del Pero receded into forest. Trees arched overhead, hiding the sun. Nico soon became disoriented by the many twists and turns, but his horsed detected a scent that let it track with no difficulty. Nico loosened the reins and put his confidence in the animal.

30

PIETRA ALTA

The soldiers posted at Pietra Alta by knight Rufio Scalari were experienced, high trained, and well-disciplined, but many days camping in a field outside the town were taking a toll. All chores fell to them. They had no young recruits to hunt and scavenge for their food, and no cook to turn the raw ingredients into tasty meals. For bathing, they had no tubs of warm water, only a cold stream. Boring days waiting for the knight to return extended into boring weeks. Rainy days tested their resolve in the extreme. Even simple tasks such as cooking, eating, and caring for their horses became miserable chores under heavy rain.

The knight positioned his troops where they would be visible as a constant threat to everyone in town. Scalari found pleasure intimidating peasants, and by his measure, everyone in Pietra Alta was a peasant. When the men tired of hunting and trapping game, they started sneaking into barns and live-stock pens to pilfer foodstuffs, chickens, and goats. The knight had ordered them to avoid contact with people of the town, so they made their surreptitious raids only at night.

Lack of female companionship was their greatest hardship. They longed to return to a real army installation where pleasure could always be found in the beds of camp followers and prostitutes. In lieu of physical contact, they spent their waking hours leering at the women of the town. Their discussions often turned into debates about which woman had the biggest or the shapeliest breasts. On other days their attention focused on the size and shape of buttocks. The men memorized the daily work schedules of the women who, in their opinions, had the most desirable physical attributes. The highpoint of their day was when the girl they called 'the bouncer' rode through a pasture to exercise her horse. They welcomed the sight of her atop the horse as it walked from the barn to the field, but they became absolutely transfixed when she let the horse run, and her breasts rose and fell with the animal's every step.

Eventually, the isolation exceeded the self-control of the youngest soldier, a private named Soli. He learned that the first job done every morning by 'the bouncer' was to milk the family's two goats. At first light, he positioned himself in a stand of trees where he could observe the girl leave her house and enter the barn. So focused were his senses that he heard nothing, not the roosters crowing, and he saw nothing, not the flock of birds swooping overhead, until the door opened, and the girl emerged from the house with milk pail in hand. He let her enter the barn before leaving his hiding place and making his way quietly through a bramble thicket toward the barn. He moved around the far side of the barn so he could not be seen by anyone in the house. Soli saw her on a stool beside one of the goats as soon as he stepped into the barn. The spongy dirt floor muffled his footsteps as he approached her from behind. When he drew close, he heard her singing softly, either to herself or to the goat.

Soli bent low and inhaled deeply to absorb her scent. Then

in a smooth motion, he slid a hand around her, up under her shirt, and reached for her breast. For an instant, the girl was too startled to react. Then in the same moment that she opened her mouth to scream, Soli grasped her hair with his other hand and pulled her head back, intending to kiss her on the lips. The sudden move stifled her scream into a gasp. In desperation, she swung the milking pail upward in a wide arc, splashing the warm liquid onto his face. He pulled his hands away, jumped back, and began rubbing frantically to clear his eyes. Now, free of his hold, the girl swung the pail again and landed it forcefully against the side of Soli's head. He staggered backward, giving her a chance to slip past him and escape from the barn. Her father and two neighbors responded to her screams; however, when they reached the barn Soli was gone, and all that remained from the incident was a dented milk pail stained with a smear of blood.

Word of the offense spread quickly through the town. Although the soldier was the one who initiated the confrontation by attacking the girl, her response had injured the attacker, so everyone in town believed the soldiers would retaliate. In Fapane's absence, the two remaining priors convened a town meeting to discuss the situation.

"I am not surprised that this happened. I have been expecting it," one voice said. "They eye our women constantly, even the youngest girls."

Another echoed the sentiment. "Lust has turned those men into animals."

All agreed it was no longer safe for women to be seen. The town's blacksmith suggested that the women remain locked in their homes. His idea garnered some support, but ultimately it was decided that a stronger measure was needed. That the women should leave the town entirely until the soldiers' intentions became clear.

On a high bluff outside of town, construction was underway on a building that would become a church for the faithful of Pietra Alta. The church would be visible from town when the steeple was completed, but until then, the structure was masked by a ring of trees. It might not be as comfortable as their homes, but it would serve to keep the women safe. The women waited in their homes until nightfall, then under cover of darkness, they vanished.

31

THE ROAD TO PIETRA ALTA

Early the following morning, a courier dispatched from the Province of Rimini by knight Rufio Scalari guided his horse through the Apennine Mountains toward Pieta Alta. At his destination he expected to find a pristine military encampment. Instead, he found a site littered with refuse. Its sour stench, a mixture of garbage, sweat, and urine, stung his nostrils. The soldiers who greeted him were unshaven and wore the coarse tunics of laborers rather than crisp white uniforms. They almost did not notice his arrival because they were busy arming themselves with daggers and long swords as if preparing for battle. They wore no insignias of rank, so the courier could not identify who among them was the superior officer. His only recourse was to announce his message to all.

"I am sent to advise you that Sir Scalari will arrive here before sundown. You will present yourselves for his inspection at that time."

Soli spoke, even though he lacked any authority to do so. "We have business in the town. There are people there who need to be punished. And there is a bitch who needs to learn that men deserve respect."

The courier scanned the filthy camp site before replying, "When Sir Scalari sees this pigsty, it is you who will be punished."

"Our business with the town must wait," the troop leader announced with conviction.

His men watched him unbuckle his weapons and set them on a table. For those who had witnessed Scalari's wrath in the past, the choice was clear. Their time must be spent restoring the camp and themselves to respectability. One standout, Soli, remained obstinate.

"I need no help. I will go myself and return with the girl. She thinks me soft, but I will show her how hard I can be."

The leader grabbed Soli by his collar and shoved him backward into a chair with such force that the chair collapsed to the ground, with Soli splayed across its broken pieces.

"Keep your pants on, stronzo. I will make sure that when Scalari asks who defied his order by going into town and assaulting the girl, it will be your ass that receives his punishment."

Fapane entered the town on a rarely used road that rose into the mountains from Arezzo. He did not notice the absence of workers in the fields of the normally active town. He rode directly to his house, eager to reunite with his wife and son. Disappointment descended on him when he entered his house and found it empty. In mid-afternoon household chores usually kept his wife busy, although it was possible, he reasoned, that she had gone to visit a neighbor. A rustling sound from outside caught his attention. In a garden behind the house, his son, Tommaso, struggled with an apricot tree that was reluctant to release its fruit. Fapane rushed to the boy and enveloped him in loving arms. For several long moments, Fapane said nothing while he absorbed his son's presence. Then he stepped back and looked at the boy.

"I have been away for only a few days, and in that short time you have grown. How is that possible?"

Without giving Tommaso time to respond, he asked, "Where is your mother?"

"She is at the church. All the women are at the church."

"At the church? What are they doing at the church?"

"One of the soldiers attacked Maria," Tommaso replied, only adding to Fapane's confusion.

"Maria? Maria Scorcesi? What do you mean a soldier attacked her? What happened?"

"I do not know exactly what happened. No one will tell me. There was a town meeting. Everyone is worried that the soldiers will return, so they sent the women away. That is why they are at the church. They are hiding."

A hundred more questions flooded into Fapane's mind. He was torn between seeking answers to the questions and wanting to see his wife.

His fellow priors were wise in taking quick action to protect the women and girls. When men lose control over their savage instincts, there is no limit to their depravity. Fapane worried about the safety of others, especially the young boys.

"Come with me," he said to his son.

Fapane locked his house. Then he led Tommaso on a circuitous route through the woods to a path that would take them to the church.

Knight Scalari arrived in Pietra Alta with a small detachment of loyal followers. They traveled the same road used by the courier earlier in the day. When traveling through insecure territory, military procedures called for two scouts to ride ahead of the leader to guard against ambushes. Scalari deployed no scouts on the journey to Pietra Alta. "I have no fear of those backward peasants," he had told his men.

Unlike Fapane, Scalari did notice that the town seemed deserted.

"Where in hell is everyone?"

His question fell to the first soldier that Scalari met as he approached the camp. That soldier was not the troop leader, nor was he skilled in offering tactful answers to those in power. He simply blurted out, "There was an unfortunate incident."

The Knight did not believe in fortune, good or bad. The word 'unfortunate' meant nothing to him, and the phrase 'unfortunate incident' was a completely unacceptable explanation. In a move that could have ended as self-sacrificing bravery, the troop leader stepped forward to elaborate.

"Young recruit Soli went into town and confronted a girl."

"He disobeyed my command and entered the town?"

Scalari had no concern for the girl, but defiance of his orders was intolerable. His ears brightened to crimson. His eyes narrowed to slits, and the muscles in his neck tightened. In words spit out through clenched teeth, he said, "Bring him to me."

Two soldiers seized Soli by his arms and propelled him forward. The Knight scrutinized the now trembling recruit.

To Soli, he said, "You dress like a soldier, but you are not fit to wear a soldier's uniform."

Then to the restrainers, he bellowed, "Remove his uniform."

Each man grasped Soli's tunic. A third soldier shoved Soli from behind, tearing the tunic free and driving Soli face first into the dirt.

"Finish it. Finish it," Scalari barked.

The two soldiers lifted Soli's legs into the air, pulled off his boots and pants, and dropped him again to the dirt. The Knight urged his horse forward until he was over the hapless recruit. He bent his head forward and spit.

"You want to be with peasants. Go be with them. Never come here. Never enter my sight again."

Soli pushed himself up to a kneeling position. He swept his eyes around, looking for compassion from other members of his troop. He found none. All his former colleagues stood rigid, looking straight ahead and avoiding eye contact with their disgraced cohort. When Soli's scan reached Scalari, he saw the Knight reaching for his long sword. Soli understood that signal. Wearing only his underclothes, he ran into the woods.

With that matter resolved, Scalari returned to his earlier concern.

"Now I ask again, where are the peasants?"

The troop leader again responded, "The men are in town, but the women have disappeared."

"Women do not disappear. The men must know where they are. We will make them tell us. But first, the time has come to collect the tax from these peasants. We will take gold. And if they have too little gold, then we will take women as payment."

Fapane had returned from the church and was searching for his fellow priors when the soldiers, led by Scalari, reached the center of town. The Knight brought his horse so close to Fapane that the horse's hot breath swirled around Fapane's head.

"I promised to return to collect the tax, and here I am. The time is now," the Knight boasted.

"The Papal Archive determined that Pietra Alta is not part of Rimini," Fapane protested.

That statement brought a roar of laughter from Scalari.

"Do you think I care what the Papal Archive says? Those fools in Rome are worthless."

Fapane continued his protestation. "A tribunal in Perugia ruled that no taxes are due to Rimini. Pietra Alta is an independent commune."

The Knight's reaction transformed from bemusement to anger. Once again, his ears colored, this time becoming purple. His hands balled into trembling fists.

Fapane continued, "It was a military tribunal. The Papal Army will enforce the ruling."

Scalari pointed to Tommaso. "Who is this boy?"

"He is my son."

"Look around, boy. Tell me, do you see a Papal Army?"

Tommaso shook his head.

"That is right. There is none. Maybe you are not as stupid as your father. He speaks of armies where there are none."

The Knight addressed his second in command. "Have the men bind this peasant. Then send them through the town to collect gold. Gather all the gold they find. They must visit every house."

Fapane, Tommaso, and Scalari listened as the soldiers swept across the town. They heard doors being broken, shouts of men voicing resistance, and screams of pain as the resistors were cast aside. The gold haul was meager.

"These people have little," the Knight's aide reported.

"If they cannot pay with gold, they can pay with flesh."

Scalari turned to Tommaso. "Where is your mother, boy?"

Tommaso looked to his father before giving a meek reply. "I do not know, sir."

"I think you do. Tell me, do you like birds?"

Surprised by the strange question, Tommaso simply nodded.

"Watch as I draw a picture of a bird for you."

Scalari walked to where Fapane was bound. He pulled his dagger from its sheath and used it to tear Fapane's shirt open. He pressed his dagger against the bare chest until a drop of blood appeared at the dagger's point.

"Tell me what kind of bird to draw?"

He hesitated until fear danced in the boy's eyes.

"Or would you rather tell me where your mother is hiding?"

Tommaso watched the stream of blood now flowing down his father's chest. Tears welled up in his eyes. In a soft quivering voice, Tommaso said, "She is at the church."

"Have the women brought here," Scalari ordered.

32

THE CHURCH AT PIETRA ALTA

Eight monks, brothers in the Priors of Constantine, guided Nico Argenti through mountain trails from Palazzo del Pero to Pietra Alta. The trails they followed were little more than animal tracks and known only to those who had lived their entire lives in the high mountains. Their first view of the town was a cluster of homesteads, and in the distance, a column of soldiers heading out from the town. The first dwelling they reached had fragments of a broken door scattered in the front yard. The sound of someone moaning drew them into the house where they found a man lying on the floor. Blood was coagulated on his forehead and in his matted hair. One of his arms was pinned under him and twisted to an unnatural angle. A monk knelt next to him to treat his injuries.

When the man was able to talk, Nico learned that the town was under siege, and the column of soldiers was heading to the location where the women and girls of the town had been secreted. Nico and the monks agreed that their priority should be aiding the women. The monks felt certain they would prevail if they engaged the soldiers directly, although Nico did not understand the reason for their confidence. The soldiers were well trained, experienced in combat, and equipped with weapons such as long swords. In contrast, the monks carried only long wooden poles fitted with a heavy metal hook at one end. They called the weapon a guisarme. Nico knew of similar pole weapons used by horsemen, but he had never seen one in the style carried by the monks. It was not clear whether they had ever faced any real opponents with their guisarme.

The monks had offered to furnish Nico with a sword or other weapons, but he declined. Instead, he opted for a pouch filled with wood ash. Nico had no skill with a sword, but in the past, he had defended himself against a mugger by throwing a handful of oat flour into the eyes of his aggressor. That instance led him to assert that he was experienced in the technique of surprise warfare, a claim that always brought forth laughter from family and friends.

When Nico and the monks reached the church, shrieks coming from the building confirmed that the soldiers were already inside. The monks wanted to enter the building to engage the soldiers without delay, but Nico persuaded them that fighting in the confines of the church would put the women in danger. He surmised that the soldiers were sent to collect the women and return them to the town, not to harm them. His plan was to wait until the soldiers exited the building.

"The doorway will force only one or two of them to pass through the portal at a time," he argued.

As Nico anticipated, when the door opened, a group of girls emerged, followed by two soldiers. The soldiers' swords were sheathed. They controlled the girls by pushing the laggards and shoving others. Their attention was focused on the girls, so they did not notice the monks standing on either side of the doorway. In unison, the monks swung their guisarme weapons in arcs that struck the soldiers' heads with sufficient force to push the limp bodies away from the panicked girls. The strikes were so sudden and quiet that the girls were unaware their minders had been eliminated.

Nico's plan worked flawlessly until the number of women massed together outside the doorway crowded against the monks and restricted their movement. At the same time, what began as whispering among the women grew in volume until the soldiers still inside the building became aware that something was amiss.

Three soldiers burst out through the doorway with swords drawn. Two of the soldiers targeted monks that were positioned away from the group of women. The third soldier's advance was hindered by a group of girls in his path. He charged forward, his blade only inches from the throat of a small dark-haired girl. Fear froze her in place. Nico lunged. With one hand he grabbed the girl and pulled her aside. His other hand reached into the pouch he carried and withdrew a handful of wood ash. He tossed the ash into the air, spraying it across the soldier's face. Ash burned the victim's eyes and filled his nostrils. He coughed uncontrollably as his body tried to eject a mouthful of the blackened grit.

One of the women retrieved the dropped sword and thrust it forward, slicing through the soldier's tunic and into his flesh. Had Nico not taken hold of her arm to restrain her, she would have pressed the blade to its hilt. Other women joined the action by binding the soldiers that had been subdued by the monks with twine the women had been using to make baskets. The conflict was brief. The one soldier stabbed with the sword was the only casualty, and his wound proved to be minor.

Two women remained at the church to guard the prisoners and to comfort the young girls who were distressed by the ordeal. Several older girls were chosen to run from house-to-house to search for any men who might have been injured when the soldiers invaded the homes. Houses in Pietra Alta were widely separated from each other by fields and livestock pens, so the most athletic girls were given this task. All the other women accompanied Nico and the monks to reclaim their town. Having seen how effectively Nico disabled a soldier using only a handful of ash, the women decided to adopt his 'surprise warfare' tactic. They gathered up fistfuls of ash from an old cooking fire and loose dirt from the forest floor.

The plan was for Nico and the women to proceed to the center of town to intercept the knight and the remaining soldiers. When the soldiers came into view, the women started chanting and singing to draw the attention of the soldiers. This diversion allowed the monks to sneak around behind the soldiers.

The soldiers were expecting the women to be returned to town, but they were puzzled by the absence of their colleagues who had been sent to collect the women. The appearance of defenseless and seemingly amiable women did not give the soldiers reason to draw their weapons. Even the sole man with them, Nico, was unarmed. By the time the women neared the soldiers, the monks had skirted the group and were moving into position behind the soldiers. The women spread out to make each soldier feel that he was being graced by female attention. Any tension felt by the soldiers quickly dissipated and many smiled.

At the exact moment when one of the soldiers reached out to squeeze the buttock of a nearby woman, Nico shouted, "Now!"

On cue, each woman hurled the material clutched in her fist upward toward the nearest soldier. The air seemed to explode in a cloud of ash and dirt. When the cloud dissipated, the women opened their eyes to witness soldiers struggling to recover from the debris that covered their faces. The men were quickly disarmed and then wrapped in twine like prey in a spider's web. As they had done at the church, the women bound the men hand, foot, and to each other. The monks had no role except to stand aside and enjoy the spectacle.

The defeated line of men let their heads hang in shame. How could they admit to colleagues in Rimini that they were overcome by a band of unruly women who kept them from drawing a single weapon or landing a single blow?

"What will happen to the soldiers?" Nico asked Fapane.

"As you know, we have no lawyers here in Pietra Alta. Would you like to remain here to defend them?"

Fapane smiled broadly as he voiced the question. Nico responded only with his own dismissive smile.

"Although we have neither lawyers nor magistrates in Pietra Alta, we do believe in justice. There is always work to be done in our town. I am certain we can find enough work to compensate for their crimes," Fapane declared.

33

THE UCCELLO, FLORENCE

Six men were already seated when Nico arrived at the Uccello. It was a Tuesday, the day of their regular weekly luncheon. But this Tuesday was special because they had invited a seventh person, a guest, to join them. Fortunately, the large round table where they sat had ample space to accommodate an additional person without crowding the diners together. Comfort was important to the men. They especially relished the Uccello's wide padded chairs that let them settle back during their long leisurely meals.

The first man to see Nico was the butcher. He waved to draw Nico's attention and gestured to the empty chair where Nico was to join them. The men already knew part of the Pietra Alta story from Vittorio, one of their own who had accompanied Nico on the first leg of his journey. They were eager to hear the rest of the saga.

Vittorio had been physically assaulted when he and Nico were in Arezzo. He still walked with a limp resulting from that attack, and maybe that injury would prove to be permanent. Vittorio's wife told what she knew of the story to all of her friends, and they spread her account widely. Before long, everyone in Florence seemed to view Vittorio as a minor hero.

Only fragments of Nico's role were widely known because Nico and his acquaintances were discreet in revealing information. Those who had learned the fragments held some suspicions that Nico might be the major hero. Nico was eager to be inducted into the Notaries and Magistrates Guild so he could begin his law career. He was not eager to become a hero, and therefore he evaded questions about his actions. But Nico realized evasion would not be possible with these men. He agreed to attend their luncheon because Vittorio deserved to learn what had happened since he had put himself at risk.

Instead of taking his place at the table, Nico stood behind the empty chair and asked, "Vittorio, can you come with me for a moment? I have something to give you."

Nico intended to bring Vittorio to an empty section of the restaurant. Vittorio remained seated and scanned the package Nico was carrying. "If you have something for me, you can give it to me here. These men are my closest friends."

The jeweler, already on his third glass of wine, looked to Vittorio and began laughing as he remarked, "We are your only friends."

"It is somewhat ..." Nico hesitated briefly, searching for the right word. "Gruesome. It is somewhat gruesome."

"Do we look like children?" the butcher said. "I spend my days pulling organs from dead sheep. That is gruesome. I doubt that whatever you have compares with sheep entrails."

Nico ceded to their plea. He slid into the chair and unfolded the silk wrapping from the object before him.

"It is a dagger," announced the surprised baker.

"And a damned fine one," added the jeweler. "The handle is inlaid with gold."

"Is that blood on the point?" asked the stable owner.

Nico began the story.

"This dagger belonged to Rufio Scalari, a knight from Rimini. He is the person who led soldiers to Pietra Alta, the town where Vittorio's brother-in-law Fapane is a prior. That is Fapane's blood on the point. He still bears a scar from the cut. The wound would have been deeper, he would have been killed, were it not for a painful choice made by his brave son Tommaso."

A sudden pang of guilt made Vittorio shudder. He knew Fapane had a son, but he had never met the boy. He had not even known the boy's name, yet Tommaso was his nephew, he was family.

The men ate delicious food and drank vintage wine through the next hour while Nico told of his journey. In his account, Fapane and Tommaso were the major heroes. The women of Pietra Alta were minor heroes. Marco, the young lawyer in Perugia, and Giulio, the teacher and apprentice architect from Citta di Castello, contributed greatly to the pursuit of justice. Nico chose to omit any involvement by the Priors of Constantine. He respected their wish to remain in the shadows. In his account, Nico Argenti was merely an observer of events as they unfolded.

Enjoy chapter I of Nico's next adventure

Assignment Milan

Andrea Mozzi, First Chair of The Ten of War, arrived early for the meeting, the one that he had convened. At the appointed hour, his five invitees entered the grand salon at Palazzo Strozzi: Scala the Chancellor, Pucci and Cino, both representatives of the Signoria, and Corsini the First Chair of The Eight of Guard, the agency responsible for the police and the safety of Florentine citizens.

When the last man was seated, Mozzi began. "Thank you all for being here." Mozzi had considered his invitation as a request, but the others regarded the message from the First Chair of The Ten of War as a summons.

Meetings organized by Mozzi were always efficient and without distraction. He wasted no time stating its purpose. "Recently, Chancellor Scala received disturbing news from our embassy in Milan." He turned his head to face Scala. "Chancellor, please summarize the report."

Scala leaned forward and rested his hands on the table. "Two of our embassy staffers were having dinner at a restaurant when they overheard a conversation among the Duke's advisors and an agent of a Genovese shipping company. The agent mentioned negotiations underway between his company and the Duchy of Milan that would have all wool fleece brought to Italy in Genovese ships. Our embassy workers recognized the importance of that claim, so they reported it to our chancery."

"Ten years past Milan would not have been negotiating maritime agreements because Milan has no seaports," Mozzi said. "But now it controls Genoa, which has excellent ports, so an alliance between Milan and Genovese shippers is conceivable."

With alarm in his voice, Pucci protested, "We cannot let this happen. There are maritime treaties that govern the shipment of wool. Those treaties protect the rights of Florentine ships carrying goods to Pisa. My woolen mills depend on imported fleece. Any arrangement that would give foreigners exclusive rights to transport fleece would violate the treaties. What if they impose exorbitant taxes on products they deliver? They might even deprive my mills of the materials we depend upon. If this happens, I will be ruined."

Cino voiced an even broader concern. "Nearly half of all Florentine people work in the woolen shops. If the Milanese disrupt that industry, it could ruin our entire economy."

"This event in Milan is but one of several recent incidents that could grow to threaten the security of our Republic. There are others," Mozzi said. "When Cosimo was alive, Milan was a strong ally, but now they are becoming brazen. And what makes this situation most serious is that we have no means to investigate and remedy these threats. I believe there is need for a special commission to deal with suspicious reports such as this."

Heads nodded around the table in agreement with Mozzi's proposal. All the men were familiar with stories of foreign nations plotting to subvert Florence's riches. Mozzi, who had given serious consideration to a solution, described his plan. "My recommendation is for us to form a commission with the mission of stemming these threats. I believe that initially the commission will need at least three members: an investigator skilled in gathering information, a lawyer to seek legal recourse when the evidence warrants, and someone with military experience who can bring force when necessary."

Pucci responded first. "I know of a distinguished army

officer who serves the Republic with honor, Sergeant Massimo Leoni. Leoni joined the Florentine militia in his seventeenth year to help oppose the incursion by Alfonso of Aragon at Maremma. The courage he displayed in that battle earned him the Citation for Valor for entering a burning building to rescue a fellow patriot. Leoni dispatched an enemy soldier with his short sword while carrying the wounded man to safety on his shoulders."

"He's exactly the kind of person we need," Mozzi said.

Corsini raised a hand to gain the attention of the other men. "There is an investigator in the Guardia with an impressive ability to discover evidence that others overlook. Everyone in the Guardia regards him highly. His reputation even extends beyond Florence. Recently, officials in Prato requested his aid in apprehending a band of thieves raising havoc in that city. I believe that Vittorio Colombo is well qualified to be the Commission's investigator."

Mozzi signaled for Scala to speak next. "Nico Argenti is a recent graduate of the University of Bologna law school," Scala began. "I followed his career during his time at the University. He received outstanding evaluations from all of his professors, and at graduation, his fellow students nominated him to the list of superior students."

Cino, who was a consul of the Magistrates Guild, said, "I know that name. Argenti is scheduled to join the Guild at our forthcoming induction ceremony. Our proconsul knew Argenti's father. It is sad that young Argenti's father and mother were both taken by the plague when he was just a boy."

From the corner of his eye, Scala caught Mozzi's expression. Mozzi wanted Scala to mention Nico's exploits since he returned from the University. Taking Mozzi's cue, Scala said, "I am sure you recall the attempted assassination of the hospital directors in Siena. Argenti was the one who uncovered the plot, identified the intended victims, and enlisted the support of Sienese officials to confront the assassin."

Pucci brightened. "Yes, of course. I remember that vicious scheme. I thought the name Argenti sounded familiar when you first mentioned it. That was a remarkable accomplishment for one so young." Pucci spread his hands widely in an encompassing gesture and continued, "These men all have impressive credentials. I support all three for membership on the Commission."

"Are we agreed then with having Leoni, Colombo, and Argenti being the three Commission candidates, or are there other nominees?" Mozzi asked. He looked from man to man as each one signified his approval of the candidates.

After the slate was accepted, Pucci asked, "Will you, Signor Mozzi, discuss the proposed commission and their roles in it with the nominees?"

"Before doing that we need authorization from the Signoria to establish the Commission," Mozzi replied.

Cino, one delegate from the Signoria, said, "I feel confident we can secure the approval of the Signoria. I will request its concurrence at our meeting tomorrow." He glanced at Pucci, the other Signoria delegate, who showed that he agreed. Then Cino asked, "How optimistic are you that these candidates will accept an appointment to the new Commission?"

The question caused Mozzi to chuckle. "I will leave the challenge of recruiting the men to Chancellor Scala. His tongue is cast from a much finer grade of silver than mine."

Times have changed, Scala thought. No longer do states rely on armies to steal their neighbors' lands. Instead, they scheme to plunder wealth and undermine the prosperity of other nations. The men we appoint to the Commission for External Security will face tough challenges.

Get your copy of Assignment in Milan now!

What was life like at a Renaissance university?

Get your FREE download of *Nico's Story*, a recounting of Nico's path through the University of Bologna by signing up for our newsletter at

https://www.KenTentarelli.com/nicos-story

ABOUT THE AUTHOR

Ken Tentarelli is a frequent visitor to Italy. In travels from the Alps to the southern coast of Sicily he developed a love for its history and its people. He has studied Italian culture and language in Rome and Perugia. At home he has taught courses in Italian history spanning time from the Etruscans to the Renaissance. When not traveling, Ken and his wife live in New Hampshire.

ALSO BY KEN TENTARELLI

The Laureate: Mystery in Renaissance Italy

(Nico Argenti series book 1)

When Nico Argenti returns from the university, he is drawn into the turmoil gripping his beloved city of Florence.

Assignment Milan

(Nico Argenti series book 3)

Nico races to uncover the plot targeting the Florentine Republic when a Florentine banker goes missing in Milan.

Conspiracy in Bologna

(Nico Argenti series book 4)

Nico is dispatched to Bologna to thwart a vengeful renegade and rogue mercenaries.

Rebels in Pisa

(Nico Argenti series book 5)

When Nico is sent to Pisa to find and stop insurrectionists, he uncovers smuggling murder and kidnapping.